"Here, tell me what you think."

She held her wrist near his face. He bent to sniff, his lips accidentally touching her warm skin.

He jerked away. Crouching this close to her was hard enough, but his lips touching her? Even a spot as innocent as her wrist, with her blood beating warmly just below the surface.

"What change did I make to my perfume today?"

Wary, because his lust threatened to undo him, but also curious, he leaned close again, damn careful not to make contact.

"Spice. Incredibly subtle." He sniffed again. "Cinnamon. No, cloves."

Her smile enhanced the loveliness of the day. "How do you do that? You're right. It's cloves. Not much, though, because its scent can overpower everything else."

She dropped her arm into her lap and he missed her nearness, even though he knelt right beside her. How incredible must it feel to *lie* beside her?

Dear Reader,

I have always loved stories about the attraction of opposites, about those people who knock us off our feet no matter how hard we resist! We know we shouldn't be attracted, but *sigh* we are.

Monica and Noah appeared as secondary characters in *In from the Cold*. I wanted them to have their own stories, but with each other? Never! They were wily, though. They started sneaking around behind my back, then demanded that I write their romance.

Monica is all about designer clothing; Noah wears Birkenstocks and army surplus. She loves fashion magazines; he reads Kierkegaard. She is refined and elegant; he is an environment-loving farmer.

Despite all of his efforts to the contrary, Noah is in love with Monica. The more Monica gets to know Noah, the more trouble she has resisting him. In the end, they fall in love. The attraction of opposites triumphs again.

I hope you enjoy this story! I loved writing it.

Mary Sullivan

MARY SULLIVAN

Safe in Noah's Arms

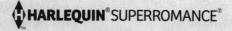
HARLEQUIN® SUPERROMANCE®

Recycling programs
for this product may
not exist in your area.

ISBN-13: 978-0-373-60925-3

Safe in Noah's Arms

Copyright © 2015 by Mary Sullivan

Printed in U.S.A.

Despite growing up in a large city, **Mary Sullivan** loves to write about small towns. Maybe because of the countless hours spent as a child listening to her mother's fascinating stories about life in rural Newfoundland. Since her days working in commercial darkrooms, Mary has gravitated toward careers that require creativity, alone in her own private space. Her interests are simple: cooking, entertaining, reading and long walks on nature trails. And puzzles! She can't get enough of cryptic crosswords! She loves to hear from readers and can be reached through her website, www.marysullivanbooks.com, where readers can also sign up for her newsletter.

Books by Mary Sullivan

HARLEQUIN SUPERROMANCE

No Ordinary Cowboy
A Cowboy's Plan
This Cowboy's Son
Beyond Ordinary
These Ties That Bind
No Ordinary Sheriff
In from the Cold
Home to Laura
Because of Audrey
Always Emily
No Ordinary Home

Visit the Author Profile page
at Harlequin.com for more titles

CHAPTER ONE

Standing amid the hustle and bustle swirling around her like a colorful carousel, Monica Accord thought back to when it all started. She wasn't a violent person, but she thanked her lucky stars that she broke Noah Cameron's arm all of those years ago.

THERE WERE THREE kinds of days in Monica Accord's life—days when she didn't care, days when she knew she should care and the odd, rare day when she actually did care.

This morning, driving onto Noah Cameron's organic farm outside of Accord, Colorado, she cared.

Too bad. Life would be easier if she didn't have a conscience.

She parked beside Noah's ancient pickup truck, which was next to a big old farmhouse that appeared to be abandoned. White paint peeled from the railing on the veranda. One eaves trough hung askew—it was a forgotten house, the owner off to parts unknown without a backward glance.

Was she at the wrong place? She had understood it to be a working farm.

Yesterday, the court's directions to the farm had been clear. The address was correct. This had to be the right place, but she couldn't be sure. Situated as it was down the highway that ran south from Accord, instead of north toward the attraction of Denver's shopping centers, it ran counter to Monica's internal compass. She rarely drove out this way.

And no one came out of the farmhouse to greet her.

She glanced at her watch—7:00 a.m. Maybe Noah was already up and out in the fields, or maybe he was already in town at his store. Maybe she wouldn't have to face him this morning.

She could live with that. The shame burning a hole through her stomach concurred. Though at least the shame was better than emptiness. Something, anything, was better than nothing.

Bewildered, she glanced toward the fields. Ah. *There* was the proof of a working farm. Meticulously and perfectly tended, and an obvious indication of where the owner put his energy—the fields were cared for a heck of a lot better than the house.

She stepped out of the car and studied the yard. Sorry-looking place.

In yesterday's courtroom when Judge Easton had intoned, "Guilty of a wet reckless," and had sentenced her to two hundred hours of community service, she'd thought she would be talking to high school kids about the dangers of drinking and driving.

She would have taken that on happily. Because what she had done last Friday night had been beyond reckless—there was no excuse for drinking and driving.

As her daddy had said after the verdict, "You don't

make mistakes often, sweetheart, but when you do, they sure are doozies." He'd softened it with a hug before walking out and leaving her to pay her five-hundred-dollar fine. Fair enough. It had been her mistake and hers alone.

Lecturing kids would have made sense.

But *no-o-o-o*. Judge Easton had given her a far tougher sentence.

This whole terrible experience had moved with mind-numbing speed, as though she was caught in a vortex. Was she the only person who'd done something wrong last weekend? She'd committed a crime on Friday night and, boom, she was in a courtroom a few days later. She'd barely had time to hire herself a lawyer, but then, the facts were not in dispute. She had been drinking. She had run down Noah on his bike and had broken his arm. She'd heard he also had plenty of scrapes and bruises.

She shivered. She was lucky she hadn't killed the man.

The judge sentenced her yesterday and, boom, she was to start right away. Today. Was it a slow point in crime or did Noah have some kind of pull with the courts?

The whole town knew Noah as an ethical guy. Truly, she didn't think he'd do anything like pull strings.

If anyone had *pull*, it was the Accords, not the Camerons. Not that they'd ever used it. She strongly doubted the justice system in Montana was corruptible.

Was this rush because of the time of year and the fact that Noah needed help immediately? She imagined June must be a busy month for a farmer. Maybe that was the real and simple answer.

So here she was, serving all two hundred hours on Noah's farm, near him, with him. Crazy old judge. What did he think Monica knew about farming?

She'd expected to have to atone, but with Noah? Pure, simple torture.

Why couldn't it have been anyone other than arrogant, holier-than-thou Noah Cameron on that dark road last Friday night, he of the *über*-huge brain who lorded it over others every chance he got?

They had gone to high school together, him one year behind her, but even then she'd been intimidated by the massive mind lurking inside the hippie exterior.

From her youngest days, she'd been made to feel inadequate by him.

Even worse, these days she worked for his mother. And Olivia Cameron wasn't the least bit happy that Monica had hurt her precious Noah.

Didn't anyone—the judge, Olivia, Noah, the townspeople—get that she would never intentionally hurt anyone, least of all someone she would happily never have to deal with for the rest of her life?

For years, she'd pushed the guy off her radar, but now she couldn't avoid him. She had to spend the next couple of months with him—*her entire summer*—all because of a mistake fueled by loneliness. Still, she knew there were no excuses.

She approached the nearest field with trepidation. *Ha!* She'd bet Noah would never believe she even knew a word like *trepidation*, let alone its meaning and how to use it properly.

Stepping over a couple of puddles, more miserable than she'd been at any time in the five years since Billy's death, she moaned low in her throat. A bird somewhere nearby sang in response.

She should have worn sturdier shoes. Rubber boots, maybe. Problem was, she didn't own any. Until yesterday, she'd never owned a pair of jeans, either. She didn't do denim.

Across a long field of swirling dirt in leftover patches of early-morning mist, to a stand of trees in the distance, plants dotted rows of dark earthen hills like tiny green hieroglyphics, a foreign language she would have to learn by immersion—and fast. Sink or swim.

She used to be that new, that green and full of promise, like those plants. Where had it all gone?

Fascinated by their burgeoning vulnerable beauty, she squatted and rubbed a tender leaf between her fingers, both the plant and the soil still cool in the early day.

Babies scared her. Small helpless creatures terrified her. These soft plants intimidated her. What if she killed them?

If she bent over and walked down the rows with

her palms outstretched, she could read them like braille, but she still wouldn't understand their needs, or how to keep them alive. She still wouldn't know how to farm.

Her lawyer had told her not to worry, that Noah would guide her.

She wouldn't be surprised if Noah kicked her off the farm upon first sight. In the pit of her stomach, that blasted recurring shame stabbed at her with a hot poker. Her tummy had been doing somersaults all morning.

She didn't want to be here, to have to face the man she'd hurt.

She touched the plant closest to her.

"How do I help you to grow?" she whispered.

Against the bright green, her hands screamed "pampered," her nails manicured with OPI's Not So Bora Bora-ing Pink. These hands that had never gardened—had never even tended a houseplant—had to learn how to dig around in the dirt.

What had the judge been thinking?

What on earth did one night of loneliness and one drink too many have to do with farming?

She spotted Noah across the field, watching her, red hair blazing in the sunlight. Noah, she'd noticed, presented two faces to the world—the happy, easy-going hippie and the *über*-intelligent, fierce activist.

At the moment, he'd added a third. Angry farmer—directed at her.

The heat that had roiled in her belly all morning crawled up her chest and into her throat, choking her.

Her mind refused to remember what she saw Friday night, but echoing sounds gathered, drowning out the nearby bird's sweet melody. The screech of her tires on wet pavement. The awful thud of Noah hitting her car. The shattering of her windshield and tinkling of glass raining down on her in the driver's seat.

The silence of Noah's prone body.

She didn't want to be here.

A WILDFIRE RAGED inside of Noah.

His right arm ached from overuse.

His left arm itched inside the cast.

He needed to be able to work whole, unhindered. Almost as badly, he needed to wring that pampered, rich, entitled woman's neck.

Since last Friday night, he'd cursed Monica Accord from here to the Pacific Ocean, but his anger still hadn't cooled.

He didn't want to see her today, didn't want her on his farm infecting the goodness here with her shallowness, but what choice did he have?

The prosecutor had consulted with him before requesting the sentence for Monica; otherwise, they would have been inflicting the offender on the poor, hapless victim. Which wouldn't have been right. And he'd agreed with their decision.

He might not want Monica here, but he needed

her, *and* he found the sentence fitting, forcing her to learn exactly how hard this job was, and how much her selfish act of drinking and then getting behind the wheel of her car had set him back.

He had told the courts that, yes, he would have her here to serve her community service.

Let her get her precious hands dirty for a change. Daddy couldn't buy her way out of this fix.

He knew he was being hard on her, but he had a right to be.

He tore out a couple of weeds and tossed them into the pail by his side, seething with an anger that hadn't abated even a fraction since the accident.

He hated this. He wasn't an angry man. Passionate? Oh, yeah. Angry? Nah. He left that for other people. He was a lover, not a fighter, but man, he wished he had a heavy bag to punch for an hour or two. He needed to vent, badly.

Trouble was, it would amplify that he had only one useful arm.

He flexed his neck to ease the tension that had lodged there like a recalcitrant tree stump, going nowhere no matter how hard he tried to yank it out.

Stop. This doesn't do you any good.

Filling his lungs with the fresh scent of morning dew, he tried to clear his mind. Usually, not much got him down at this glorious time of day—not worries, not memories.

He'd already been out here weeding for two hours, the drill usually as calming as yoga or meditation.

Even so, rage flexed its fists in his chest, pummeling his ribs, beating up on him from the inside out.

He didn't need this.

An engine sounded in the distance, then in his driveway. He heard it because he'd been waiting for it.

She was here.

He dropped his spade and stood—it was a real struggle to rein in his emotions. Useless exercise. Fury flooded his veins. Every last item of produce he grew was destined for a food kitchen in Denver, or for families living miles around who had fallen on hard times.

Now this—a broken left arm and too much work to do alone in his current state. Whatever didn't get grown and harvested couldn't be eaten by those in need.

Why couldn't it be anyone but Monica here to help him? At the moment, he'd take aid from a goat if it was a viable option to get more accomplished. He really didn't want to deal with that woman.

Court-appointed or not, help was help. He glanced toward the driveway and his breath backed up in his throat.

Monica Accord stepped out of her baby blue BMW convertible, cool and composed, pale blond hair in place, long legs encased in designer jeans, a Victoria's Secret model and *Sports Illustrated* swimsuit-issue model rolled into one. A classy one.

Monica Accord could no more do trashy than the Pope could break-dance.

She walked toward one of his fields, stepping close to his rows of new radish plants, a puzzled frown furrowing her otherwise perfect brow. He tracked her progress, 'cause the thing with Monica was that *walk* was too normal a verb to describe her movement. Monica did nothing so mundane as walk. She glided, floating with a lithe elegance that mere mortals couldn't imitate.

God, she was gorgeous with the sun running warm rays over her skin as though infatuated with her.

Who wasn't?

His heart boomeranged inside his chest, beating hard enough to hurt. Twenty years after leaving high school, she was still the golden girl, and he was still the guy who had an unrequited crush on her—disgusting in a rational thirty-seven-year-old man.

He tossed his spade into the pail with the weeds.

Still a fool.

He needed his wits about him. Sure, he was a smart guy, but Monica Accord could scramble his brain in creative ways.

She bent over and touched a plant. Her lips moved. She was *talking* to it? Wasn't that a little New Agey for Monica?

Wrapping his anger around himself like a protective shield, he approached. She noticed him. He glared and watched guilt heat a path up her neck and into her cheeks. Good. She was the reason he was in this hellish predicament.

A swift glance at the cast on his arm had color infusing her face. When she noticed the healing scabs on his forehead, she winced.

When he reached her, she said, "I'm truly sorry." No "hi" or "how's it going?" She sounded abject and looked miserable. Good. She had screwed him royally.

There wasn't one ounce of compassion or forgiveness in him for her.

"Y-y-y-ou have any id-d-d—" He hissed in a breath, furious. Not this again! *Stuttering*, for God's sake. He'd worked his butt off to overcome his affliction, but a split second in Monica's rarefied company and a bad case of stupefying adoration threatened to lock his tongue.

Steeling his nerves, he pulled himself together and started again.

"You have any idea what you've done to me?" He hated the victim-like sound of that "to me," but said it anyway, skipping the niceties and gesturing with the cast. "You have any idea how much trouble you've caused me?"

"I can only imagine, Noah."

"No, you can't," he snapped and was gratified when she flinched. He'd pierced her cool elegance. Since early adolescence, her effortless physical grace had mocked his gangly limbs, old clothes and wild hair. He'd grown up since then, had added muscle in all the right places, courtesy of hard work. His thin face had matured; his jaw had hardened. He refused to cater to fashion or vanity and yet, women found him attractive. Except for Monica, of course. He had the worst desire to crash through her facade and break down her boundaries, to make her as human as the rest of the world.

As human as me.

"I can't get my work done." Bitterness churned up from his belly like acid reflux. "You've screwed me at my busiest time of year."

Had she ever once in her life thought of anyone other than herself?

"You've got *big* amends to make. Huge."

Hurt lingered in her eyes and he fought the urge to soften his words because he wasn't mad at just her. He was furious with himself because even after the nightmare of her hitting him with her car and breaking part of his body, his knee-jerk, teenaged reaction to her was to turn to jelly.

Some boys never grew up where some girls were concerned.

Those boyhood memories, those significant moments of teenage mortification, rose too close to the surface. She had never been intentionally cruel. He just hadn't existed for her, in her world—not even on the periphery of it. What boy wants to be invisible to a beautiful girl?

Back then he'd been a tall redhead, growing like

a weed. How could he possibly have been invisible to her?

That wasn't all of the truth, though, was it? There had been that one time when she'd seen him and had been cruel. Intentionally? He didn't know.

There'd been a gaggle of pretty girls standing in the hallway at their lockers when he had walked by. He had thought of them as worldly fourteen-year-olds to his thirteen-year-old unsophisticated self, aggressive in his opinions because without them he was just…awkward.

Monica—tall, gorgeous and perfect in every way—had been in the center of the whirling vortex of giggling femininity.

One of the girls had pointed to him and whispered something to Monica. She'd glanced his way, coolly, because that's how she did everything—with calm self-assurance.

His ever-hopeful young self had thought, *This is it. Monica Accord is finally going to acknowledge me, and talk to me!*

After that one brief glance, she had turned away, dismissing him and leaving him to feel invisible again. And after a word to her friends that had set them off giggling, he became worse than invisible. He was shunned and ignored and left to feel worthless.

He didn't know what mean or unkind remark she had said about him, but his hatred of her had started that day. Problem was, it was worse than pure hatred.

It was love-hate from afar and he was a fool for still falling under her spell, especially when he clearly still meant nothing to her.

He knew he meant less than nothing to her because, since high school, she'd spent the better part of her adult life ignoring him, except for that damned polite little smile the odd time when their paths crossed. And that he could do without.

In the grand scheme of things, this was peanuts. In his work with the poor and needy, especially in New Orleans after Katrina, he had seen true hardship. He had no illusions this wasn't on the list of the worst things that could happen to a guy, he knew that, but it had happened during those impressionable, early adolescent years, a time fraught with raging new feelings.

As it turned out, it had been a pivotal event that had shaped his life for years to come.

Her behavior on the previous weekend, drinking and driving, cemented what he had always known about her—Monica Accord was still as self-centered and self-indulgent as ever. The town might accept her goody-two-shoes image, but he knew better.

The cast on his arm and his bruised ribs told a more accurate story.

So, no, he had no use for her, but today he required her help. No choice. It put him in the impossible position of needing her, but not wanting her.

Her gaze dropped, and then shot back to his face. "You're wearing socks…with sandals."

"So what?"

"It's so unfashionable."

"Seriously?" Still an airhead, believing that fashion was more important than anything. What about poverty? Need? What about war? What about—? Ah, hell, none of it mattered to Monica.

"It's chilly in the mornings." That he sounded defensive further inflamed his irritation. "My toes freeze if I don't wear socks." Crazy woman. What the heck difference did it make? "So? How many hours did they give you for a DWAI?"

"Two hundred for a wet reckless."

"They dropped the driving with ability impaired?" he asked, incredulous. Once again the rich got favors while the common man was screwed. *"Why?* Did you get a break because you're one of the mighty Accords?"

The delicacy of her frown bothered him. Was there *anything* Monica did that wasn't attractive? "Not exactly, Noah. In fact, Dad wasn't happy when Judge Easton took his seat to preside over my sentencing. He said I was lucky he hadn't made things worse, not better." She fiddled with the hem of her shirt. She was nervous? Couldn't be. Not Monica. "I don't know why it got knocked down. You'd have to ask my lawyer how he reduced the charge. He worked it all out."

Despite what Monica's father had told her, he and the judge were cronies. Had to be. What else would it have been? Once again, money talked, and that made him livid. "*Your* lawyer? Don't you mean your daddy's lawyer?" He was being sarcastic and cutting, and he didn't like that in himself, but God, he was mad. At a time when he needed to be strong in order to get massive amounts of work done, she'd turned him into half a man. Helplessness fueled his outrage.

As an awkward kid trying to come to grips with bones that were growing too quickly for his muscles to keep up, he'd been beat on by a group of nasty boys, repeatedly. Day in and day out, they would hold him down while Kenny Rickard whaled on him.

Helpless to defend himself, he'd grown to hate that feeling.

He wouldn't complain, though. He'd never once snitched.

Over time, he had grown into his bones and his gangly limbs had filled out. These days, at six-one and two hundred pounds of lean muscle, he could fight anyone who tried to hurt him, but Monica Accord could still bring him to his knees with nothing more than a glance. Plus, she'd handicapped him physically.

Worst thing she could have done to him was to make him feel helpless.

"You broke my arm." *Lame. She already knows that, Cameron.*

Her pretty lips thinned. "For God's sake, not on purpose." She sounded angry.

Good. *Welcome to my world.*

He stepped closer. "Let's get something straight.

I'm not happy about you being here, but you caused this—" he pointed to the cast "—so I'm going to work the daylights out of you. Farming is a tough, physical business, so be prepared to work like you've never worked before for your *mandated* two hundred hours."

A woman like Monica would never have volunteered for such a job.

Disgusted, he growled, "Let's get started. Follow me."

He turned away, but she touched his good hand to stop him. Fireworks zinged up his arm.

"Okay, Noah, you want to clear the air? Fine." He'd never heard her sound so hard. "I'm not any happier about this than you are. I hate that I broke your arm. I don't like hurting people."

She took a deep breath, to calm herself he assumed, but what the hell did she have to be angry about? *She* hadn't been injured in the accident. "I've never driven drunk before—*never*—but as my lawyer said, it takes only one time for something bad to happen. I'm sorry I hit you. I will pay to replace your bicycle. I've already offered more than once."

"It was vintage. It can't be replaced."

"Well, I'm going to try. Give me all the details you can and I'll track one down." She tilted her head to one side. "Or can yours be fixed?"

"It's in bad shape. You really hit me hard. We're both lucky all I got was a broken arm. You could have killed me."

He wasn't sure, but he thought she shivered.

"Maybe you have a conscience, after all," he conceded. "In my experience, rich people rarely do."

"Stereotype much, Noah?"

"As I said, I've come by it honestly. Through experience."

One long-fingered hand rubbed her stomach. What was that about? "I am really, truly sorry. I don't know how many more times I can say it. Let's move forward from here, okay? Show me what I need to do to help you."

So, the spoiled girl knew how to be reasonable. Okay, he could be, too.

"Do you know how to farm?"

"Nope."

"Do you keep houseplants?"

"Never."

"Do you know *any*thing about plants?"

"Nada."

"Oh, crap." Visions of how useful she would be to him evaporated like the last vestiges of morning dew dried up by the sun. He stared at Monica in her designer jeans and absolutely useless loafers.

His silly dreams of a capable helper came to a screeching halt. She was going to be useless to him—even less so than he'd imagined.

None of his friends or family had the time to help him out, and he couldn't afford to hire employees.

Instead, he was stuck with Monica Accord.

What made it all truly rotten was that despite

despising everything that Monica stood for—her princess-in-an-ivory-tower lifestyle, her frivolity, her designer clothing that embodied crass consumerism, her *uselessness*—Noah still felt those awful pangs, the ones he'd had in high school that had been worse than the growing pains in his long legs, worse than the way the other kids made fun of his retro clothing and taunted him his fervent fights to save the environment. He still felt those awful, unwelcome and debilitating pangs of unrequited puppy love.

For two hundred long, long hours, he would be stuck with Monica, golden goddess, former cheerleader and prettiest prom queen Accord High had ever seen.

As he led her around to the back porch of the house to hunt down a pair of rubber boots that might fit her, he said it again, with feeling. "Oh, *crap*."

FOR THE FOURTH time in the two hours Monica had been weeding, Noah yelled at her.

"What are you doing?" Along with his harsh shout came a shadow that cut off light.

Behind his head, the sun created a halo around Noah's too-long red hair. Wisps of it had escaped his ponytail and curled in the heat.

"That's not a weed," he cried. "It's a radish."

Rats. She'd screwed up again. Cramming it back into the earth, she shoved soil around the roots with shaking hands. She'd been pulling up too many plants. She just couldn't tell them apart. She wished she could. Contrary to what Noah seemed to think, she didn't like screwing up, especially when he'd drilled into her that she was wasting food.

"It will be okay." She picked up the pail beside her and watered the radish. "Honest, I'll check it again tomorrow to make sure it survived."

He crouched down, too close. Noah had grown up well. Really well. His eyes sparkled like bright green gems. The man exuded a lot of heat. His mouth, a flat slash that divided his red mustache and beard, signaled his disapproval. Usually when she saw him around town, his lips were full and on the verge of an ever-ready smile—not that she'd noticed.

"No, Monica, it won't recover from being yanked out of the soil when it's still so young. Would *you* recover?"

Abruptly, he stood and stomped away, clearly agitated, but spun back and moved close to her again. "Every plant that dies is food that doesn't make it to someone's plate. Understand?"

"I *know*. You've already told me a million times since I got here."

"You know nothing about hunger or poverty. All you've ever known is privilege."

Why did he take such pleasure in making her feel ashamed of who she was? "I *get* it, Noah. I truly do." Monica stood, because she didn't like that he was taller than her at the best of times, let alone when she was kneeling in the dirt. "Whether or not you choose to believe me, I'm trying my hardest to do a good job."

She took off her sun hat and wiped her forehead with her sleeve. It came away damp with sweat. "You have to understand how new this is to me, Noah." She touched his arm, but he pulled away, so she dropped her hand to her side. Even before she'd hit him on Friday night, he'd always seemed to go out of his way to avoid her. Why did he dislike her so much? "I want to get this right. I really do. Okay?"

"Okay," he muttered, but she had the sense it wasn't, that there was something going on beneath the surface that Noah wasn't explaining to her—something she couldn't figure out on her own.

It messed with her nerves so she gave up trying. "I have to leave. I start work in forty-five minutes and I have to wash up first." She took a small pink notebook and matching pen out of her back pocket and wrote down a sentence indicating she'd put in her first two hours of her sentence. She handed the book to him. "Initial here, please."

"Aren't you the organized little beaver?" Ignoring the pen, he fished a pencil stub out of his jeans and scrawled his initials across the page, a messy slash beside her tidy script.

She held back a knee-jerk response, totally getting that he had a right to be angry, but his sarcasm hurt. She rose above it by ignoring it. One of them had to be the adult here.

"Write down all of the details about your bike, too."

When he'd finished and handed the notebook back to her, she said, "I'll be back tomorrow morning at the same time."

She trudged to her car, tired already, and she still had to put in a full day at work.

With Noah's hot gaze burning through the shirt on her back, she started the car and drove away.

Once in town, she detoured to her apartment to shower and change for work. It wasn't quite ten and here she was having her second shower of the day.

She threw on a bit of makeup then ran out the door.

For over a year now, Monica had been working at The Palette, the only art shop in town. She stepped through the doorway and found the gallery cool, a godsend after the past two hours spent under the hot sun.

The owner, Olivia Cameron, Noah's mom, stood talking to one of the sculptors whose work they stocked. Gorgeous Aiden McQuorrie had his focus squarely centered on Olivia. Even though she was fifteen years his senior, she held him in sway. Monica sighed. So romantic. Everyone in town knew they were getting it on every chance they got. In the year since Olivia had started to date Aiden, after much persuasion on Aiden's part to get her over her reluctance because of their age difference, she had blossomed.

Monica smiled. Understandably, Aiden was Olivia's favorite sculptor.

When Aiden stepped past Monica to leave, his glance sympathetic—he knew how angry Olivia was with her—he squeezed her arm then left the gallery.

Olivia approached, every beautifully dyed strand of hair in place, her peach suit expensive and understated—her sophisticated demeanor a sharp contrast to Aiden's rough-hewn, restless energy.

Another case of the attraction of opposites, like me and Billy.

Olivia, a former housewife, had started the art gallery years ago and, through determination and sheer grit, had nurtured it into a successful enterprise.

Oh, how Monica admired her. She would love to be a businesswoman, but had no idea what kind of business she would start.

Working on commission in an art gallery and living on a small widow's benefit, Monica didn't have a lot of money, wasn't married and didn't have children, nor did she really have a career. In short, she was floating through life, about as aimless as a leaf drifting on the surface of a stream.

She certainly wasn't directing her life toward any place she wanted to go.

Olivia glared at Monica. It was all too much—first her son and now her. Monica's nerves jangled like someone plucking loose guitar strings. Olivia had been cool with her since she'd run down her son last week.

It made Monica's heart ache because she truly liked Olivia. They'd become good friends. Monica had—dare she think it?—begun to see Olivia as a mother figure.

Now the relationship suffered because of Monica's flawed decisions on Friday night. Monica couldn't be more grateful to Olivia for giving her a job, for showing faith in her, but Olivia had also gifted her with friendship…only to now withdraw it.

It hurt.

Monica stifled her longing for things to be normal. She had loved spending time with Olivia on their monthly spa days. She would secretly pretend she had a mom she could hang out with.

The sadness of that loss overwhelmed her. It left a heaviness in her heart more burdensome than the guilt she felt when she was with Noah. She wanted her affectionate relationship with Olivia back. She turned away to surreptitiously wipe her damp eyes.

Struggling to make amends, she said, "I'm sorry I'm late, Olivia."

"How did it go in court yesterday?" Olivia asked, her tone too cold for Monica's liking. "Everything okay?"

"I have to perform two hundred hours of community service."

Monica straightened a painting. She genuinely loved the shop and the art they sold. A little more challenge in her job wouldn't hurt, but at least this brought in a paycheck. "My lawyer plea-bargained down from a driving with ability impaired to a wet reckless."

Olivia's mouth thinned. She didn't like the break Monica's lawyer had managed to negotiate any better than Noah had, but then she was a mother bear concerned for her cub. Monica just wished Mama Bear wasn't also her boss.

"Community service?" Olivia asked. "There's nothing like that available in Accord. Where do you have to go? Denver?"

"Noah's farm. I have to grow plants."

A mean little smile tugged at the corners of Olivia's mouth. "You have to farm?"

Oh, dear. It looked like Olivia was going to enjoy Monica's discomfort just as much as Noah. "I don't know a thing about farming and now I have to help Noah grow his vegetables. Yes. I have to farm."

Olivia's glance took in the sleeveless sage linen dress and the rose pumps Monica had donned in a hurry a few minutes ago.

"Good luck." The hard edge of Olivia's voice saddened Monica even while she tried to cut Olivia some slack.

"I was already there this morning pulling up plants instead of weeds. They all look the same to me. Noah was angry." Monica crossed her arms and grasped her elbows. She knew she sounded unhappy, but there wasn't much she could do about it. What had the judge been thinking? She needed to talk to Daddy, to find out why he'd groaned when Judge Easton had entered the courtroom yesterday morning. Unless Monica had it wrong, there was history between the two of them—and now she was paying the price.

Olivia's glance skimmed Monica again. "Do you even own a pair of jeans?"

"Of course," she said, but relented and told the truth. "I bought a pair yesterday after I left the courtroom."

"You'll still need to keep your full-time hours."

"I'll put in all of my hours. No problem, Olivia." She didn't ask her dad for help these days. She was trying really hard to get by on her own. It had taken her years to learn that self-sufficiency provided rewards far greater than material goods.

She'd stopped shopping as a hobby a couple of years ago. The dress and shoes she wore today were a few years old. Fortunately, her style was classic and she took care of her clothes.

Olivia led her to the office in the back. "Noah works on his farm for four hours every morning before he comes into town to open the army surplus store."

That ugly old thing. The town should demolish it. Force it to shut down. All of the other shops on Main Street had spruced up their storefronts to bring in tourists. Why shouldn't he have to, as well?

Her mind went back to what Olivia had said. So Noah had already been out weeding for a couple of hours before Monica had arrived this morning? Insane. "Four hours? *Before* he opens the store? What time does he get up?"

"As far as I know about five."

"As in a.m.?"

Compelled, she did the math. Two hundred hours. If she went to the farm for two hours in the morning before coming to work—no way was she getting up at five—it would take her one hundred days to complete her service, if she worked there *every* day. More than three months, and she would have to work longer hours on her days off to make up the time faster. A little faint, she leaned against the wall.

Olivia grasped Monica's arm. "You try real hard to make it work, to make up for how much you hurt him." She picked up her purse. "I'm running across the street for a coffee."

The slamming front door put an exclamation point to her exit.

She'd left without offering to bring back something for Monica, unheard of in their relationship to date.

As Monica had already done a dozen times this morning, she rubbed a hand over her roiling tummy.

Making amends was a heck of a lot harder than it looked.

CHAPTER TWO

"CAN YOU BELIEVE this whole cockeyed situation?" Noah asked Audrey and Laura when he arrived at Laura's café for lunch. They were crowded into Laura's office in the back behind the kitchen. "I'm stuck with Monica Accord on the farm."

He and his best friend, Audrey Stone, ate together most days, either at her flower shop or at Noah's Army Surplus, and took turns bringing food. He'd chosen the bakery today so he could vent to both his best friend and his sister.

"She broke your arm," Laura said, patting her brother's cast. "It was the best solution. She can be of use to you on the farm."

"Ha! She threw a bunch of weeds onto the compost heap even after I'd told her they belong in the garbage. How is that useful?"

"She might become better at it than you think." Laura pushed her long hair back over her shoulder. She'd inherited a more subdued version of their father's red hair than Noah had.

"Are you kidding? She overwatered the turnips so I can't water them tomorrow. She didn't water the radishes enough, so I have to water them again this evening. I need less work, not more." He banged his fist on Laura's desk, rattling a bunch of papers, a soup ladle and a bag of cloth diapers delivered by her service. "The woman's too stupid to know a rake from a curling iron."

Laura stood abruptly and picked up the diapers. "I have to go. It's feeding time and I'm ready to burst."

Noah perked up. "How's Pearl doing?" Flat-out chuffed to be a brand-new uncle, his curiosity about and fascination with his niece grew with each passing day.

"Growing by leaps and bounds." Laura tucked the diapers under her arm and picked up the soup ladle to return it to the kitchen. "Who left this here?"

"Probably you." Noah laughed. Laura left a trail of cooking utensils wherever she went. The woman was as passionate about preparing food as he was about growing it.

"You two stay here and finish your lunch." Resting her hand on Noah's shoulder, Laura said, "Give Monica a chance. I almost lost Nick by judging on appearances and past behavior. People grow, Noah. They change."

After Laura left the room, Noah finished his quinoa salad and felt Audrey watching him the whole time. He knew why. Monica used to be married to Audrey's brother, Billy Stone, until he died in Afghanistan. She probably felt some kind of loyalty to Monica.

"I'd rather do anything this summer than teach spoiled Monica to farm," he said, disgust coloring his tone far more than the situation warranted. "It's distasteful to me."

"I understand, Noah, but be careful you don't make assumptions that are unfounded," she said. "Or based on clichés about rich women and Monica's blond good looks. You've had a bad string of luck with women."

When he opened his mouth to object, she raised her hand. "Don't worry. I won't bring up the elephant in the room."

The elephant in the room was that Noah had always chosen women who had an uncanny resemblance to Monica, and who were just as wealthy.

It confounded him that he would choose women like her. "That's all been nothing more than coincidence."

"Really? Deirdre? New Orleans? A dead ringer for Monica."

Noah was angry instantly. He'd put a lot of energy into forgetting Deirdre and her betrayal. He didn't need Audrey bringing it up now.

"Don't go there, Audrey."

"Deirdre might have looked like Monica, but Monica is nothing like that woman."

"Okay, so I showed poor judgment. I won't again. Okay?"

Unfazed by his anger, Audrey urged, "Everybody underestimates Monica. Just don't let your bias have you judging her wrongly."

Both Audrey and Noah had been on the receiving end of the false assumptions that people made based on flimsy evidence—Audrey because of the way she chose to dress in retro forties and fifties clothing, and Noah because of the same thing—the way he chose to dress—and also because of the green, organic lifestyle he lived. He would probably fit in better in a big city than in rural Colorado.

But in Colorado, he got to *grow* things, to plant seeds and produce something out of nothing that could feed those in need…and it was the best feeling on earth.

In high school, he and Audrey had bonded as the misfits who didn't dress like others. They'd been best buds ever since.

"Noah, you weren't too hard on her, were you?"

With one hand, he wrestled his empty Mason jar into his cooler bag, avoiding her gaze. "I wasn't patient with her," he admitted, but, compelled to defend himself continued, "For Pete's sake, Audrey, every time I look at her I still get tongue-tied. When she showed up at the farm this morning, I actually stuttered!"

Her eyebrows shot up. "That bad? Still?"

"Yeah. It's still that bad. When's the last time you heard me stutter? It's like I'm thirteen years old again! And for what? For a spoiled, ditzy blonde." So, yeah, he'd been harsh, but that was a whole lot better than stuttering.

"Noah, don't call her names. You forget that Monica is family," Audrey admonished.

Chastened, he calmed himself and said, "I do. I often forget. I'm sorry. It's just that I've never understood how you two could be so different and yet get along so well."

"First, it's because she's not quite who you think she is, and second, because we both lost our mothers when we were so young. Mine when I was five, but poor Monica in childbirth. She never even knew hers."

"And this helped how?"

When Audrey hesitated to share, Noah bumped her shoulder with his. "I'm just trying to understand this space alien who's tearing up my radishes."

Audrey huffed out a laugh and then grew serious. "Okay. Here goes. Losing a parent so early leaves a hollow spot in your life along with a low-grade sadness. It doesn't matter how deeply you bury the sadness, it's still there. Often, you feel like you don't have anyone to talk to about it, even your other parent. My dad was grieving, too, but didn't know how to express it."

"What about Billy?"

"I think he dealt with it by ignoring it, by surrounding himself with friends. By becoming the class clown and making sure that everyone, including himself, was always laughing. Plus, when it happened, he was older and less dependent on Mom than I was."

"That makes sense." Noah picked at his egg sandwich. "Monica felt that way, too?"

"Yes. She also understood that it makes you different from your classmates and friends who still have both parents. Mother's Day is particularly hard."

Finished with her salad, Audrey passed him her empty jar. "Knowing that someone else in the world understood how I felt gave me a measure of comfort, even though I was already a teenager by then."

"Okay," Noah conceded. "She might have more depth than I've given her credit for, but she pulled up eight of my baby radishes before I caught her. It frustrates me, Audrey. That's food that won't make it onto some hungry person's plate."

Audrey sobered. He knew she admired his passion for feeding the needy. Of all of the people in his life, she truly understood him.

"She said she thought they were weeds," he continued. "They *were* the only plants in a row I'd already weeded."

"Sounds like a problem with communication."

"Yeah, there was definitely a problem. *I* communicated. *She* didn't listen."

He stared at Audrey, begging her to understand how screwed he was.

"What am I going to do about her, Audrey? I'm thirty-seven years old, a sane and reasonable grown man, but I'll be seeing her nearly every day this summer and I might as well be back in high school." He added miserably, "Déjà vu all over again."

AT LUNCHTIME, MONICA headed to the bar at the end of Main Street, knowing her father had his midday meal there every day. She wanted to question him about his relationship with the judge.

She'd tried to contact him last night, but he'd been out and hadn't been answering his cell, leaving her with the strange suspicion he was avoiding her.

In the courtroom yesterday, she'd been upset by the judge's lack of professionalism. His sly looks, the pleasure he seemed to take in convicting her, had irked her and yet, he had agreed to the plea bargain that got her sentence reduced. So confusing. She meant to get to the bottom of it.

The scents of fried food made her mouth water, but Monica was watching her figure.

When she slid into the booth across from her dad, he didn't seem surprised to see her.

She ordered a cup of coffee with skim milk and a toasted bagel with light cream cheese. Her father picked up his glass of Scotch to drain its contents, looking everywhere but at her. Curious.

"What was that all about?" Monica asked.

"What?" He stared at a point behind her left shoulder.

"You know what, Daddy. I heard the noise you made when Judge Easton entered the courtroom and sat on the bench. When he passed down my sentence, he actually smirked."

Milton Ian Accord rattled the ice cubes in his glass. He hated his first name. Everyone in town knew him as Ian. Why on earth the Accord family used such old-fashioned names was beyond Monica. Monica. Case in point. An old-fashioned name.

They used names of ancestors that had been

handed down from generation to generation. She supposed it was simply tradition.

Ian carried his age well, but signs of unhappiness, of discontentment, hovered around a sullen mouth. Whatever was bothering him had come on lately, but he wouldn't share it with her.

She stared at him hard. She wasn't going away. He finally gave in. "Gord Easton and I went to high school together."

"High school?" That old man and her dad?

He nodded.

"Same grade?"

Another nod.

"That's hard to believe. He looks a lot older than you."

"Gord likes sun, whiskey and cigars, and has the money to indulge as much as he wants." Tone derisive, he glanced around as though checking to make sure the man wasn't sitting nearby. Was the drink making him paranoid? Lately, there'd been a lot of this furtive checking-his-surroundings behavior. He wouldn't respond to direct questions about it, though, and Monica had run out of ideas to get out of him what was going on.

"He pampers himself with regular visits to the spa," Ian continued, "but with his lifestyle, it's like throwing a coat of paint on a house that's about to keel over. He owns a boat in Florida and spends all of his spare time on it."

"That explains his too-tanned skin—the alcohol

and cigars explain how dull it is. The guy needs a good diet and exercise regimen."

Her dad laughed. "That isn't going to happen."

"So you went to school together. That doesn't explain his animosity toward you."

Dad raised his glass and signaled the waitress for another. He ran his finger around wet rings of condensation on the table then said quietly, "It started in high school, but got worse over the years. We're both competitive. I seem to have a golden touch where investments are concerned, a real knack that Gord lacks. He envies my skill."

"But how would that have started in high school? You were already investing back then?"

"No. It wasn't that. In school, we were both in love with the same girl."

"Mom?" On a dime, Monica's mood became wistful. She wished she'd known her. Mom had died giving birth to her, and didn't that just leave her feeling bad, even all of these years later. Monica figured that was the thing that continually felt missing from her life—her mom.

With a philosophical shrug, her dad said, "I won the fair maiden's hand in marriage. And that's where the competition started. Gord was angry for years afterward. But how could we know the joke would be on the two of us?"

When Monica realized her dad was slurring his words, her already low spirits plummeted further. How could he be drunk at only one in the afternoon? This was so recent, she didn't know what to make of it.

"Mom's death was a joke?" she asked, her voice a sharp knife cutting the air.

Ian reared back. "God, no. Of course not."

He didn't elaborate. He'd been making a lot of cryptic remarks lately, but whenever she asked for clarification, he would change the subject.

"Well, what do you mean?" she queried. "What joke?"

His gaze had become unfocused. "Huh?"

"What joke was on you and Judge Easton?"

He shook his head and shuttered his expression. "Nothing."

She knew that closed look. No trespassing. This part of the discussion was over. She knew her dad well enough to understand she wouldn't get any more out of him. Okay, then she would change her tack.

"So he was getting revenge on losing Mom by sending your daughter farming? How does that make sense?"

"You never knew…your mother's parents died when you were still a toddler. Do you remember them?"

She shook her head.

"Your mother grew up on a farm. She and her family were the products of generations of farmers." When the waitress brought Monica's food, she also brought her dad another drink. Monica frowned, but he ignored it. "Gord thinks it's funny for my pampered daughter to now have to work on the land."

Monica's hackles raised at being called pampered, but only briefly. She was and she knew it. Or had been. Daddy had always given her everything she'd ever wanted.

Those days were gone because of her self-imposed austerity plan. By hook or by crook, she was supporting herself from now on.

She lifted the coffee to her lips.

Dad sipped his drink then said, "The farm Noah owns? The one Judge Easton sent you to?"

"What about it?" She took a sip.

"Used to be your mother's."

Monica finished choking on her coffee then wiped her mouth with her serviette. "Mom grew up on that farm and you never told me?"

"There was no point in mentioning it." Dad swirled his Scotch in his glass.

To a daughter craving every detail about a mother who had never actually existed in her life, Monica disagreed.

Why had Daddy felt it necessary to hide it from her? Or had he just never thought that her heritage mattered to her?

It did. She already knew all there was to know about the Accords. Talk about heritage. Dad had been super proud of his.

His great-grandfather Ian Accord had been a railway baron, had made his fortune building spur lines all over the West. Then he'd settled in the big Victorian that was now the town's B-and-B and bought up the surrounding land. When settlers flocked to the area, he sold that land at inflated prices, increasing his fortune. He spent his life nurturing and building his wealth for future generations.

Apparently, Daddy came by his business acumen honestly.

Ian had built schools and the bank and the library, along with an impressive city hall.

Then he had married a woman from back east named Maisie Hamilton and had started a dynasty.

Daddy had finished it.

Or maybe Monica had.

The likelihood of her having a family was slim to none.

She'd never worried about it until now.

"There's been a lot of death in our family, hasn't there?" she asked quietly, thinking of grandparents on both sides dying too young. With Mom's parents, it had been a car accident. With Dad's, a plane crash in the Rockies, with her grandfather at the controls in bad weather. Within weeks, her extended family had been decimated. No wonder Dad had been a heavy drinker for a while back then, or so she'd heard. Seems he was at it again. She wondered for the umpteenth time what was going on.

"Yes," her dad agreed soberly. "Far too much death."

"It's just you and me, Dad. We don't have any

other family left. Lots of deaths and too many only children." Dad had been an only child, like her. She missed having aunts and uncles.

"Yeah," he said shortly, his gaze sliding away, and Monica wondered what that was about.

Where was the history on her mother's side? Who were the Montgomerys? When she had asked him questions, he'd been vague at times, loquacious but nonspecific at others. He'd talked about Mom's character, her personality as bright as a new penny, her laughter that lit up a room, but nothing about her background.

Mom used to live on that farm.

When she asked, "So I'll be farming where Mom grew up?" she heard the yearning in her own voice.

Her father's lips compressed into a hard line. "Yep."

"So," she mused, "Judge Easton thinks it's poetic justice to send me off to my mother's farm to muck around in the soil and get my hands dirty."

"Essentially, yes. He probably agreed to the lesser charge to avoid jail time, to get you onto the farm."

She should be angry. In fact, a flash of refreshing righteousness passed through her, but was quickly replaced by curiosity. Mom had lived on Noah's farm. Monica would be putting her hands into the same earth her mother probably had.

Monica had relied on Daddy through the years to make her mother real for her. She did so again now.

"Tell me about her."

Ian Accord glanced away too swiftly and Monica

wondered yet again what his action meant. Dad was shifty today. Indirect.

In the next moment, though, a sad, sweet smile spread across his face and he opened his mouth to speak, bringing Monica into that dreamy state she entered before going to sleep at night.

"Did I ever tell you about the time she put a frog down the back of my pants? I was only ten, and she did it at school. I ran around the schoolyard like a chicken with its head cut off, trying to get that thing to shake out of one of my pant legs."

He laughed. "I pretended to be angry with her, but I wasn't really. I was already halfway to being in love with the girl."

Daddy's memories about Monica's mother had always been a lonely little girl's favorite bedtime stories.

That evening when she got home from work, she reached for the only photo she had of her mother. Her mood threatened to turn melancholy. That troublesome loneliness dogged her again. Look how it had gotten her into trouble last week. She couldn't let it get to her tonight.

Best to shake it off.

One thing she could do was make amends to Noah as best she could.

She turned on her computer and went online to search for vintage bikes. She had told Noah she would replace his bike and she meant to. He might not think her useful or smart, but there were two things she knew well—shopping and vintage anything.

Two hours later, she was ready to admit defeat. Who knew vintage bikes would be so hard to come by?

The only lead she found was a man in California who rebuilt bikes from parts. Tomorrow morning, she would get Noah's wrecked bike from him.

MONICA ROLLED OVER in bed onto her back and stared at the ceiling, motivation to get up and start another day eluding her. Her radio alarm had gone off at 6:00 a.m. and the same questions she faced every morning troubled her.

Do I care? Should I care? Why *should I care?*

On the radio, a female sang a bright and chirpy song. The falsely engineered cheer passed over her like a specter.

She spread a hand across the empty side of the bed, across the sheets that had been washed hundreds of times since Billy had gone to war. His pillowcase, though? That she hadn't changed or washed since he'd left for Afghanistan. For many nights afterward, she had curled herself around his pillow, drinking in his scent and missing him.

She changed and washed the sheets every week, turned and flipped the mattress twice a year, vacuumed under the bed, but never, ever, washed her late husband's pillow or pillowcase.

I miss you, Billy.

He'd been dead five years. Shouldn't the pain have eased by now? Why couldn't she let go of the grief?

You already know, don't you? What would you replace it with? What would fill your emptiness without your grief for your dead husband?

She hated when her smart-alecky brain or psyche or common sense, or whatever it was, knew the answers to questions she didn't really want solved.

The vacancy on Billy's side of the bed represented the gap in her life, in her soul, but then, it had always been there, hadn't it? Even long before hormones had kicked in and she'd started looking at cute, funny Billy Stone differently, she'd been empty. He'd become the most magical creature she'd ever known. He'd made her laugh.

He'd been everything. Her first, her one and only. He'd made love like an oversized puppy dog, with enthusiasm and greed and joy. Even in bed, they'd had a lot of fun.

She'd never slept with another man. She wouldn't even know how to approach sex with someone else.

He'd filled in the hollow, hungry holes that had been part of her for as far back as she could remember. Now he was gone and those holes were back, and she didn't have a clue how to fill them.

She reached over and flicked off the radio, cutting off some irritating song that would be played half a dozen more times before the day was over. The ensuing silence closed in on her, broken only by the tick of the ormolu clock on the mantel in the living room.

She hated the silence, hated all silence, had always hated that void that needed filling, and the feeling that something was missing. There was too much quiet and emptiness in her life these days.

On Friday night when she'd gone out drinking, she'd been going bonkers in this apartment. She'd been sick of the sound of her own voice, of the irritating ticking of the clock, of the useless, mind-numbing junk on TV.

Billy used to keep the void at bay. His practical jokes, wisecracks and ceaseless banter used to destroy the silence. Used to annihilate it. Now it was back in full force and Monica was lost.

No wonder she'd gone drinking when the silence of her apartment had made her climb the walls. She just shouldn't have driven home afterward.

She crawled out of bed with the energy of an old woman, reluctant to face Noah's wrath when she pulled plants instead of weeds. They all looked the same to her.

Then she remembered she was going to the farm her mom had grown up on.

Okay, maybe today she cared a little.

NOAH WALKED ALONG the row of green peppers to check on Monica and found her with her back to him, bent over at the waist plucking something from the earth.

Gold stitching on the back pockets of her blue jeans hugged the curves of her perfect derriere. Why,

oh why, couldn't he lust after a normal woman, someone with as much depth as the people he admired
in life? But no, he had to be as shallow as the next
man and want the one woman in town with the least
depth of character.

Audrey's voice rang in his memory. *Everybody
underestimates her.*

He tried to soften his stance. Hard to do when he
desired a woman he didn't respect. Cripes, he wished
she would squat to weed instead of bending over.

She straightened, noticed him watching her and
pointed to the pile beside her. "See? Only weeds."

"That's great."

"Before I leave today, will you put your wrecked
bike into the trunk of my car?"

"Sure, but why?"

"I'm going to take care of it."

It was useless to him. She could do what she liked
with it. "Listen, are you going in to work today?"

"No. Your mom and Aiden are both there. I have
today off because I'll be working on Saturday."

"Good." He hated to ask, didn't want Monica anywhere near this task, but had no choice. He needed
her two good arms. "We have to leave the farm, to
help some locals."

"What kind of help?"

"Feeding their families. I need you to come with
me."

"You mean as part of my sentence?"

Heaven forbid she should give of herself unless

someone forced her to. "Yeah, as part of your community service. I have to pack and deliver food, but I can't do it with this bum arm."

"Okay, show me what to do."

"Let's fill this first." He pulled from behind him an ancient child's wagon.

"That looks old."

"I guess it is," he answered with a shrug. All he cared about was that the thing was useful. "I found it in the shed."

She grasped his arm. "That's a Radio Flyer."

"So?"

"So, it's a vintage children's wagon. I love vintage."

She did? He would have never guessed she'd like old stuff. "Never mind that. We need to harvest some of the spring vegetables today."

"There are vegetables ready this early? Which ones?"

"Spring onions. Garlic scapes. Asparagus. Broccoli rabe. A little watercress."

"I lo-o-ove asparagus. I could eat it year-round."

The way she said *lo-o-ove* made him crazy, horny. Angry at his knee-jerk response, he reined himself in. He wasn't a randy teenager, for God's sake.

"It's amazing in risotto. There's this recipe I use—"

"You cook?"

She reacted to his surprise with a snooty lift of her chin. "Of course. Why wouldn't I?"

"I've just never thought of you as being, I don't know, domestic?"

Judging by the defiance in her expression, he'd offended her. "Cooking is one of my favorite hobbies."

Noah just managed to bite his tongue before blurting *cook for me.* He liked food, but couldn't bring himself to spend enough time in the kitchen to make really great, tasty stuff. Healthy, yes. Gourmet? No.

"It brings me joy," she continued. "So to whom are you taking these veggies?"

He stared at her. *To whom?* Who used that kind of grammar anymore?

"Will they know what to do with garlic scapes?" she asked.

"Do *you*?"

"Yes. In fact, may I buy some from you? There aren't any in the shops yet."

"I can't sell them. I'm a nonprofit."

"Hmmm." She set a finger, with its pink nail, against her chin. "How can we get around that? I'd really like some for dinner tonight. Can I make a donation to a charity in your name or something?"

"Yeah. We can work out something like that. You can make a donation to the food bank in Denver."

She smiled and his world became a brighter, ever-expanding thing. "Great! I'll take some asparagus, too. Anyway, you didn't answer my question. Will the people you're taking these to know how to use scapes? They're kind of a new trend. Most people just use straight garlic."

He shrugged. "You can ask when we get there."

She smiled…slyly, he thought. "You're going to let me come inside when you deliver the groceries? You're not going to make me sit in the truck?"

He'd wanted to do just that, but he couldn't carry in the produce on his own. How had she known?

"Of course. Why wouldn't I invite you in?"

"Because you don't want to harm your holier-than-thou reputation by being seen with an airhead like me?"

She'd skewered him, her assessment so dead-on it left him speechless.

She waved a hand. "Never mind. Let's move on. What should I pick?"

He pointed to one row. "Let's start with the green onions. You pull up about half of this row. I'll go cut down a row of asparagus."

When the wagon was full, Noah led the way to the barn. "These are the boxes I fill." He pointed to a bunch of plastic crates stacked neatly against one wall.

She started to fill one, but he stopped her. "Let's take them to the truck. If you fill them first, you won't be able to lift them."

"Oh, Noah, give me a break. I can lift a crate full of these veggies. Potatoes, turnips, maybe not. Green onions and garlic scapes? Can do."

Together, they filled the crates, fitting vegetables in for minimum bruising. When they were done, Monica bent at the knees, put her arms around the first one and stood. Noah watched as she carried it to the back of the truck, impressed despite his misgivings.

"How are you so strong?"

"I work out four times a week. I never let anything get in the way. Workouts have been my lifesaver."

He followed her back to the barn. "Lifesaver?"

"After Billy died, I needed something to do to work through the grief." She mentioned her grief matter-of-factly, without self-pity. Cool.

Funny, he'd never really considered how much she would grieve for Billy. He'd thought she'd go out shopping and that would be that. Man, he could be an idiot sometimes.

"When things got really bad…" She paused to pick up a full crate.

Things had gotten bad for her. He'd never given her much thought at that time outside of the standard expressions of compassion, but she'd lost her husband, for God's sake.

He had spent his adult life avoiding contact with her and didn't really know who she was, outside of someone who would drink and drive. Who would knock him off his bike. And ruin his bike. And break his arm. And prevent him from getting his work done. There was all of that that was still wrong with her.

"Gabe Jordan taught me how to lift weights." She returned to what she'd been saying. "And how to set up a good running program."

Gabe. Billy's best friend. For a while after Billy's death, the town had speculated that something might be forming between Gabe and Monica. Next thing they heard, Gabe was marrying the new woman in town, Callie MacKintosh.

Subdued because he had indeed underestimated her, he said, "Let's fill a couple more and head out."

Before they left, she returned the tools she'd been using to the shed, as he'd taught her. He had to maintain his tools meticulously since he didn't have money to replace any that weren't cared for properly. Nice to see she was paying attention to him.

"Should I take my own car?"

He was tempted to say yes to give his libido a rest, but the thought of the two of them driving separate vehicles to the same places went so far against the grain with his need to conserve, that he couldn't let it happen, not even if it meant spending time with her in the too-tight cab of his ancient truck.

"We have to come back here to pick scapes and asparagus for you anyway, so ride along in the truck with me."

She slipped off the big old rubber boots she was still borrowing from him and into the baby blue suede loafers she'd been wearing when she got here this morning.

"Where is your bike?" She joined him at the truck. "The one I wrecked?"

"In the back stall of the barn."

"I'll put it in my trunk now so I don't forget it."

Curious. "What are you going to do with it?"

"I'm going to try to get it fixed."

"I don't think you can."

"Let me be the judge of that."

As if she knew anything about bikes. She helped him retrieve it from the barn anyway, along with the parts that had been knocked off, and then she loaded it into her car trunk.

It was a mess. He didn't expect to see it again.

They drove for a couple of miles in silence, mileage underscored by the constant rolling hum of tires on pavement. He wracked his brain for something to say to this woman he barely knew even though they'd grown up in the same town, had attended the same schools, had witnessed the same births, deaths and marriages. How could a couple of people who'd shared so much also have shared so little? They were neither friends nor strangers.

What did he expect? That's what came of living in the same town but avoiding each other—of him avoiding her, that is. He didn't know what had been going on in her head all of those years. And he was becoming curious.

CHAPTER THREE

"DON'T YOU EVER TALK?" Monica's question cut through the tension in the cab.

"Huh?"

"Why are you so quiet? Don't you believe in casual conversation?"

He bristled. He talked all the time to people with whom he was comfortable. He was not comfortable with Monica. Not by a long shot.

He thought of all of the times in high school when he'd wanted more from her—not more attention, but *any* attention. She hadn't even noticed him. Now *she* wanted more from *him*? In his book, his respect had to be earned.

It wasn't something she deserved just because her name happened to be the same as that of the town's founding father. Nor because she had money and he didn't. She had no right to his conversation or his inner thoughts because she hadn't earned them.

"I talk when I have something important to say." Damn. He hadn't meant to sound so cold.

He felt her withdraw. He needed to monitor his responses and treat her better. He wasn't mean-spirited. Not usually. Her scent, so different from his own, filled the cab. "Why do you smell different today than yesterday?"

"You noticed?" She sounded surprised. "I thought it was a subtle change."

"It is subtle. I mean, it's like you changed your perfume, but didn't. Like it's the same perfume, but slightly different. Yesterday, it smelled more citrusy, like lemon, and today it's more…not quite floral, but sort of like bergamot."

When she didn't respond, he glanced away from the road for a second to find her staring at him with her mouth open.

"I'm impressed, Noah." She nodded slowly. "Seriously impressed. You have a sensitive nose. That's exactly the change I made."

"Say what? The change *you* made? What do you mean?"

"I make my own perfume."

"You do?" She kept surprising him, piquing his curiosity. "I've never known anyone who made their own perfume."

"I've been experimenting with different essential and natural oils."

"Why? There are a million perfumes on the market."

"I know, but I haven't found one that suited me perfectly. There's always something wrong with them, or something missing. Or, they're way too strong. I like concocting original, personal scents."

"So you added bergamot to the perfume you were wearing yesterday?"

"I have a base perfume that I've been slowly working on. I have several different mixtures going at any given time."

"Why bergamot?"

"Because I like it in Earl Grey tea. It's fragrant and floral without being sickly sweet."

"You know, I have wildflowers in my fields."

"What kind?"

"All kinds. You should check them out."

"May I steal some?" *May* I, not *can* I. Perfect grammar again. He liked it.

"Of course. I also grow herbs."

"You do? You grow them fresh on the farm?" She sounded excited.

"Yep."

She was silent for a while and then asked, "Will you teach me about them? Help me learn to recognize them?"

"Sure."

Silence fell again.

"May I turn on the radio?"

He nodded and she fiddled with the knobs. The cab filled with music, but she kept the volume turned low, sort of as background filler.

"So these are people who don't have enough money to buy their own groceries?" Monica asked as they approached the small Keil ranch.

"The Keils are having trouble making ends meet right now."

"Why? Is the father crippled or something?"

Noah tensed. "Nothing so Dickensian. Robert has been hanging onto his small ranch for years. He's a hard worker, by the way." A note of defensiveness had crept in.

Flatly, Monica replied, "I didn't say he wasn't."

"Rich people—" he glanced swiftly down at the designer jeans she wore "—often assume that anyone out of work or hungry is just lazy."

She stared out the window, but said, voice low and quiet, "Noah, please stop making assumptions about me. You don't know me."

His conscience pricked, he relented. "Fair enough. I'm sorry." He found he was sorry in truth. They had to get along—they were stuck with each other. And this roller coaster of flaring and abating tension would exhaust them both.

She deserved an explanation. Maybe then she would understand how a simple family managing all right could suddenly find themselves in dire straits through no fault of their own. A reversal of fortune could happen to anyone. As he thought about it more, he realized that Monica probably would understand, because hadn't Billy's death been a reversal of fortune for her? Her fortune being her happiness?

"Robert was hanging on, doing all right for himself and his family, when his wife got ovarian cancer. Kayla beat it. She's in remission. But the medical bills just about bankrupted them. I imagine they'll be paying for years."

"Oh." Monica's voice sounded small. "I remember Kayla from high school. She was a year or two behind me." Then she appeared to have a thought. "They own land. Why can't they grow their own vegetables?"

A reasonable question. "Kayla kept a large kitchen garden before the cancer, but the illness depleted her energy stores. She's just now getting back to a semblance of normalcy. There's only so much Robert can do. He has his own chores caring for the cattle and planting the big fields with feed. He can't also be maintaining the kitchen garden."

She seemed to be thinking hard.

"The problem for most people," he explained, "especially small farmers and ranchers, is that they live close to the edge. If something happens, a child gets sick, or we have a really dry summer, they have no buffer. Nothing to fall back on."

"Are there lots of families like that around?"

"More than you'd think. Things got real bad in 2009 with the recession. Economy's picked up a bit since then, but not enough. People have their pride, too—which is another problem. They don't always ask for help, then suddenly you hear they've gone bankrupt, or lost the ranch, or moved away for no apparent reason. I don't want to see that happen to the Keils. They're good people who've lived here for generations."

He turned up the long driveway. The house and grounds were clean and tidy.

The last time Noah had been here was late last autumn when he'd brought a couple of boxes of root vegetables to get them through the winter. He'd helped Robert fill the old root cellar. They'd have surely eaten those vegetables by now.

He glimpsed the herd in the pasture, noticeably smaller than last summer. Robert was either selling off cattle, or slaughtering and eating them. Probably both. You can't make money on slaughtered cattle, but a family's got to eat.

Monica retrieved one of the boxes of food from the back.

"You sure you don't want to wait here?" Noah held his breath. Now that she'd put him in his place, he found he was doing a one-eighty. He wanted her to visit with the Keils, wanted to make these people real to her, make this more than court-ordered community work. He needed her to understand why this was important.

"I'll come in."

Yes. Noah released his breath. Monica had more backbone than he'd given her credit for. Or maybe it was just morbid curiosity.

Robert and Kayla greeted them at the front door with their three young children.

Like the house, the children were clean, but their clothing had seen better days.

Kayla was thin. She used to be a round, jolly woman. Now, her blouse hung from too-slim shoulders, but she offered them a smile and a welcome.

Noah noticed Kayla checking out Monica's clothes and wished she'd worn something other than designer jeans and suede loafers. Even her attire for the farm was more expensive than the average person's. Did Monica own anything cheap? Not likely.

At least she smiled at Kayla and said hi.

Despite Kayla's discomfort—she looked intimidated by Monica—the woman invited them in for coffee. Some people never failed to impress Noah. This was why he raised crops for those less fortunate than himself—because of grace, and because these were good people who deserved a break.

After setting the box of food on the kitchen counter, Monica accepted a cup of coffee. Kayla handed Noah a cup and he sipped. Weak as dishwater.

They all sat at the kitchen table. Conversation was scarce and awkward. Monica gave Kayla surprisingly good ideas for using the garlic scapes, nothing that would cost the family much to implement.

Kayla blurted, "I've been looking for work, Noah. Robert and I won't have to depend on you forever."

"Hey, that's great. What kind of job are you looking for?"

Kayla's fingers worried the hem of her blouse. "Simple things. I was a cashier at the grocery store when I married Robert. I've been home with the kids ever since."

Noah didn't respond, didn't want to dash Kayla's hopes. She'd been out of the market for, at a guess, ten or so years, and her skills were limited.

Monica and Noah rose to leave.

Noah said goodbye and left the house. Monica

whispered something to Kayla before she followed him to the car.

Whatever she'd said to Kayla had put a smile on the woman's face.

In the truck, he asked, "What was that about?"

She fiddled with the air vents to get a breeze blowing her way and flicked on the radio again, with the volume low. "What was what about?"

"What did you whisper to Kayla to make her so happy?"

"I told her I had a dress I didn't want anymore and I would bring it out to her for her job interviews." She buckled herself in and they left the property, driving down the highway toward the next delivery. "I'll bring her some makeup, too."

"That's really something." Noah couldn't hide his surprise. "That's really nice of you."

"I'm not the monster you think I am."

He tensed. "I never said you were a monster."

"Oh, please, Noah," she scoffed. "You think I'm vain and selfish."

"Yeah. So?"

He expected her to take offense, but she chuffed out a laugh. So, Miss Monica had a certain level of self-awareness of how she was perceived by others. "Honestly, Noah, you're too blunt. Thanks for the boost to my ego."

The interior of the truck heated with the goodwill emanating from Monica. She had a sense of humor about herself. Noah would have never guessed. He

liked teasing her. "Hey, I believe in being honest."
He softened that with a smile in his voice.

"I like good clothes and nice things, but I'm not
selfish."

"No, I guess not." Noah smiled at her, momentarily in harmony with a woman who wasn't as bad
as he had assumed.

His perception of Monica shifted.

The next family they visited had had a string of
hard-luck events that had left them destitute.

"This damned economy." Back in the truck after
the visit, Noah pounded his fist on the steering wheel.
"When will this recession end?"

Monica remained silent, a thoughtful frown furrowing her brow.

They made one more stop, again staying for coffee.

Truck empty and produce gone, they headed home.

Monica stared out the passenger window at the
passing scenery.

Noah hoped she'd learned a few good lessons
today.

As though she sensed his regard, she met his gaze.
"You're doing this all wrong."

He choked on his saliva. When he finished cough-
ing, he stared at her. "*Wrong?* What the hell are you
talking about?" Honest to God, he was a peace-
loving guy, but she made his blood boil.

Frowning, she admonished, "Watch your language."

He ignored that, dealing instead with the salient
points. "I feed the hungry. I work my fingers to the

bone to help the poor. I wear cheap clothes, not designer duds." His disgusted glance raked her body.

"Keep your eyes on the road," she said, calm despite his raised voice. "It isn't safe to look at your passenger while you're driving."

"Says Ms. DWAI. Oh, pardon me, Ms. Wet Reckless."

She pressed her hand against her stomach. "That's a low blow. I told you I've never done it before and I never will again."

"I don't care. Why did you say I'm doing this all wrong? What, in your not-so-humble opinion, am I not doing right?"

"First of all, we shouldn't have had coffee at those houses."

"Oh, that. Yeah, I'm wired on caffeine, but I don't want to hurt their feelings by saying no."

"I don't mean that." She flipped hair out of her face with an impatient hand. "Coffee and tea are expensive. If they can't afford vegetables, they certainly can't afford to replace whatever meager supplies of coffee they might have. We're robbing them of a treat for themselves."

He hadn't thought of that. She was right. Both were expensive commodities. Suddenly he got a terrible feeling maybe they kept them on hand just for his visits.

"Also…"

"There's more I'm doing wrong?" He didn't bother to quell the sarcasm in his voice. He didn't believe in sarcasm, liked to deal with people honestly, but she'd just blown his decency out of the water. *Doing it all wrong, my ass.*

"You shouldn't deliver the groceries to them—"

"Some families are too embarrassed to drive into Denver to the food bank, not to mention using gas."

"I can imagine. I would be, too. What I meant to say, before you interrupted me so rudely, was that you shouldn't deliver the groceries when they're home. Deliver them when they're sleeping or when they're at work or church or something."

She'd snagged his curiosity. "Why?"

"Those visits were brutally difficult. All of that awkward small talk. We're not meeting them as equals. It's not a social visit. They were chagrined that we were there delivering charity to them."

"So?"

"So-o-o…" She exaggerated the word, as though speaking to a child. The woman knew how to get his dander up. "If the visits are hard for us, imagine how hard they are for them. If you're delivering food once every week or two, then you're drinking their coffee and embarrassing them on a regular basis."

Even though it hurt his pride, he admitted she was making sense.

"Plus," she said with such emphasis he grew wary, "you're not doing enough."

"What?" She'd poleaxed him again. Swear words bounced around inside his head like pinballs. *"Are*

you kidding me? How can you say that? I work from dawn 'til midnight every day. I'm doing all I can."

"I know you work hard." She patted his arm.

"Don't condescend to me." He sounded fierce.

"Sorry. I hate when people do that to me. I won't do it again." She removed her hand. "You do great work, Noah, but you could do more."

"More?" Heat blazing through him like a bonfire, his tone could char toast. Her criticism was so damned unfair. "I work my butt off fourteen hours a day. I do the work that everyone *should* be doing, but hardly anyone does—caring for my fellow man and the environment. This stuff should be universal. It should come naturally to everyone. But I'm the only one in this community out here doing it day in and day out." He poked himself in the chest so hard it hurt.

She opened her mouth to speak, but he ran roughshod over her. *Not doing enough, my patootie.*

"If that sounds arrogant or self-righteous, too bad. I have more passion about these issues in my baby finger than you do in your whole body. I believe in peace and love and communal property and service for the greater good. You believe in clothes, fancy cars, Calvin Klein—"

She gasped. "I *never* wear Calvin Klein—"

"—and rampant consumerism. You're the most shallow person I know."

Only when silence filled the quiet cab did Noah realize he'd been shouting, his last sentence ringing like the bong of a brass bell, its echo still reverberating like a heartbeat.

Oh, geez, that was bad. He shouldn't have been so harsh. Honesty was a good thing, but not when it devastated another soul...

Tentatively, he glanced at Monica.

She stared out the passenger window, her blond hair falling forward and hiding her face.

Oh, sweet freaking crap. He'd hurt her. He didn't do that to people.

Noah struggled to calm his thundering pulse. Sure, he had no patience for excess and waste and hunger and poverty, but he never lashed out at individuals unless they were doing truly egregious things. He never spoke this harshly. He never insulted people or called them names.

She'd been getting under his skin since she'd stepped onto his farm and started ripping out tender plants instead of weeds.

He'd learned, as Audrey had said, that it was easy to underestimate Monica. While she might have an uncomplicated soul, she wasn't stupid. On the other hand, she had no right to criticize him. He did a world of good for those in need while she sat at home and painted her fingernails pink or, worse, paid someone else to do it.

While Kayla struggled to feed her family, Monica probably had weekly manis, pedis and whatever else people did at spas.

Breathing deeply of the warm air flowing through

his open window, he pulled himself under control. His anger was doing neither of them any good.

He heard her sniff and a surge of remorse flooded him.

He placed his fingers on the cool skin of her arm, but she jerked it away from him and shrank against the car door.

"I'm sorry. Really. Don't cry."

She rounded on him, red spots on her high cheekbones. "I'm not crying. I'm angry." She leaned toward him, straining against her seat belt. "I do a lot more than you give me credit for. You've always thought you were better than me."

"*What?* It's the other way around," he yelled. He jabbed a finger her way. "*You* think you're better than *me*. You've got it backward."

"I do not," she responded hotly. "I think you're hardworking and smart. You think I'm lazy and stupid. So who thinks he's better than whom?"

Okay, so maybe he did think she was lazy and did nothing much outside of shopping and pampering her body. He knew she and his mom liked to go to spas together. It was like Mom had adopted her as another child. And yeah, he might think Monica was lazy. How hard could working in a gallery be?

He mimicked her in his mind. *Who thinks he's better than whom?* It was petty, but it felt good. As quickly as his indignation flared, it abated. Her shot had been a bull's-eye. He did think himself superior to her, and to all of her kind.

And that was wrong. He needed to see her as an individual, and he needed to remember that he trusted Audrey's opinion. If she saw more in Monica than what was on the surface, he should, too. Besides, he *had* seen glimmers of depth in her today.

His righteousness deflated.

"Tell me," he said quietly.

"Tell you what?" Her body language still screamed that she was a prickly, angry woman.

Other than eating crow, which he wouldn't do, the only way to appease her was to listen. "What else could I be doing?"

For a long time she sat without speaking and he feared he'd hurt her so much she wouldn't respond. Now that the heat of his anger was spent, he wanted to know what she thought.

"Tell me," he urged, touching her arm again, and this time she didn't pull away. Her soft skin warmed his fingertips. "I want to know."

"Fund-raise," she said. "Raise money so you can deliver meat and diapers and lots of other stuff with the vegetables and eggs, including a few luxuries like coffee and tea. Maybe even deliver seeds in the spring so they can grow their own stuff."

She was right, damn her.

"I don't think I'm qualified to fund-raise," he responded.

"I am," she said and he heard in her a confidence that was missing on the farm.

"How so?"

"I was tutored by the best fund-raiser around."

When he looked at her questioningly, she said, "Believe it or not, my dad. He might look like he does nothing but sit around all day and have lunch at the country club, but boy, does that guy know how to network." She lifted the hair from the back of her neck where a sheen of sweat glistened, her arms strong and firm, and her breasts high. Noah glanced away before he started some pretty hot daydreaming. "When I was little, he took me with him everywhere. I watched and listened and learned. I could set up a charity event in Denver that would bring in big bucks."

Noah snorted.

Monica shot him a look. "Really, Noah, that's uncouth. If you don't believe me, just say so."

"I don't believe you can do it."

"I can." She sounded huffy, indignant, and he found it far too cute, so cute he wanted to provoke her further.

"How do I know it wouldn't be a waste of time?"

"You'd have to trust me."

Ah, there was the rub. He'd trusted before and where had it gotten him? Screwed, royally, by a woman just like Monica, a woman who walked, talked and spoke like Monica...and who schemed like the devil.

"Wouldn't it be a lot of work?"

"Yes. Dad worked his tail off when he raised funds, but he also had a host of women organizing

the events, women with wealthy husbands, who do-
nated their days to running charities. Lucky for you,
I still know all of them."

The desire to do more and feed more people
threaded tentacles of temptation through him. "You
would do all of that work for my charity?"

She looked surprised. "Of course. Why wouldn't
I? I like this helping-people business, Noah."

A gentle, satisfied smile spread across Noah's face.
"So do I." And it felt fabulous to share that with
someone. So good, in fact, he was willing to eat
crow after all and admit he had a thing or two to
learn about charity from Monica. In his hubris, he'd
thought the learning would go only one way.

ON MAIN STREET, Monica headed for the organic
market, Tonio's, hoping to figure out what she'd have
for dinner.

Until a year ago, it had been called the Organic
Bud, but the Colantonios had since bought it. Now,
along with local organic produce, they had introduced a lot of international products.

Monica loved shopping here.

As an Accord living in the town named for the
founding father, her ancestor, she had always felt
apart from most people. She had never had Billy's
easygoing personality that drew people to him.

Her natural reserve had gotten in the way of her
being a real part of this town. She could never figure out whether people liked *her*, or were awed by

her background, or wanted to cozy up to her father's wealth.

But the owner of Tonio's was a friend, Maria Colantonio, a woman not much older than her with whom Monica had formed a bond over a love of good food. With Maria, she felt at ease. Maria liked her for herself, no doubt about it. For that, Maria had Monica's undying affection.

"Hey, Maria," she called to the open indoor window of the office through which Maria watched the store. "What's good today? I have fresh asparagus and garlic scapes."

Short, round Maria ran down the four steps out of the office, clapping her hands. An attractive woman, her deep-set brown bedroom eyes lit up. "You have scapes already? Where did you get them?"

"Noah Cameron's farm."

"Oh, that guy." Maria flipped her hand in a disparaging gesture.

"He's a good guy." After watching what Noah did for local families, and seeing how much they appreciated him, Monica felt compelled to defend him. Lord knew why, except that maybe she was developing an appreciation for his charity, even if he was doing it all wrong. "He does good work."

"Oh, I know. He's wonderful."

"Then why do you seem disgusted by him?"

"Because he won't sell me his lovely vegetables! He's the only one around here growing organic. He could make a fortune selling to me, but he gives it all away."

"For the needy." A swell of warm, fuzzy pride arose in Monica that she was helping him. But she was also proud of Noah, that he had the guts to buck financial common sense and everyone who screamed at him that he could be making money, so he could feed people in need. She smiled. "He's a decent guy."

Maria sighed. "Oh, I know, I know, but you have garlic scapes and I don't and I'm jealous." She laughed and directed Monica toward the meat counter.

"Joseph," she called to her husband. He came out from the back, where he butchered meat. Big and handsome, he carried his dark Italian good looks humbly.

Maria surveyed the meat on display and ordered, "Give Monica a couple of those nice thick center-cut pork chops."

"I live to serve." Despite the sarcasm, Joseph's tone was also filled with amused affection. Monica had seen him give his wife a pat on her butt or place an arm around her waist when he thought no one was looking.

When Joseph handed Monica the wrapped meat, she blew him a kiss. He slammed his hands against his large chest, over his heart. "My day is complete."

Maria laughed. "You two are shameless. Monica, stop flirting with my husband. Joseph, stop playing to the balcony."

"Me and Monica, we're running away together."

Maria drew Monica toward the front of the store, stating loudly enough over her shoulder for her husband to hear, "You can have him, Monica. He's more trouble than he's worth."

"Ha! I'm the guy who puts up with a wife with a sharp tongue."

Monica giggled. "If anyone tried to come between you and Joseph, you would fight her tooth and nail."

Maria grinned. "True, but don't tell my Joseph that. It's good to keep him on his toes."

Monica became serious. "Maria, is there any way you would be able to hire a friend of mine?"

"To do what?"

"Anything. Working on cash, or filling produce bins, or stocking shelves." She explained about Kayla Keil's situation.

Maria tsked. "The poor woman. Every day I thank my lucky stars that I have a good life. Problem is, I can only hire part-time right now."

"Maria, trust me, Kayla will take anything."

"Okay, send her to me then."

Monica paid for her items then walked down to her lawyer's office. Maybe having two part-time jobs would work for Kayla.

Just inside the lawyer's doorway, she stared at the empty receptionist's desk. She glanced at her watch. Of course. It was after hours. But the office should have been closed and the front door locked. She called, "Hello?"

John Spade stepped out of his office, brows raised. A warm smile blossomed when he saw her. He took both of her hands in his and kissed her cheeks, cloaking her with a sophisticated aftershave he had applied with a light hand. Nice.

She liked the scent. Maybe she should try to develop men's colognes.

A handsome man, polished and well-dressed, John had asked Monica out in the past. She had gone out with him on several dates, but there had never been enough chemistry between them. There was, however, plenty of respect and affection.

Many in town thought him cold. She hadn't had that experience with him. She'd bet the man could be as cutthroat as he needed to be in business, though.

"Working so late in the evening, John?"

"Of course. The clock never stops."

And didn't that sum up John Spade in a nutshell? She explained about Kayla needing part-time work, but having few skills. "Unless you can give her full-time hours?"

"No. My receptionist, Linda, is more than capable." He tapped her empty desk. "Though she has been missing work lately because her grandmother is sick. She's running behind on a few things. I'm sure she could use support with filing, answering the phone, or filling in when she has to take her grandmother for appointments. We can start Kayla on simple stuff, a few hours a week, and train her to do more."

"John, thank you. I mean it. Kayla needs this badly."

He delivered one caveat. "She will have to dress well. I have an image to maintain."

"She will. Not to worry. May I bring her in tomorrow morning for an interview?" She crossed her fingers that Kayla would be available. She wanted to get her out and earning a paycheck as quickly as possible.

"Yes. I'll be here."

Before she left, Monica said, "John, she'll be nervous in her interview, especially with you."

"Me? Why?"

"You're polished, attractive and rich. She's a farm girl. She will be intimidated, guaranteed. Go easy on her."

"I'll be gentle," he promised.

Satisfied, Monica stepped out of his office and took her groceries home. Once there, she got on the phone to a delivery company and arranged for them to not only pick up the bike and parts, but to also bring a box large enough for her to package it in.

By dinnertime, it was on its way to California. Monica crossed her fingers that the repairman would be able to fix it. It was the least she could do for Noah.

After dinner, she got Kayla's number through directory assistance and phoned her.

During their conversation, she made the determination that Kayla would love two part-time jobs as long as she could work the hours out with both employers.

As far as clothing went, Kayla thought she might have something nice enough to work in a grocery store, but not a law office.

When the young woman started to fret, Monica assured her, "No problem, Kayla. Let me handle that part. I have to be at work by ten tomorrow. Can I come out to your place before eight?"

After she hung up, she searched her closet for something that didn't look too expensive. She chose one simple gray dress, sleeveless with classic lines, which she'd always worn with a pair of stunning Stuart Weitzmans shoes, but the shoes would look too dressy for a job interview.

She spotted a navy blue wrap dress that would look good with Kayla's dark hair. Both dresses would be about an inch too long for Kayla, but that was no big deal.

A plain white blouse and black pencil skirt rounded out the wardrobe. She tucked them all into a suit bag then loaded a cosmetic bag with shades of makeup she thought might suit Kayla, along with other items she suspected the woman would need. In her jewelry box, she found a simple gold chain and a bangle bracelet.

She had one pair of black ballet flats that Kayla could wear with all three outfits. They would have to do for now. Once Kayla made some money, she could fill out her wardrobe herself.

CHAPTER FOUR

THE FOLLOWING MORNING, Monica showered, put everything into the car and drove out to the Keil farm. She carried her goodies to the door.

When Kayla answered her knock, her flat expression quickly turned into a smile. "I didn't think you would really come."

"Of course I came," Monica replied. "I said I would, didn't I?"

"This is so kind of you."

Monica waved away that comment. "You need a little help. I can give it." She stepped into the house while Kayla eyed her packages.

"Can we go to your bedroom so you can try this stuff on?"

"Yes! Follow me."

Once upstairs in Kayla's very tidy bedroom, Monica took the clothes out of their plastic sleeve. Kayla gasped.

"Oh, this is beautiful. It's all so classy." She touched the linen of one dress reverently. "Too classy for me. This will never work."

"Strip," Monica ordered. "Let's see how it looks on you before we decide whether it works."

The dress pulled a bit tightly at Kayla's middle—she'd had three children, after all—but other than that, it fit.

Noah was right. With the cancer, she'd lost the

plumpness that had made her so pretty. But all was not lost. Monica knew her way around hair and makeup. She could bring out Kayla's beauty.

Monica slipped the simple gold chain over Kayla's neck and then added the bangle to her wrist. "If you have a dressy little watch, wear it. Otherwise, if what you have looks too old, keep it in your purse. Personally, I don't like watches, but we have to be on time for work, don't we?"

Shell-shocked, Kayla nodded.

"Try on the shoes. I hope they fit."

Kayla slipped them on. They were slightly too long. Monica stuffed the toes with tissues. "This will have to do until you can afford to buy a pair."

Kayla stared at herself in the cheap full-length mirror on the back of the bedroom door.

"Oh," Kayla breathed. "I look so good. I'll have to buy pantyhose."

"No," Monica ordered after a horrified gasp. "Never, ever, wear pantyhose in the summertime."

"But my legs are so pale."

"That's okay. Use baking soda to exfoliate then moisturize. Cheap skin cream will do for your legs. Just make sure they shine. Got it?"

Kayla smiled. "Got it, boss."

A small grin tugged at Monica's mouth. She liked Kayla's pluckiness.

"How long may I borrow all of this?" Kayla smoothed the dress over her hips. "It will take me a few weeks to be able to purchase an outfit. We have heavy debts."

"Oh, I'm not lending it to you. It's yours to keep." Monica picked up the bag of makeup she'd packed and stepped toward the hallway to find the washroom. When Kayla didn't follow, she stopped.

"You can't," Kayla said.

"I can't what?"

"You can't just give all of this to me. It's too expensive."

Monica set down the stuff she'd been fiddling with. "Okay, listen, Kayla. Every day I'm aware of how fortunate I am. The worst thing that ever happened to me was Billy's death."

She sat down on the bed, because she couldn't talk about him without getting sad. Kayla sat beside her and tentatively put her arm around Monica's shoulders. Monica leaned into her for a moment and then rallied. "But I have a roof over my head and enough food to eat. I have nice clothes because my dad used to spoil me. I don't let him anymore. These days, I'm making my own way in the world."

She touched Kayla's knee. "But you…you are dealing with hardships I hope I never have to face. You should be given a helping hand. What Noah is doing for you is wonderful, but it isn't enough. You need big changes to see you through to a better future and I'm trying to see that you get them."

Kayla's eyes were glazed with unshed tears.

Monica's vision blurred. Too much emotion. She stood abruptly.

"Do you wear makeup?"

"Never."

"I thought so. I brought some. I'll show you how to apply it so you don't look overdone. Where's your bathroom?" Kayla led her down the hallway, where she turned on the lights over the mirror despite sunlight pouring in through the sole window.

"You have good skin," Monica observed. "Let's skip foundation. It can look awful if it isn't applied properly."

She took a small jar of cream out of the bag. "Even though your skin is good, you need to moisturize like crazy. Use this every night before bed, got it?"

Kayla smiled softly and held the jar with the reverence a cream that expensive deserved. "You are amazing."

Monica welled up. No one ever said nice things about her. Noah thought the worst of her, Gabe Jordan had chosen another woman over her, and most people thought she wasn't really that smart, but Kayla was looking at her as though she hung the moon and the stars. This helping-people business was amazing.

"Okay, on to the makeup," she said briskly, blinking a lot because of moisture in her eyes messing with her eyesight. "Light and natural will suit you best."

Ten minutes later, she'd taught Kayla everything

she needed to know about applying makeup for both interviews and at work.

She studied Kayla's hair, understanding there was no money for either a haircut or coloring.

"Okay, this is what we're going to do." She pulled out her natural bristle brush and brushed Kayla's short hair until it shone.

"It grew in all right," Kayla said. "After the cancer, I thought it would never come back, but it eventually did."

"It looks healthy. See how it shines?"

Kayla's sad smile was also proud. "When you don't have money for junk food, when you have to prepare all of your food naturally, it's good for your skin and hair, I guess. Maybe that's the only good thing that's come out of the past few years."

Kayla's bittersweet smile hit Monica in the solar plexus. On impulse, she threw her arms around the woman. Monica might not be demonstrative, might not hand out hugs easily, but Kayla deserved one so much.

"The really good thing that happened was that you stayed alive." When Monica pulled back, they were both teary. "Don't ruin your makeup. Suck in a big breath."

They both did and when they exhaled at the same time, they laughed. Monica had made a new friend. All she had done was put herself out a little and she'd won the lottery.

Was this how Noah felt when he did things for

people? Was the result always so rewarding? She should ask him.

"Let's finish your hair." Monica filled her palm with hair putty and rubbed it between her hands before applying it to Kayla's hair. She scrunched clumps of it between her fingers and arranged it artfully to frame the woman's face.

Kayla stared at herself in the mirror, wide-eyed and happy. "I look beautiful. I don't look like myself at all."

"Nonsense," Monica said. "The benefit of makeup when it's applied well is that you look *more* like yourself."

She packed the makeup back into the bag. "Hide this somewhere so your children don't get into it. Kids love makeup."

"Kids love *everything* they shouldn't." Something had clicked and come alive in Kayla. She positively glowed.

"Let's go," Monica said. "Can you drive yourself into town behind me? I won't have time to drive you home afterward."

"Of course."

They walked downstairs just as Robert entered the house. When he saw his wife, his jaw dropped.

"Robert," Kayla said, voice full of laughter, "what do you think?"

"You look…amazing. So pretty."

As Monica passed Robert on her way out, noting the patent desire and admiration for his wife, she said, "Don't you two go making any more babies tonight. Three are enough!"

Kayla kissed Robert's cheek and stepped toward the front door. "Wish me luck on my job interviews…and on our old clunker actually getting me into town!"

Robert nodded, his eyes never leaving his wife.

In Accord, they went to Tonio's first—it had already been open for an hour—where Monica introduced Kayla to Maria. They had a chat that seemed to consist more of talking about children than about job qualifications, then Maria stated, "We can definitely find things for you to do here. When can you start?"

"Right away. Right now."

"First we have to see John Spade," Monica interjected. "I've set up an interview with him. Kayla will need two part-time jobs. Can you work out her hours around whatever John can give her?"

Maria patted Kayla's arm. "We'll make it work."

Walking along Main to the only legal office in town, Kayla said, "I've never been inside Tonio's before. I used to grow most of our fresh produce and then shopped for everything else at the discount grocery store. I can't afford Tonio's, but what an amazing place. They have all kinds of products I've never seen before. And Maria is so nice!"

As Monica opened John's front door, she waggled her eyebrows at Kayla, knowing she looked comical, but she was totally okay with it. She needed to get Kayla loosened up. "Maybe you'll get a discount as an employee."

Kayla laughed. Good. She was in great spirits. Maybe she wouldn't be intimidated by John.

Monica greeted his receptionist, who alerted her boss.

As handsome as ever, even though he'd probably burned the midnight oil last night, John approached, hand outstretched toward Kayla.

"John," Monica asked, "have you met Kayla before?"

He shook her hand. "I've seen you around town."

John was older than both Kayla and Monica. They hadn't been in high school at the same time.

"Step into my office and we'll chat. Monica, can I offer you coffee while you wait?"

"I'm good, thanks, John." She sat on a small leather love seat. John ushered Kayla ahead of himself. Just before he entered his office, he glanced back at Monica. She mouthed *be kind*.

He winked.

Ten minutes later, Kayla came out with a wide grin. "I got the job," she whispered.

Of course she did. Once John had promised Monica he'd give Kayla a job, he would follow through, unless Kayla was thoroughly unsuitable, which she wasn't. She was eager, willing and intelligent. She could learn whatever needed to be learned.

And apparently, for the next two days she would be learning the ropes at John Spade's office.

They went back to the market.

"Okay," Maria said. "We can operate around John's hours, but if he can let us have you on Saturdays, it would help us a lot."

"I'll ask him," Kayla said, her fingers threaded nervously.

"No, you won't," Monica said. "I'll stop in and ask him on my way to work. Speaking of which, we'd better go."

They stepped out of the store and nearly collided with Noah.

When he saw her, his expression darkened. Completely ignoring Kayla's presence—or not even seeing her there—he addressed Monica. "Where were you this morning?" His harsh tone cut through Monica with the heat of an acetylene torch. "Do you think farming is like shopping? You do it only when you feel like it?"

"No, I—"

"It's a day-in, day-out necessity. Plants need to be watered whether you feel like getting out of bed early or not. The work needs to be done even if you aren't in the mood."

Foul man. Monica wanted to bite off his head. "The courts made no mention that I had to be at the farm every day. I guess they assumed you would tell me when you needed me. You told me *nothing*."

"I assumed you would be smart enough to know that farming is done every day, rain or shine, whether or not you feel like showing up. I assumed you would be responsible enough to act on it."

"If you *assume*, you make an ass out of *you* and *me*. Next time, tell me what you want. This was your mistake, Noah, not mine, but from now on I'll be there every single dam— Every morning, okay?"

Noah seemed taken aback by Monica and her acid tone. Good. He should be afraid. She wouldn't let him walk all over her, especially not after she'd spent her morning helping someone.

"Listen, I—"

Monica ignored whatever Noah was about to say, hugged Kayla goodbye and walked away. Noah Cameron could rot in hell for all she cared.

The courts had told her to report in on the farm when Noah needed her. He hadn't shared his schedule with her. Was he hoping she would fail? What did he want? For her to go to jail?

Just inside the gallery door, she drew up short, letting the door nudge her back. Her pulse pounded and her hands shook. The man made her so mad she could spit.

Olivia peeked her head out of her office to see who had entered the gallery.

"You're five minutes late." The hard edge in her voice undid Monica.

"Not today, Olivia." She'd never spoken to her boss harshly. In fact, she had always been unfailingly polite.

Olivia's mouth fell open.

"I will work my butt off while I'm here today, *boss*, just as I've always done. But how many times over the past year have I been late? Twice! Both times this week. I'm sick to death of you and your son coming down on me. I made a mistake. I apologized. I'm paying my dues."

She approached the office. Wide-eyed, Olivia stepped out of the way to let her pass inside.

"I thank you heartily, Olivia, for giving me this job, but if you can't appreciate me as I am then I will leave. Is that clear?"

Olivia nodded.

Monica tossed her purse into the bottom drawer of Olivia's desk, where they kept their personal belongings. "Good. I'm glad we have that settled."

She stepped into the back room to finish baling boxes in which artwork had been delivered yesterday, not too careful today about whether she might snag her dress or tear a nail, ripping them apart with her hands rather than using box cutters, happily imagining tearing Noah limb from limb.

"NOAH?" THROUGH THE red haze of his fury, Noah heard a woman's voice and tried to focus on her.

For the first time since bumping into Monica, he noticed Kayla standing in the doorway of Tonio's, smiling hesitantly. She wore a tasteful dress and makeup. She'd done something funky and fun with her hair. "You're—you're lovely. You look amazing."

How long had she been standing there? Had she

heard him give Monica hell? He didn't haul people across the carpet in public, but then, Monica hadn't shown up this morning when he'd needed her and he'd gone nuclear.

He tried speaking normally, but his hot blood was slow to switch gears. "I've never seen you wear makeup before."

"I know. Monica showed me how to apply it."

"Monica?" The woman's name came out on a faint gust of air. Kayla had been with Monica. She'd been standing there all along. Monica had hugged someone before storming off, but Noah had been too intent on her and his own indignation that he hadn't noticed who the other woman was.

"Uh-huh. She's amazing, Noah. She got me two jobs."

"Monica? *Two* jobs? Where?"

"I'm working for John Spade. Just real basic work, but he said if I'm willing to take a computer course then he'll give me more hours and responsibility, and pay me more."

"I'm kind of speechless. I didn't think Spade had that much heart."

"I'm not sure he does, but judging by the way he looks at Monica, I think he would do whatever she asks." He didn't like the spurt of jealousy at the thought of Monica and Spade together, not that it made any sense.

"Where's the other job?"

"In here." She gestured over her shoulder. "At

Tonio's. I'll be working a lot on weekends, but that doesn't bother me. I'm so excited, Noah. We'll actually have money coming in."

"I hope they're both paying you an honest wage."

"I forgot to ask. These are good people, Noah. I'm sure everything will be fine. Besides, I can make a dollar stretch for miles. I've been doing it all of my married life."

Kayla touched Noah's arm, tentatively. "What's going on between you and Monica? Why did you yell at her?"

He scrubbed his scalp, working like a demon to bring himself under control. "Monica really got you two jobs?"

"Uh-huh."

"Since yesterday?"

"Yes. Can you imagine? Plus, she gave me a couple of gorgeous dresses and a blouse and skirt to wear until I can buy more for myself. She *gave* them to me, Noah. I need to dress professionally in Mr. Spade's office."

She leaned close. "Now that he's my boss, I have to remember to not think of him as just John."

"Wait. Go back. I'm still processing that Monica Accord got you work and gave you clothes."

She stuck out her foot and pointed down. "These gorgeous shoes, too."

"Shoes," Noah said weakly. "But isn't all of that out of character?"

"How so?" Clearly puzzled, Kayla asked, "Why would you say that?"

"You know. Self-involved ice queen." Like the girl who'd made fun of him with her friends, who'd turned her back on him and walked down the hall like a princess with her entourage. She had never given him the time of day in high school, and had ignored him for all of her adult life until she'd gotten drunk and hit him with her car.

"Noah, sometimes you can be so blind and so full of your own worldview." Kayla put her hands on her hips, obviously ready to defend the woman who had just gotten her two jobs. "That has not been my experience with Monica at all."

Intrigued, he asked, "What *was* your experience?"

"In high school, I never thought she would give someone like me attention. You know how beautiful she was. The popular kids liked her. When I tried out for the cheerleading squad and didn't make it, I was devastated. Of all of the older girls on the squad, Monica was the only one who came over after tryouts and was *so* nice." She transferred her big purse from one shoulder to the other. "Here was this gorgeous older girl not only giving me the time of day, but trying to make me feel better. I wasn't a cool kid, but Monica consoled me and then told me everything she'd liked about my routine. She was kind, classy. That's when I realized there was more to her than she let on. Also, it's strange, but I got the strong impression maybe she was more shy than she showed."

Monica? Shy? Impossible.

"Why were you angry with her just now? I mean *really* angry, Noah. I've never see you like that before."

No, he didn't usually eviscerate people. "She's supposed to be doing community service at the farm. You know she did this?" He raised his left arm in its cast.

"Yeah. Word travels."

"Her sentence was two hundred hours helping me out."

"That's why she came with you yesterday?"

He nodded. "I needed her to fill and carry the food crates. I was angry with her this morning because she didn't show up. I thought she'd just slept in."

"Nope. She was helping me. I don't know how I can ever repay her."

Noah rubbed his beard, 'cause that's what he did when life threw him for a loop.

"If you'll excuse me," Kayla said, "I have to get back to John's, I mean Mr. Spade's, office to work out my hours. Monica was going to stop in for me, but I think she forgot. I guess she was too upset."

Just before she left, she said, "Don't be too hard on her, Noah. She did a good thing today."

No fooling. Monica had done more than he ever had to further the Keils' long-term welfare.

He had a lot to think about. Had his own prejudices, his own insecurities, clouded his judgment and closed his mind to who Monica might really be?

He wasn't stupid or narrow-minded. Everyone in town knew him as a fair-minded guy. So what was it with Monica?

There were undercurrents here that he didn't understand, and something else going on besides him being close-minded where Monica was concerned.

Common sense told him he should open his store, but he didn't like not understanding what was going on inside of himself, or who the real Monica was. He could afford a few minutes to get to the bottom of this.

Besides, it's not like there would be a mob of people waiting outside the army surplus to pick up waterproof matches and bug spray.

He walked down Main, stopping to peer in through John Spade's window. Kayla gave him a thumbs-up—Kayla, who had a new hero. Heroine.

That bugged him.

He was being unfair, but so what?

He busted his butt to grow food, but all Monica had had to do was to ask favors of a couple of friends and suddenly she was this bright, shining star.

It shouldn't bother him.

It did.

He stopped at the gallery and found his mom dusting paintings. When he entered, she looked at him curiously.

"What?" he asked.

"How are you doing?" She gestured toward his broken arm. "Getting by?"

"Yeah. Listen, is Monica here?"

His mother's expression changed. Mom could be a hard-ass and was afraid of no one, but she looked uneasy. "Maybe you should come back later."

"Why?"

"I don't know what you did to Monica, but she's furious. I've never seen her like this."

Crap.

"I'd like to talk to her anyway."

His mom looked at him as though he was crazy and then shrugged. "It's your funeral. She's in the back putting together the recycling."

When Noah entered the back room, Monica didn't stop what she was doing even though he had the sense she knew he was there. With his size, and being a redhead to boot, he wasn't exactly invisible. Even so, she ignored him and kept ripping apart cardboard boxes. Shredding them, really, with her bare hands. Her biceps actually flexed. The woman was strong.

No trace of the ice princess here today. A volcano burned inside of Monica, and it was Noah who'd set her lava flowing.

The room was small and he towered over her, but today Monica had all the power. Heat radiated from her in fragrant bergamot-scented waves.

Big mistake coming here. When he made to step back out of the room, she ordered, "Stay where you are. Don't you dare weasel out of this."

Weasel? Who, him? Yeah, him. Intensely uncomfortable, he wanted to be anywhere else, but Monica's anger snared him, like a mongoose paralyzed by a cobra.

He'd never seen her so wound up.

"You made terrible assumptions about me this morning, Noah."

"Yes, I did. I sure did." He shuffled his feet. "Er... what assumptions?"

"That I was being lazy. That I hadn't come to the farm because I was sleeping in."

"Yeah. Yeah, I did think that."

"I was up and out at Kayla's farm by eight. I helped her get ready for her interviews. I brought her into town and waited while she did both. I knew she would be nervous and thought she might like the support."

"I'm sure she did."

"Don't patronize me."

He held his hands out in the most placating gesture he could manage. There were no right answers here for him today. This was one of those woman-mad-at-a-man moments when he wouldn't be able to do anything right, other than eat humble pie, that is. "Sorry. I didn't mean to patronize."

"I did a very good thing for Kayla and then I had to take sh—" She closed her eyes and took a deep breath. "I had to take crap from you."

As mad as she was, she wouldn't swear. Noah smiled then hid it when she glared at him.

"You shouldn't have had to take crap from me,"

he agreed lickety-split so he could get out of here in one piece.

He cleared his throat, trying to force himself to admit what was so hard for him, but he could do no less than tell her the truth when he'd given her such a hard time this morning. "What you did for Kayla was beyond awesome." He was sincere. "You gave Kayla an amazing gift."

"Thanks." Terse. Still angry, she accepted his appreciation grudgingly.

"Can I ask you a favor?"

"What?" Not giving an inch.

"Just tell me when you can't come out to the farm, okay? So I can rearrange what needs to be done, like heavy lifting, for when you can be there to help me? Okay?"

With one quick nod, she stepped outside into the laneway with a pile of cardboard, effectively dismissing him.

Ice? The woman was blazing hot. It was a wonder the gallery hadn't ignited and burned to the ground.

Scorched, Noah left the store fully chastened, but also…strangely turned on.

ON SUNDAY MORNING, they rushed through their chores, because Noah was taking six children from town fishing.

When she heard that he needed her to help with the task, Monica decided to forgive Noah for his rudeness yesterday. Besides, she'd always been terrible at holding a grudge, a fact Billy had used to get away with murder sometimes. Remembering how cheeky and sure of her forgiveness he always was, she smiled.

"What's that smile for?" Noah stood beside her in the kitchen, filling an ancient, hard-sided cooler with drinks. He smelled earthy and maybe a little like mothballs. Making a scent for a guy like Noah would be a challenge. It would have to be spicy to cover that mothball scent.

If she did design a scent just for him, would he wear it? Good question. And why was she even considering what would suit him? Another good question, one for which she didn't have an answer.

She liked his heat beside her, though. The morning had been chilly.

Monica handed him the sandwiches she'd made so far and he put them on top of the drinks.

She stood at the counter making peanut butter sandwiches, wrapping them in waxed paper and then snapping elastic bands around them. Noah wouldn't let Monica use plastic wrap. Apparently, he didn't even own any.

Her smile broadened—thinking about Billy in the good times brightened her mood. "I was smiling because I was remembering how Billy knew I forgave easily and, boy, did he use it to his advantage."

"I gotta admit, after yesterday I was sure you were gonna still be a volcano ready to blow this morning."

"No. I heat up quickly and I'm slow to cool down, but I don't hold grudges."

"Good, 'cause today would have been brutal if you were still mad."

"I'm glad you asked me to help with the children. I like the whole idea. Do you do this often? Take kids out fishing?"

"As often as I can, when I can afford the time. I like to get them away from tablets and computer screens and out into nature."

"Are these kids needy? Is there a reason why their parents can't do this?"

When Noah bristled, she said, "Relax, Noah. You always assume I'm being judgmental, but I'm not. I really want to know why you do this."

His shoulders, which had seemed to ratchet up to his ears, relaxed. "For some, both of their parents work. Some are from single-parent families. Some are just kids who want to come for the fun of it. I do this for whoever has an interest. For any kid at any economic level, at any age. I want to nurture an appreciation of the outdoors in as many of our youth as possible. Fishing is a fun way to do that."

"What do you fish for?"

"Brook trout. Then we bring our catch back to the house and cook it for an early dinner."

Trout. One of her favorites. "What if you don't catch enough to eat?"

He fell back against the ancient refrigerator with his hand against his heart, mock offended. Monica laughed. The man could be funny when he wasn't being intense.

"You wound my ego and my skill." He grasped one of the handles of the cooler and she took the other. "We'll catch enough. Come on. Let's go."

Just as they'd finished loading the truck with the cooler and fishing supplies, a van turned into the driveway. Four young boys and two girls got out. Monica guessed their ages at maybe nine through eleven.

Three of them got into the pickup, and the other three joined Monica in her car. Monica followed Noah but winced when he turned onto Gabe Jordan's land.

She'd managed to avoid Gabe since his marriage, but apparently not today.

Her heart sank.

Pulling into the huge yard of the pretty house Gabe and his new wife, Callie, had built over the past year, Monica parked beside Noah's truck.

Gabe stepped out of the house onto the porch, as handsome as ever. He had been Billy's best friend, and had been in Afghanistan with him when her husband had been killed by an IED. Monica knew full well how devastated Gabe had been by Billy's death. In that awful first year, she had leaned on him and he'd helped her grieve, so well in fact she'd thought there was something developing between them.

Too late, Monica had learned that, while Gabe might have felt affection for her, he'd never loved her. In the end, he'd married someone else. At least, she hoped there'd been affection. What if it had been only pity? Afraid that it had been exactly that, she'd avoided him since.

When he saw her, Gabe broke into a broad grin. "Monica! How are you?"

He jumped from the porch, approached with long, exuberant strides, still with that huge smile, and wrapped her in an all-encompassing hug that blocked out everything around them. *Gabe, you gem.* His arms locked around her waist, lifting her feet off the ground. He spun her around.

Joy filled her. It hadn't been pity and she hadn't lost a dear friend. For the past year, she'd missed him, had missed his big, tender hugs.

While she'd been avoiding him, he had given her the room she needed to get used to him being married. In a flash, she understood that now.

During the year of her self-imposed Gabe-avoidance, she had come to understand that, while they'd had a lot of affection for each other, it hadn't been a passionate love, on either side.

Gabe had been wise to find himself a woman he could love.

He set her on her feet, his hands on her arms warm. She smiled. His admiration felt good.

"How have you been?" he asked, brow furrowed. "Are you good?"

She understood that he was really asking, "Are you over Billy's death?"

"I'm getting there, Gabe." She smiled to reassure him and he squeezed her hands.

Not only had she been living in silence for too long, but she'd also been going along without touch. She felt color fill her, rise into her flushed face. She needed more of this.

No wonder she'd gone drinking on that Friday night. Her life was barren. She needed to find something. Gabe had gotten past his grief and now thrived. Surely she could, too.

At least here this morning, in his hug, she found a consolation...true warm-hearted kindness and friendship.

"You're fishing with us today?" he asked. "I had no idea you knew how."

"I don't. I'm game, though."

Gabe turned to Noah, who, Monica noticed, didn't look happy. "Hey, man, what happened to your arm?"

Monica froze. He hadn't heard? She thought the whole town, no the whole *world*, knew, judging by the comments she'd heard everywhere she went.

She might be put off by Noah's attitude, but the townspeople sure liked him and didn't want to see him hurt.

"Sorry I've been out of touch." Gabe smiled. "I've been preoccupied with Callie's pregnancy. We've had a couple of false alarms. She's close."

Monica watched Noah. He raised one red eyebrow her way, as if asking, "Should I tell him or should you?"

Time to own up. The shame that had been burning in her tummy the first morning she'd gone to Noah's farm returned, setting off fire alarms in her stomach.

"I did it."

Gabe stared down at her, uncomprehending. "Did it? Did what?"

She pointed to Noah's cast. "That."

"How on earth could you have broken Noah's arm?"

She hated to tell him. Gabe, with his overdeveloped sense of right and wrong, would never understand falling so low, feeling so alone, that he would go out and drink…and then get into his car.

She steeled herself and blurted, "I drove home from the bar after too many drinks and I hit him." She might as well come completely clean. "Noah was on his bike. I ruined it. It was vintage."

Gabe's head swiveled between the two of them like the balls in a Newton's cradle. Noah probably wouldn't believe she knew what one was. "You drove drunk? I don't believe it."

"As my lawyer said, it only takes once to make a mistake of that magnitude and get caught."

"She hit me like a ton of bricks," Noah said, his tone hard, as though Gabe asking about it had reminded him of his outrage.

All of the lovely camaraderie she'd been feeling with Noah in the kitchen this morning evaporated like morning mist. He was still angry with her.

Rightly so. He should be, and yet, when could they get past this?

She didn't get why Noah's attitude toward her boomeranged so much.

Gabe rubbed the back of his neck, as though having trouble wrapping his head around everything. Then he settled his heavy hand on her shoulder and her shame eased. Commiseration. Sympathy.

Thank you, she mouthed.

The front door of the house opened and Callie stepped outside, her cropped red hair and sassy smile a contrast to Monica's own conservative demeanor.

She approached—waddled really, because of her big pregnant belly. Monica envied her that belly. She would love to have children.

Callie stood beside Noah, subtly aligning herself with him. "I heard about the accident, Noah. Can I autograph that thing?"

"You knew about this and didn't tell me?" Gabe asked.

"I only just heard yesterday. I was so tired last night I forgot to share."

"I don't know if you can sign this type of cast." Noah gestured with his broken wing. "It's a new-fangled material. Not like the old plaster casts." He smiled at Callie.

Monica didn't like that smile. It was sweet and affectionate and unlike anything he shared with her. Not that she cared who Noah smiled at, or how.

Anyway, what really mattered in this moment

was that Gabe's show of affection toward her had changed Monica's emotions, morphed them into something more positive than envy. Her regret that Gabe couldn't love her and any jealousy she'd felt toward Callie eased. She was better than this. It was time to accept things as they were. Gabe deserved love.

"Congratulations on your imminent birth, Callie," she said. "I hope all goes well in delivery."

She found she meant it and added a smile.

Caught off guard, Callie hesitated and then said, "Thank you." Perhaps sensing the sincerity of Monica's sentiment, she returned the smile.

The kids hovered in the background, not quite understanding the complex emotions, good and bad, swirling among the adults.

Noah took care of that, his natural exuberance reasserting itself once he'd collected all of the fishing equipment from the truck.

Callie went back into the house. She was taking it easy so close to her delivery date. Monica pulled the cooler from the back of the truck, but Gabe was right beside her in an instant to grab it.

"I can do it," she protested.

"I don't doubt it, but it's a fair hike to the river. You look good, Monica. Strong. I see you've been keeping up the workouts I taught you."

"Religiously. They've helped a lot, Gabe. They were a lifesaver."

"Good." She followed when he stepped into the woods. "What's with the drinking and driving?"

"It was only one time, last Friday night." She explained about being lonely.

"You need to find something to do with your life, Monica."

"You used to tell me that all the time. I didn't get it then. I do now. I just haven't found what that might be."

"No ideas?"

A flare of excitement arose in her. "Actually, I would *love* to have my own business. I watched you with your dogsledding. You get so much, I don't know, *juice* out of running it and giving children joy."

Gabe grinned. "*Juice* is a good word for it. Earning a living doing something you love is rewarding, but being your own boss is even better. Couple that with teaching kids from the city about nature and how to take care of animals is the best feeling on earth."

"Yeah, I can see that. I've noticed how much pride Olivia has in her gallery, too. I love working there, but I really want something of my own. I just don't know *what*." Her frustration bled through. "I mean, look at the things I love. Fashion is already a crowded industry. What could I possibly do in Accord that would attract a clientele anyway?"

Gabe looked thoughtful, but had no answers.

"Both of Main Street's lingerie and clothing shops are doing well," she continued. "Another store like that would cut that market in half. Even with our healthy summer tourist trade, it wouldn't work."

"I'm happy to see you trying to come up with ideas. Even if you haven't figured out what exactly it is you want to do, you have the desire. It's only a matter of time before you do."

His faith warmed her.

"So what are you doing here today with Noah? How did this come about?"

She reached forward and held a branch out of their way while Gabe passed, his hands full with the heavy cooler. She explained about the community service and how the experience had been going so far.

"Things will ease with Noah. He's just frustrated that he's hindered when he needs to get his work done."

"I understand his hostility, but it's just hard to live with him constantly glaring at me." That wasn't true, though. There'd been those compelling moments when they'd talked about fund-raising, when she'd felt it could be a shared passion. His moods turned on a dime, though. She didn't understand him.

"Look," she said as they approached the bank of the river where Noah and the kids waited. "He's glaring again."

After a protracted incisive stare at his friend, Gabe laughed. "Don't worry, Monica. It'll pass. My buddy's just got stuff to work through right now."

Monica wasn't sure what kind of *stuff* Noah had

to work through, but she wished he'd hurry up and deal with it, thank you very much. Because it was definitely no laughing matter.

CHAPTER FIVE

NOAH GOT EVERYONE set up with rods and lures then began teaching the kids about everything that popped into his head. Or so it seemed to Monica.

The man was an encyclopedia of the outdoors. Gabe wasn't so bad, either. Between the two of them, they taught the children a lot. Monica was impressed.

She watched Noah with the kids. Despite her pique and her doubts about where she stood with him, she liked how he treated the children—like gold.

The kids really liked him. She knew the townspeople respected him, too. Why was it only her to whom Noah offered so little of the best of himself? He'd always gone out of his way to ignore her, long before the accident.

While Gabe showed Monica how to hold the rod properly, Noah moved onto what seemed to be his favorite theme—the environment.

"Okay, kids, this might sound preachy, but I'm going to say it anyway. Convince your parents to stop using bleach. Okay? It's hard on our ecosystem and really hard on fish once that bleach leaches into their habitat."

Monica must have been doing something wrong because Gabe wrapped his arms around her from behind and murmured, "Hold it like this. You'll have more luck."

It was too bad for Monica that Noah happened to glance at her at that moment. Oh, dear.

He glared at her, and it got her back up. Did he actually think she had something going on with Gabe? She couldn't seem to do anything right where this guy was concerned and she was tired of defending herself.

He wasn't perfect, either.

Then she heard Gabe laughing. She turned around and narrowed her eyes when she saw the twinkle in his eye. "What are you up to?"

"Just stirring the pot a little."

"Stirring what pot?"

He chuckled and walked away to help one of the kids.

"How is my mom supposed to get our clothes white if she doesn't use bleach?" That was from one of the girls.

"Vinegar. Washing soda. Lemon juice. Hydrogen peroxide." Noah might have been answering Becca, but he was watching Monica, and he didn't look happy.

She looked around at the children. They were taking Noah seriously. Some of them apparently had a case of hero worship where Noah was concerned. How could they not when he took an entire day out of his busy schedule to take them fishing?

It was almost a guarantee they would each go home and demand that their parents stop using bleach.

Before she had finished the thought, Noah pointed to her nails. "That nail polish?"

Every child directed their attention her way. She held up her hands and studied her pink polish. "What about it?"

"Main ingredient is formaldehyde."

Monica recoiled. "You're just trying to scare me."

"I am, yeah, but it's true."

"Ewww," Becca said. "You have formaldehyde on your hands? Remember the frogs we had to dissect? They reeked. The teacher said it was the formaldehyde that preserved them that stank so much. I'm never wearing nail polish."

Shannon wrapped her arm across Becca's shoulder. "Me either!"

Great. In the car on the drive over, Monica and the two girls had enjoyed a lovely chat, but now they glared at her as though she were the enemy. *Thanks, Noah.*

Try as she might, Monica couldn't stop herself from feeling wounded by Noah's obvious disdain.

She stared at her hands. How was she supposed to have known about the ingredients in her nail polish? There must be polish out there with fewer chemicals. She would research it online tonight.

Many long hours later, with a catch of fish that would make an awesome dinner, and the sandwiches and juice all gone, Gabe led the kids back to the vehicles, with Noah and Monica bringing up the rear.

"Noah, you have to find a better way to educate

people about all of this environmental stuff—guide, teach, whatever. I know you're passionate, but don't preach. You come off as self-righteous and unforgiving, and it makes people feel bad about themselves."

He startled. "The kids? I hurt their feelings?"

Emboldened by the concern on his face, she continued, "Not them. Me."

"Oh. You."

The way he said it with such casual disdain, the way he *dismissed* her as though she was of no consequence, as though the kids deserved his respect but she didn't, burned a hole right through her.

"How dare you?"

He stopped dead in his tracks and stared at her. "How dare I what?"

"How dare you treat me as though I mean less than those kids? I'm a human being as worthy of respect as anyone."

"I don't—"

She railroaded over him. "You treat me like crap. I broke your arm. I'm sorry. Okay? I didn't do it on purpose. I'm sure if you canvassed the entire town you'd have a hard time finding anyone I've hurt in my thirty-eight years."

"Yeah, you're a real saint, getting people jobs. Lift one finger and John Spade falls all over himself to do your bidding. Right? Meanwhile I bust my butt year-round for these people. You know what you are? You're a princess living in an ivory tower. You don't know the first thing about real life."

She jabbed him in the chest. "I'm as good as you are. I am as worthy. You think you're better than me? Well, guess what, Noah, I wish you would go to hell."

Tears blurring her vision, she marched ahead of him only to run headfirst into a hard body. Strong hands gripped her shoulders. Gabe's concerned face hovered in her blurry vision.

"What's up?"

She dashed tears from her cheeks. "Nothing of importance." She glanced over her shoulder at Noah. "Absolutely *nothing.*"

DIDN'T THAT JUST put him in his place? Just as Noah had always thought, Monica assigned no importance to his person whatsoever.

She marched off after the children while Gabe walked back to him.

"What's going on with you two? You've been shooting daggers at Monica since you got here this morning. At first I figured you had the hots for her. I thought it was funny, so I played up teaching Monica how to fish. I thought you were jealous. Now I don't know. You've really upset her. What's your problem?"

"What do you think? This!" He shoved his left arm into Gabe's face. "She screwed me up, man."

She screwed you up, all right, but this is about a heck of a lot more than your arm.

Aw, shut up.

No, you didn't like when Monica and Gabe

hugged. When Monica looked at the man like he was a god, you hated it. When you saw Gabe holding her, you wanted to be that man.

"I'm sorry she broke you arm, Noah, but you know that kind of behavior is out of character for Monica."

"Is it?"

Gabe responded with a quelling look.

"Okay," Noah admitted. "It wasn't like her to go drinking and driving, but I'm the one suffering the consequences."

"I wouldn't say you're the only one. You just left her in tears."

He pulled up on the path. He'd hurt her that badly? "She was crying?"

"When she bumped into me, yeah. After I brought Billy's body home, she cried once and that was it." They both climbed over a tree trunk that had fallen across the path. "But I'm pretty sure she cried her heart out whenever she was alone, probably every night judging by how puffy her eyes were some mornings, but the rest of the time she put on a good face. No more crying in public, not even at his funeral."

Noah wondered what had been going on in his own life that he hadn't really noticed Monica during that time. Again he realized how much he underestimated her.

Gabe slowed down to put more distance between them and the kids. "She's stronger than she thinks she is, and a hell of a lot stronger than she looks.

That's why I'm wondering what you did to upset her so much that she would cry in public."

Guilt put him on the defensive. "Why are you taking her side? She just said some nasty things to me, too." He realized he sounded childish, but he couldn't help it.

"Like what? I heard the whole conversation."

"Not possible. You were at the front of the pack."

"The woods are quiet. The kids are tired and growing hungry again. They're not talking much. We all heard everything. I came back to try to get you two to tone it down." He dipped below a low-hanging branch. "She said she's as good as you are. That she's a worthy person. All true. What did she say that was so bad?"

"She said I'm of absolutely no importance."

"Come on, man. You pissed the woman off. Of course she's gonna get in a parting shot. Doesn't mean she thinks you mean nothing to anyone."

Of course he meant a lot to plenty of people, but when Monica said he meant nothing to her, he believed her. And it hurt. When Noah didn't respond, Gabe glanced at him sharply. "She really did hurt your feelings. Why? I've heard the things people have hurled at you during protests. You've got thick skin."

Still, Noah remained silent, unwilling to share with Gabe how easily Monica could wound him. Gabe might get the impression that he cared about the woman.

Gabe stopped him with a hand on his arm while

putting enough distance between them and the kids that Monica couldn't possibly hear. "It's because it's Monica, isn't it? I mean, specifically Monica. You really do find her attractive, but it's more than that, isn't it?" he asked softly.

Damn the man. He saw too much. Noah couldn't even pretend to lie.

"Have you just got the hots for her?" Gabe swung around to stand in front of Noah. "Or do you care for her?"

Noah gritted his teeth. The two men had become good buddies since Gabe had come home from Afghanistan and they'd discovered a shared love of nature and outdoor sports. In the winter, Noah often helped Gabe with his dogsledding business, when things were slow at the shop.

Yet Gabe had never guessed how Noah felt about Monica until now. The only other person who knew was Audrey, and she would take his secret to the grave.

But so would Gabe. Salt of the earth didn't begin to describe the man. The guy had depth and honor.

A gust of air exploded out of Noah and he scrubbed his beard. "Yeah. I like her. Too much. I have since high school. Since middle grade. Okay? Satisfied?"

Gabe didn't retreat. He stood his ground with a puzzled frown. "So why don't you go after her?"

"Are you kidding?" Noah raked a hand down his own body. "Take a good look at me. Then look at her.

Notice any differences? We're about as opposite as two people can be."

Gabe nodded thoughtfully. "Yeah, but that doesn't preclude attraction. Right now she's upset, but maybe she's not entirely indifferent."

"No way. She goes out of her way to ignore me. Then, when she does acknowledge my existence, she's cool and collected all the way."

Not completely, buddy. Remember yesterday's volcano?

"You do understand that's just her way?" Gabe said. "That it's nothing personal?"

"No, I don't."

"Or maybe that's it, isn't it? You *want* it to be personal." Gabe pointed a finger at him. "You're gonna have to gather up your courage at some point and make a move. Otherwise, you'll never know how she really feels." He turned and stalked away, leaving Noah to wonder what on earth there was to learn about the woman that he hadn't already seen.

It didn't *seem* like she cared about him at all. So then why would his opinions make her so upset that she cried?

Back in the clearing in front of Gabe's house, with the children already in the cars, Monica seemed to have pulled herself together. No sign of tears.

He stepped around to go to his truck. Just before he got in, he noticed the protracted hug Monica shared with Gabe.

Apparently, Gabe was someone of importance to her.

While driving back to the farm, the kids' conversation flowing around him, he realized why he'd been so hard on Monica. He was jealous of her affection for Gabe.

He wanted a slice of that pie. And because he couldn't have what he wanted, he was being small and mean. And he felt ashamed.

HE DIDN'T ASK her to stay for dinner. Monica couldn't believe how much that hurt. Obviously she was useful to Noah in her capacity to make sandwiches and herd children, but not as herself.

The children got out of the two vehicles and unloaded the back of the truck. They returned the fishing rods to the tool shed. And all the while Noah ignored her.

When he told the children to take the fish into the house, he didn't even look her way, just followed the kids indoors. Monica stood beside her car more hurt than she thought possible.

Despite Noah's anger, it had been a good day. Even after the kerfuffle about her nail polish, the girls had come back around to being chummy with her.

In truth, it had been a wonderful day, one of the best she'd ever had—sweet, fun and educational. And now it was over—for her. Everyone else trooped inside like the best buddies on earth while she stood out here alone. Talk about being an outsider.

One of the girls ran back outside. "Monica, what're you doing out here? Noah's gonna teach us to debone the fish. Don't you want to know how?"

She shook her head slightly. "I'm going to head home now." Her throat hurt.

Shannon said, "Okay," but she sounded uncertain about this strange outcome—Monica had been there all day and now wouldn't be.

The girl slowly walked back inside. A second later, Noah barged out.

"Where are you going?"

"Home."

"Why?"

His intense gaze cut through her. So many under-currents of things—issues, emotions?— went on inside of Noah that they left her off-balance.

"What did you want? An engraved invitation just for you?"

"No," she responded quietly. "But I wasn't invited, was I, until Shannon said something?"

"Come in," he said. "Have supper with us. You caught one of the fish."

Yes, she had, and she was proud of that. She should ask for it and take it home and cook it by herself. She didn't want to be in this man's company any longer.

Shannon appeared in the doorway again, beckoning. Monica didn't have it in her to ignore Shannon. She stepped away from Noah.

Shannon ran back into the kitchen, squealing,

"She's coming." At least one person here was glad she was staying.

Then she heard the kids all say things like "Awesome" and "Great."

Her heart warmed. Noah might not want her here, but the children did and they were the only ones who mattered.

Before she stepped up onto the porch, Noah stopped her with a hand on her arm.

"Wait." He scrubbed his palms over his face. "I'm sorry. I'm being ridiculous."

"Yes, you are. What exactly is your problem, Noah? Why do you treat me so coldly?"

He studied her, looked away and then met her gaze again, confusion in his eyes. "I don't know what's wrong with me today. I'm being petty and mean-spirited. I know I can get too preachy and I am self-righteous—you nailed me good. It's behavior that's unworthy of both of us. I'm truly sorry. I'll do better."

"Thank you, Noah," she responded quietly. "I appreciate the apology."

When she made to step onto the porch again, he stopped her a second time. "You have a lot of class. I like how you rise above things."

He'd surprised her. As far as she could tell, he wasn't being facetious. He was serious. It was strange, though, that he still looked confused even while giving her a compliment.

His problem, not hers. "Thank you," she said.

"Let's go in and enjoy the rest of our time with the kids."

Inside the house, the children clustered around the fish they'd caught, which were lying dead in the sink.

"We didn't know what to do with them."

"I'll teach you how to debone them and then we'll fry them."

Monica had been thinking about the fish. Noah lived on a farm in the middle of extensive bounty. How often did these kids have a chance to eat a veggie straight from the garden?

"Why don't we pick fresh vegetables to go with the trout?" She pulled Noah aside. "The children should have vegetables. It could teach them a lot about farming, too."

"The food is for the needy, remember?"

"I know, but you have a lot of food growing in those fields. You won't miss the few vegetables we eat with dinner tonight. And we can't ignore the need here and now."

Monica subtly bent her head toward Tyler's shoes. They were scuffed bare with holes in the toes. His knees poking through tears in his jeans finished the story.

"We *need* veggies with our fish." She leaned close. Noah smelled like fresh air and sunshine. She whispered, "I gave Tyler my sandwich at lunchtime. One wasn't enough for him. He's starving, Noah."

He nodded thoughtfully. "Good point. Thanks."

She'd bet Tyler didn't often get fresh vegetables.

So they all tromped out into the fields while Noah gave them a brief lecture about farming, pointing out what could be picked early, but also what was still too young.

To complement the fish, they chose asparagus and scapes.

"Scapes?" The kids laughed at the name. "Don't let any scapes escape!"

"Wait until you taste them." Monica held a bundle in each hand. She also held her breath hoping that Noah would go for what she was about to suggest. "We need parchment paper."

"Why?" He stopped walking to regard her with suspicion.

"For the fish."

"No, we don't. We'll fry them."

"Nope. Today, we're going to teach these guys how to turn fish into ambrosia."

"What's ambrosia?" Becca asked.

"It's the nectar of the gods. It means something that tastes exquisite." She hopped over the row of radishes she'd weeded the other day. "Everyone, look."

She bent down. "This is a radish, but this—" she pointed to a small plant "—is a weed. We need to get rid of it."

When she smiled at the children, she caught a wink from Noah. A smile kicked up one corner of his mouth and she had the worst, the most insane desire to kiss that tiny smile. Where had that thought come from? She didn't find him attractive. She really didn't. Okay, maybe a little, but only when the evening sun turned his hair to fireworks.

And also maybe when his eyes crinkled at the corners when he smiled, and when that warm smile made her toes curl.

"Kids," he said, "Monica helps me out every morning on the farm. She's been learning a lot." His smile broadened. "She's been learning really well."

Oh, my. I think he's proud of me.

He'd never shown her much goodwill. She didn't know what to do with it. Flustered, she asked, "Noah, is it too early for potatoes?" Her voice sounded breathy, unlike her.

"We might get a few new ones. I'll show everyone a trick."

They waited while he got a pitchfork out of the shed and joined them where they stood beside the potato plants.

"This requires real quick work. First, look for plants that have already flowered." One of the boys pointed to a plant. "Thanks, Tyler. We'll start with that one."

Gently, with his good hand he inserted the fork into the mound of earth and extracted the whole plant. Small new potatoes clung to the roots. "Quick now. Take the taters. Gently!" The children worked quickly and when they were done Noah inserted the plant right back into the soil.

"Water," he ordered.

Back on firm, normal ground with Noah, Monica

ran and filled a bucket. By the time she returned, he'd already done the same with two more plants. They were firmly seated back into the soil and he watered them well.

"That's all we'll do. I like to leave them to grow to maturity for better yield. Same with carrots. I don't do baby vegetables. I need to get all the food that I can out of the plants I grow."

"So will those plants survive and give more potatoes?" Monica asked.

"Yep. It's early days so they'll develop more."

Apparently potato plants were hardier than radish plants. Would she ever understand this farming business?

Hands full, they all returned to the kitchen, where the kids took turns washing vegetables.

Monica wandered around the first floor, studying the books on the overflowing bookshelves. Proust. Kierkegaard. Camus. She'd heard of them all, but hadn't read them. Ken Wilber. Never heard of him. She tilted her head to read the spine. *Sex, Ecology, Spirituality.* Heavy. Next to that sat Stephen Hawking's *A Brief History of Time.*

If ever she needed proof that Noah was too smart for her, here it was. He'd been right to ridicule her all those years ago.

After that thought, she stiffened her spine. No. Wrong. No one deserved ridicule for who they were. She had many fine points, even if Noah didn't recognize them.

She wandered to the stairway to the second floor.

Her mother used to live here. A wistful knot closed her throat. How she would have liked to have known her. How strange that she'd never known of this house. She wouldn't go up to the second floor without Noah's permission—nor would she ask for it. It was enough to try to get him to let her cook the fish her way.

She returned to the kitchen, determined to get those fish cooked in parchment paper. "Noah, I'm serious." Monica gathered enough courage to push for what she wanted. "I want to cook the fish in parchment."

"Why is it so important to do it in paper? You know how I feel about wasting stuff. What's wrong with just using a frying pan?"

Monica picked up a bunch of potatoes sitting in the draining rack and dried them with a kitchen towel. How could she explain how much she wanted to be a true part of this day and feel connected to these kids? "You showed them how to fish and a little about farming. I want to teach them how to cook. The way I want to cook the fish will be an experience they might never have elsewhere in their lives. It will open their young minds to possibilities with food, and with cooking vegetables in a way they will love. One of the boys already said he hates asparagus. How much do you want to bet he'll love it cooked my way?"

Noah's thoughtful nod gave her hope. He was coming around slowly.

"Listen, you don't even have to do anything extra," she said. "I'll run into town and pick it up myself. Okay?"

"Okay. I'm giving you the benefit of the doubt, but still, I hate wasting the paper."

"I'll wash it afterward and put it in the recycling bin." She pointed to the potatoes the children had scrubbed and that she had dried. "Can you parboil these taters while I'm gone?"

"Sure. They're minuscule. Should take all of ten seconds."

By the time Monica returned from town with a roll of parchment paper, the potatoes were done and Noah and the kids were playing cards at the kitchen table.

"We need the table cleared. Come on. Quickly. Put the cards away."

"She's bossy, isn't she?" Noah remarked drily, but softened it with a smile.

"There's a method to my madness. We're going to cook the fish *en papillote*."

"On what?" one of the boys asked.

"It's French. Here. I'll show you." She snagged a scrap of paper and one of Noah's many pencil stubs and wrote it down for them. Then she pronounced it again while they read the word.

Monica taught them how to cut huge hearts out of the parchment paper. They lay a fillet on one half of each sheet. "Okay, the only items we're using today that aren't local are these lemons I just picked up. Now, squeeze some over each of your fillets."

Next, each person got two small potatoes. "Slice them thinly and layer them along the top of the fillets. Sprinkle with a little salt."

She handed them a couple of small garlic scapes each. "Slice them across into one-inch segments. The asparagus is super thin so cut it into the same length bits."

She studied the meals spread out on the big old kitchen counter and the table where everyone worked. "You guys are doing a great job. Okay, now for some dairy goodness. Put dabs of butter on top of everything. Then add some more salt and a little pepper."

She folded over the second half of the sheet. "Everyone gather around. This is the tricky part." She folded over the edges, showing them how to do it properly. Then she did it again, so the food was double-sealed. "We don't want to lose any of the amazing juices that are going to form while everything cooks."

She supervised while the kids folded their packets.

"We can't fit them all into the oven at the same time. Four of you go first and then the other two and Noah and I will follow."

"But I'm starving," Tyler said, and she believed him. "I can't wait another hour."

"Hey," Noah interjected. "The beauty of fish is how quickly it cooks. These will be in the oven for how long?" He asked the question of Monica.

"The heat is high. About twelve minutes."

In a group effort, they cleaned the counters and the table, setting it for four.

After the first batch came out, the other bundles went into the oven while the first four sat down to eat. Monica schooled them on how to open their bundles without getting scalded by steam.

"Oh, wow, this is awesome!"

"I'm glad the scapes didn't escape. I like them!"

"My mom cooked us asparagus before and I hated it. I really like it like this." Brad talked with his mouth full, but Monica didn't have the heart to scold him when he liked her food so much. "I'm gonna get her to do this at home."

Monica smiled at Noah. Mission accomplished, she thought. He'd taught them all about the outdoors, and she'd taught them how to cook what they'd caught and enjoy it. It felt incredible to contribute.

True to her word, she wiped off everyone's papers, folded them and put them into the recycle box. The kids helped Noah wash and put away dishes.

Later, after the children had been picked up—and Monica had gotten hugs from all of them!—Noah stood beside Monica in front of her car. It was past time for her to leave, but she lingered. She didn't want this thoroughly amazing day to end.

A couple of birds spoke to each other in a tree at the edge of the house. Monica didn't know what kind they were, but she heard them there whenever she came out to the farm. She should ask Noah. He would know. She kept her question to herself. She liked this stillness, this quiet moment between them.

They seemed to get their wires crossed too easily and she didn't want that to happen now.

He'd seen the way the children had reacted to the food, and judging by how he'd wolfed his down, he seemed to have a new appreciation for her. For her cooking skills, at least.

They stared at each other. Monica didn't know what she expected from him, or from herself, after such an excellent evening. She only knew that it had to end, but not *how*. She knew she didn't want it to end. Tax her brain how she might, she couldn't remember a day she'd enjoyed more and yet, something had been bothering her all evening.

She needed to get it off her chest. Because, while overall it had been a great day, parts of it had also been deeply troublesome.

"I'm not a princess, Noah. I don't live in an ivory tower. It only looks that way."

He didn't respond and that irked her. He knew only what he saw on the surface and nothing about her inner landscape.

"While it's true that I had advantages growing up, they were only financial." She wouldn't tell him about all of the hours she'd spent alone fantasizing about having friends or about how hard it was growing up without an extended family, living in an empty, echoing house. Or about all of those years when she had been the town's rich girl in a county with few wealthy residents, isolated by social conditions that had nothing to do with her. Until high school, the other children hadn't played with her. They didn't know *how* to play with the rich kid, and she hadn't known how to reach out to them. She had been shy and hadn't known how to fit in.

Then, in high school, because of her savvy fashion sense fuelled by her love of magazines, especially vintage *Vogue*—hallelujah!—she'd become a trendsetter. Whatever Monica wore, the other girls wanted to emulate. So she showed them how to do it without breaking the bank, how to use knockoffs to get the looks that she could afford.

"I've known tragedy, too. I married Billy because I lov—" She hissed in a breath on a wave of anger and pain and grief that smacked her sideways. The shock of rampant emotions arising out of nowhere left her reeling. Where was this coming from, and *why* after such a lovely evening? Maybe because it had been so lovely? She'd been robbed of years of happiness. Her husband should have lived by her side into old age.

She was scared, terrified that Billy's love for her had known boundaries while hers for him hadn't. He'd been her world. He'd been everything. Had she been worth as much to him? Apparently not. He'd left her too easily, to head off to war, of all things.

She tried to stem the tide of her flaring emotions, but whatever was inside of her wouldn't be held back. "He shouldn't have died so young," she blurted on a wave of pain. "He was full of life and happiness. It was rotten, *rotten*, that he died."

She was yelling. The grief she'd kept in check, under tight, discreet rein, spewed out of her.

"Hey." Noah touched her arm. "Oh, hey, hey."

"He shouldn't have gone to Afghanistan. He was never meant to be a soldier. I don't know what he was thinking. Trying to keep up with Gabe? I don't know. Why did he have to leave me? It got him killed."

"It seems strange that he would go just because Gabe was."

"It's true." But was it? She'd put off thinking too deeply about the issue because she didn't want to learn unpleasant truths. What if Billy had been bored with his life here? What if he'd been bored with *her*? He'd needed constant stimulation, enough that living with him could be exhausting.

What if she had been holding him back, like a dull old pair of socks when he needed black silk stockings?

The thought caused an ache in her breast.

Billy, why did you go?

She brushed her hands across her cheeks because something was tickling her skin. Her palms came away wet. She was crying. She never cried, yet she'd done it twice today. And in front of Noah, of all people.

"This is ridiculous. I'm over my grief."

"Apparently not."

This was too embarrassing. She'd held it in all these years. Why here, why now, did Mt. Vesuvius decide to erupt?

"Sounds like you have a whole lot more crying to do." In his voice, she heard empathy. She tried to get into her car, desperate to escape.

He wouldn't let her go, but instead reached for her.

"Please," she begged. "I have to leave."

Ignoring her, he wrapped his strong arms—cast and all—around her and nested her head against his comforting chest. It was her undoing.

"It's been five years," she said, her voice a whisper now, clogged with tears. "I should be all done by now. I thought I was. Men just make me so angry. *You* make me angry, Noah. Sometimes you like me and sometimes you don't." It should have come out sounding more dignified than it did, but the flannel of Noah's shirt and her stuffed-up nose made her sound childlike. In her effort to ease her pain, she couldn't seem to tunnel closely enough to this man she respected, but didn't really like. Well, not much. Okay, maybe a little.

He held her until she'd cried herself out, his heart beating a steady, calming rhythm beneath her ear. His arms across her back offered a warm hard support that didn't flag. His cast dug into her right side.

"You okay?"

She nodded, too exhausted to speak.

"You sure?"

They stayed that way for long minutes while Monica hiccuped a couple of times before finally settling into an easy silence. This version of Noah was nice. She could stay here for hours.

He felt even better than Gabe.

She brushed her hand across his shirt. "Needs fabric softener."

"What?" His voice rumbled up from deep in his torso.

"I remarked that your shirt is rough. Next time, throw a quarter of a cup of fabric softener into the wash."

When he laughed, her head bobbed against his chest. "Now I know you're back to yourself." He set her away from him.

Her embarrassment had evaporated. Maybe it was because he'd held her effortlessly without being self-conscious. Or maybe it was because he'd laughed at her about the fabric softener. In that laugh, she hadn't heard derision, but something akin to tenderness. Maybe he liked her peculiarities.

She rummaged in her purse until she found a tissue.

"You really need to start using cotton handkerchiefs—"

With a look, she silenced him. "Not now, Noah. I promise to pick some up, but I'm raw at the moment. I don't need criticism."

"Okay. You're right."

She dried the last vestiges of grief from her cheeks, feeling lighter than she had since Billy's death.

For a long while, she stared at the fields, drawing a semblance of peace from the beauty of nature, as Gabe had taught her.

She thought back to when her experience of the town had started to shift, and when the town's perception of her had changed. Sure, she'd earned respect when showing her high school friends how to dress, but the real change had come with Billy.

Billy had bought acceptance for her with the currency of his good nature and popularity, with his childish pranks and hilarious sense of humor. If he thought Monica Accord was okay, then so did everyone else.

Except Noah…

She turned to study his strong profile. After what they'd just shared, honesty was fitting. The timing was right. For once, he'd treated her like a real woman.

"Know what I think, Noah?"

He startled. Who knew what internal musings she'd interrupted? Hard to tell with him. He kept a lot to himself, sometimes hidden behind his intense frown and, at other times, submerged by his good humor. She saw more than people gave her credit for.

"No, what?" he asked.

"I think you call me princess so you don't have to treat me like a real human being. So you can treat me like a caricature…and a not very nice one."

"What do you mean?" She smiled, pleased by the hint of defensiveness in his tone—she was on the right track. There was truth in what she was saying and he didn't like her bringing it into the open.

"As long as you can think of me as a princess in

an ivory tower, with all of its attendant clichés, then you don't have to admit that I'm complex."

He tapped the fingers of his right hand on his thigh. She was hitting a nerve.

"As long as you think of me as only the shallow, blonde cheerleader from high school then you don't have to admit I have depth. That I'm a good, sensitive person who cares about others every bit as much as you do."

She glanced at him only to find his cheeks blazing red. Oh, dear goodness, she had *so* touched a nerve, but what nerve?

It hit her quickly and hard. She almost laughed aloud, but that would have hurt his feelings.

He liked her. Noah Cameron, to his utter chagrin no doubt, *liked* Monica. Oh wait, no, it was more than that. His cheeks could probably start a campfire without tinder or matches. Noah was infatuated with her. He had a crush on her.

Well, well, well. How long had this been going on?

She started to smile. He looked so acutely uncomfortable that she dropped the subject, but she turned her face away and grinned.

Why on earth that revelation mattered to her, why on earth it made her feel good, she couldn't say. She could only acknowledge that it sure did. It sure as heck did.

She wouldn't hurt his feelings by acknowledging

her suspicions. By the same token, she was tired of being put down.

"I can be hurt, Noah," she said while the birds still chirped. A mating call, maybe? It was that time of night...

"You can call me a princess, you can tell me I live in an ivory tower, but I'm not immune. I can be hurt. I'm not brainless."

He looked down at her. "I don't think you're brainless."

She smiled sadly. "Maybe not tonight, not at this moment, but you have in the past, and you probably will again."

"I won't."

"Let's make a deal," she said. "You stop thinking of me in those terms. Start to see me as a real woman with hopes, dreams and feelings, and I won't think of you in two-dimensional terms."

"How on earth could you think me two-dimensional? I'm deep. I'm caring and giving. I have a social conscience." His defensiveness made her want to laugh.

"Hippie. Tree hugger. Leftie."

To her consternation, he grinned, light from the porch lamp highlighting his red hair. Up close, she noticed freckles on his nose. "I like being all of those things," he said.

Despite her frustration, she huffed out a laugh. "You are incorrigible."

"And proud of it."

They stood in silence until Noah said, "You're right. About everything. I'm sorry. I will do better."

With his sober tone, the atmosphere changed. He meant it. A small victory, but a good one.

CHAPTER SIX

THE FOLLOWING MORNING, Noah said, "I made drawings for you."

He stood on his porch, tall and handsome, red hair beautiful in the early morning sunlight.

Monica stepped across the yard with a lighter step this morning, some of the tension between them eased by last night's talk. Funny that she didn't feel the slightest bit embarrassed by the previous evening's breakdown.

Noah had been great.

His green eyes danced as he watched her walk. She was still trying to process last night's realization that he had a crush on her.

She didn't know what to do with that info, so it was probably best to ignore it and behave normally for now. He didn't seem aware that she knew, so it was all good.

He took a sip from his cup of coffee—or whatever it was. With Noah you never knew. Maybe it was chicory. Or dandelion roots. Or some other weed. Or maybe he'd ground up yesterday's used parchment paper and brewed it. Okay, now she was being silly, but Noah lived so far outside of the box she didn't know what to expect of him.

It almost looked like Noah had been waiting for her, which was odd.

Now that she thought of it, why wasn't he already

out in the fields? Then she remembered his statement about drawings.

"What kind of drawings?"

"Of weeds. Come on inside."

She stepped into the house and stopped, yet again
silently marveling that this had belonged to her
mother.

In the kitchen, Noah asked, "Do you want coffee?"

She walked to the recycle box where the parchment paper she'd folded last night still sat. She sniffed
the air. "Oh. It *is* coffee."

"What else would it be?" He stared at her as though
she was an exotic animal he couldn't figure out.

"Nothing." She giggled. "I'm just tired."

"So? Do you want a cup or not?"

She tried not to giggle again. "Yes, I would love
a *coffee.*"

"You're strange. You know that, right?" He poured
her a cup, handed her natural sugar in a cracked bowl
and took a quart of almond milk out of the fridge.

Nuts in her coffee. Oh, joy.

"Here are the drawings." He handed her a sheaf
of papers.

"These are really good, Noah. Thank you! I'll keep
them in my pocket for reference."

"Can I ask you a question? It might just be my
imagination but…"

Wary, she said, "What is it?"

"You seem really interested in my house."

"What do you mean interested?"

"The first time you came inside, you asked how long I'd owned it and who had lived here before me. Then yesterday, you wandered around down here a couple of times, and I saw you looking upstairs, almost longingly. Just now, you stopped and looked at everything avidly. Why are you so curious?"

"It seems that my mom grew up here. This was her parents' farm."

"This farm belonged to your mom's family? Really? Why have you never been in here before?"

"My dad only just told me about the connection a few days ago. My grandparents died shortly after I was born, and I assume my dad sold the farm because the memories of my mom hurt too much. I can understand that."

Noah got an odd expression on his face, almost like a cartoonish lightbulb coming on. "Follow me." He grabbed her hand and nearly dragged her up the stairs.

When they approached a bedroom door, she balked. Where was Noah taking her?

She didn't have a lot of experience with men, since Billy had been her only boyfriend, and she wasn't always sure how to read them, but she'd had men ask her out on dates since Billy's death. Most had been honorable men. A couple hadn't been.

Noah was leading her into a bedroom.

"Noah, I, um… I don't want to go to bed with you." Was that too direct?

"Huh?" He stopped so abruptly she crashed into him. "What the heck are you talking about?"

She swallowed hard and gestured toward the bed. "I'm not sleeping with you. I won't have sex with you."

"You thought—" His face reddened.

Oh, dear. She'd misjudged his intentions. Awkward.

CRIPES, HE HADN'T brought her up here for *that*, but couldn't help his body's visceral reaction when Monica used the word *sex*, because he remembered all of those hot dreams he'd had of her in high school. He hadn't been planning to seduce her here, today, now, but he couldn't muster the indignation he knew he should feel, not when it had always been his secret dream.

The memory of last night's embrace, though, bedeviled him. She'd let him hold her for long moments that had gone on forever and had ended too soon.

Long into the night, tossing and turning in his bed, he'd been haunted by how good she'd felt. He'd slept in the T-shirt he'd worn all day, that he'd been wearing while he held her, because her singular and rare perfume lingered on it.

She wore yet another perfume today, light and lemony, like lemon balm but not as earthy, still with the floral of bergamot. Delicious. Heavenly.

"Is there a difference in your perfume today? If so, it's subtle."

"Here," she said. "Tell me what you think." She held her wrist near his face. He bent to sniff. His lips accidentally touched her warm skin where her pulse beat.

He jerked away. Just standing this close to her was hard enough, especially in his bedroom, but his lips actually touching her? Even a spot as innocent as her wrist, with her blood beating warmly just beneath the surface?

"What change did I make today?"

Wary, because his own lust threatened to undo him, but also curious, he leaned close again, damn careful not to make contact.

"Spice. Incredibly subtle." He sniffed again. "Cinnamon. No, cloves."

Her brilliant smile enhanced his longing. "How do you do that? You're right, it's cloves. Just a touch because its scent can overpower everything else."

She dropped her arm and he missed her nearness immediately, even though he still stood right beside her. How incredible must it feel to *lie* beside her? To lie on top of her? To be inside of her?

"Why do you smell like mothballs?" she asked.

He laughed because his hubris just kept catching up to him. He was having horny thoughts while she was telling him he stunk.

The irony didn't escape him. She smelled divine while he smelled not-so-good.

He pulled himself together and responded, "I don't use mothballs myself. I hate naphthalene. It's toxic and classified as possibly carcinogenic." He stepped away from her, distancing himself subtly, because he liked being close to her too, too much. "But some of the stock I buy for the shop has been stored in mothballs and I wear clothes from the store. I wash them a lot before wearing them to get out the chemicals, but it takes a ton of washes to rid the clothes of that scent."

Her brow furrowed into delicate lines. "Can't you make sure your stock hasn't been stored that way?"

"I try to vet my products before I buy them, but it isn't always possible. A lot of what I purchase is pure wool and distributors are trying to protect their investment. Less and less is stored that way, though. In time, people will learn to stop using mothballs."

"But who wants holes in their sweaters?"

"No one, but there are alternatives, like camphor."

Monica was silent for a while and then said, "You know about a lot of odd things."

Noah stiffened.

She noticed and said calmly, "I'm not criticizing, Noah. I find the weird stuff you know interesting."

"It isn't weird to me." He scratched his left wrist, working his fingers up inside of his cast as far as they would go. "You'll get used to me spouting off."

A grudging smile played around the edges of her well-defined lips.

With a sideways glance, he studied Monica. He'd always thought her cool as a cuke, that nothing much fazed her, but it was warm up here and a fine sheen of sweat coated her cheeks and her upper lip. Heat radiated from her and he smelled the barest whiff of sweat, and the fashionable, waxed and primped goddess became human. Too bad for him. She was easier to resist as a wax dummy. As a real woman, she devastated his peace of mind.

God, he was a sap where Monica was concerned, but no, he hadn't brought her to his room for sex.

"We're not here to climb into bed, Monica," he said, returning to their earlier topic. *More's the pity.* As soon as she had mentioned her grandparents, he'd remembered all of the stuff up in the attic that he'd never taken the time to deal with. "There are a bunch of boxes in the attic the former owners, who bought this place after your grandparents died, said were left here when they moved in. They never dealt with them, and I've never looked at the contents, either."

He pointed toward the corner of the bedroom. "Want to find out if they belonged to your grandparents?"

"Yes!" She dragged him forward. "How do we get up there?"

"Through that door in the ceiling."

She stared at his rumpled bed. "Wow, Noah, you really are messy. Do you know that people who start the day by making their beds tend to get more done in a day?"

"Monica," he said while he pulled down a door

in the ceiling, a ladder riding down and opening up with the action, "if I got any more done in a day than I already do, I'd be a machine."

She smiled. "True. You do work a lot."

"Come on." He carefully stepped onto the ladder and reached back for her hand with his good arm.

She batted it away. "I was a cheerleader in high school. Remember the pyramid, with me on top? If I can scramble up a bunch of girls, I can climb a ladder."

He stepped back off the ladder to allow her to go up first. Oh, yeah, he remembered her as a cheerleader, all right. All the boys in school remembered the pyramid. Her perfume wafted around him and, as she climbed higher, it became stronger. Was it on her legs?

Where else had she put it besides her wrist? Ankles? Knees? He gulped. Thighs?

Clumsily, he took the ladder, thrown off balance. In her quaint conservatism, she wasn't sexy and yet she *was*...whatever the heck that meant.

Pushing those thoughts aside, Noah made it into the attic just behind Monica and turned on the overhead light.

"Here." He dragged a large plastic container directly under the light and pried off the lid.

Inside there were quilts and linens. Noah turned to Monica with a smug smile as a scent wafted out and around them. "Smell that?"

"Yes. What is it?"

"Camphor. Whoever packed this didn't use naph-thalene."

"It sure smells a lot better than mothballs." Monica touched one of the quilts. "This is handmade." In her voice, he heard reverence.

"It looks like everything is."

"Oh, wow," she said with a breathy exhalation as she lifted up a couple of odd garments.

"What are they?" he asked.

"Homemade camisoles," she breathed, awe in her tone. "These are silk. Look at this fabulous crochet and cut-out work decorating them." She picked up another garment. "This is a bedsitting jacket. Women used to wear them if they had to go to the hospital, way back in the forties and fifties. My grandmother probably wore this after giving birth to my mom. Can you imagine that?"

She'd whispered the last with wonder.

"Thank you for this gift, Noah."

She made him feel ten feet tall. Disturbed by too much unwelcome emotion, he asked, "How do you know about old clothing like this?"

"You're not the only one who knows strange things." Her smile glowed in the dim attic, her turn to be smug. "I have a passion for all garments, for fashion throughout history, for fine craftsmanship. Whoever made these was incredible. Look at these stitches. I've never seen work so fine."

Noah watched her study more clothing and emit

oohs and aahs, breathy exclamations that, frankly, turned him on. He'd thought her cold, but that was slowly changing. Look what she had done for Kayla Keil, and she'd taught the children how to cook because of her passion for food and, apparently, for children. He'd hesitated in asking her to help out with the kids, but he'd needed her physical presence to do a lot of stuff he couldn't do with a broken arm.

And she'd treated them well—better than well. They'd reacted to her respect for them by returning it.

Also, her grief over Billy when she'd cried in Noah's arms had been heart-wrenching. He guessed that was why giving her this gift, this connection to her family, felt good.

There were ways in which he'd been wrong about Monica.

A hank of sweaty hair stuck to her cheek. The goddess had disappeared and the woman was back. Noah fell onto an old wooden chair to sit on his hands so he wouldn't reach for that hank of hair, to pull it away from her glossy cheek and lick the sweat from her skin.

MONICA RACED THROUGH her chores because she needed to see her father before going in to work. Thank goodness they'd gotten to the point that she could weed standing up using a hoe. The plants were becoming hardy enough that she wouldn't disturb their spreading roots when digging into the soil.

Once she finished her chores, she loaded a bunch

of the smaller embroidered items from the attic into her car.

Back in town, Monica stopped by her dad's house, barely able to contain her excitement. She carried a few of the bedsitting jackets with her and some exquisite, hand-embroidered handkerchiefs.

When she saw him, she frowned. He hadn't shaved and his hair stood out around his head. He used to be meticulous in his appearance, even when just at home. "You don't look so hot this morning. What's going on?"

"Nothing."

"Come on, Dad, please. I know when something's up. Talk to me."

He sipped black coffee without answering. Even from across the room, the coffee smelled bitter.

"Are you having money problems?"

He perked up a bit. "Yeah, that's it. I lost a bit with faulty investments."

That made him perk up?

She got the impression that *wasn't* it, that she should have been more insistent that he answer her on his own instead of offering him a ready-made explanation.

"Are you sure that's all of it?"

"Yep. Positive."

She waited, but he continued drinking coffee and avoiding her gaze.

"How's the work at the farm going?" he asked, clearly attempting to divert her. "You're looking tanned."

"It's good. It's strange, but I'm starting to really like it. I'm still screwing up, but helping people feels incredible.

"And something amazing happened this morning actually." She spread the garments on the table. "I found these in the attic of Noah's house. They belonged to my grandparents. He said I can keep anything I find that belonged to Mom's parents."

"That's great, honey." He reached across the table and squeezed her hand. "You finally have a connection to your mother."

Monica's eyes watered with sadness, but with joy, too. "Yes. It's too good to be true."

A thought occurred to her. "This was my heritage. Why didn't you ever retrieve it for me, for when I got older and could appreciate it?"

"I never thought to look in the attic before I sold the place. I cleared out the house, but forgot about the attic. I'm sorry."

Monica nodded, thoughtful, trying to remember things she'd heard, rumors about her dad drinking too much after her mom's death. Maybe it had just been an honest mistake. He'd lost his wife and then was responsible for clearing out and selling her parents' house soon after her death. Plus, he had an infant at home. He was probably overwhelmed.

She knew he wasn't the strongest man around when times got tough.

Monica sighed. She just wished she knew how to help him these days. *Was* it about money? Unless

Dad had remortgaged the house for some reason, that shouldn't be a concern. She knew he would survive.

Still, he sat there mute, not sharing his thoughts, and she gave up. For now.

She spread a handful of linen handkerchiefs across the table. "Look at the work on these. It's exquisite. Do you think this is all my grandmother's work?"

"Yes, certainly, and her mother's. But there were also a couple of much older maiden sisters who lived with them until they died when your mother was young."

"They had amazing skills. Yeah, maybe my great-grandmother, too. Some of this is very old. I've never seen work this elegant. I don't even know if they make needles and thread this fine anymore." Ultra-fine openwork, pulled-thread embroidery caught on a callus on her finger. Only a week into her community service and her hands were already a mess, despite wearing gloves. "I should donate these to a museum somewhere, but I'm too selfish."

"It's not selfish to hold onto your heritage when you've only just found it."

Dad had a good heart. She just wished she knew what he was holding back from her these days.

Back in her own apartment, she stored the embroidery in a small cedar chest. She got herself washed and ready for work. On the walk over along Main Street, she noticed a For Rent sign in the window of the old cigar shop that was in the process of shutting down. She peeked in through the window. Too bad she had to go to work. If she could linger until the store opened, she would love to see the interior, to check out the space. She hadn't been inside in years and had only gone in with Dad when he'd bought gifts for friends at Christmas.

She remembered mahogany countertops and stained glass pendant lamps. She could really work with that kind of atmosphere to turn it into a spectacular storefront.

If she was to start a small business, this spot would be perfect, but she didn't have a business idea, did she?

Deflated, she continued on to work. Ever since Monica had expressed her anger with both Noah and Olivia, things had been better at the gallery. She guessed her boss understood, finally, that Monica hadn't injured her son on purpose.

Either that or she was afraid of Monica. She smiled. That was okay, too. It wouldn't hurt for her boss to respect her more.

ANOTHER DAY, ANOTHER way to find Monica Accord too attractive.

This was absurd. He'd thought about Monica nonstop since their time in the attic yesterday morning. After they'd carted some of the items downstairs, Monica had hugged him hard and said, "Thank you" with the prettiest, most sincere smile, and then had run out to do her chores.

He'd stood in his front doorway dumbfounded,

the press of her body indelibly stamped on his. How was he supposed to deal with this new, warm Monica, who handed out hugs that left him rattled and wanting more?

Today he watched her straighten and walk to the end of the row, her stride both sultry and elegant. He followed her like a hound dog on the scent of a pheasant, wondering what she would look like without all of her plumage—the makeup and artifice that Monica used to put herself together every day.

The crass, shallow teenage boy still lurking inside of him wanted to see her naked.

She bent over to pick more weeds. Oh, Lord. His gaze shot away from her delectable derriere.

She let out a distressed cry. He ran to her.

"What's wrong?"

"That." She grabbed his arm, pointing with her other hand to a beet plant. A tremor of fear ran through her voice.

Noah edged closer, right into the circle of Monica's heat. He forced himself to ignore his body's traitorous reaction. *You will not, absolutely will not, desire this woman.*

Too late. His body refused to heed the message.

He followed her pointing finger. A small garter snake slept in the sun.

"It's harmless," he said.

"Kill it," she demanded, the real woman gone and the princess back on display.

Her demand inflamed his sense of injustice. He growled, "I'm not killing a harmless creature."

"But it's a snake." Real fear tinged her voice.

"Yeah, but it's harmless. Look." He picked it up and it curled around his fingers below his cast.

"Won't it bite you?"

"Not this kind. Here. Hold him."

She shrank away, backing up against the next row of plants. "Are you crazy? No way."

"Careful." He drew her away from the young seedlings. "Relax. I won't force you. I respect your fear. I just wanted to bust through some of your preconceptions about them."

"Like what? What do you think I'm thinking?"

His face only a foot away from hers, he noted how her nose had turned pink from the sun. Other than that, her skin was flawless.

"You think they're slimy," he said.

"Aren't they?"

He grinned. Bingo. She had thought exactly that. "No. Most people assume so, but they aren't. Besides, he's been basking in the sun. He'll be warm and dry."

"Seriously?"

He smiled at her, happy to hear the hint of curiosity in her voice.

"Do you want to hold him now?"

"No."

"How about touching him?"

"Mmm. Maybe."

"He is truly not slimy, and I promise that he's harmless."

"Okay, I'll try to touch him."

He took her gloved hand and held the snake over it. "Okay if I put him in your hand? You're wearing a thick glove."

"I think so. He's small. His head is sure tiny."

"Yeah. I wouldn't lay a python on you." He placed the snake on her hand, where it curled up. "You ready?"

She trembled slightly.

"You want me to take him back? I won't force you, Monica. My thing is to get people to appreciate nature, but it has to be their choice."

She stiffened. "You know what, Noah? I want to get past this fear. Up close, he's actually a cute little guy."

He smiled again. He liked her courage. "He is," he said, pulling her glove from her other hand. "Okay, now touch him."

She hesitated.

"Want me to take him back?"

"Nope." She smiled tremulously. "I'm just working up my nerve."

"You're doing well." He took her long, soft, tanned forefinger in his and directed it toward the snake's skin.

Monica jumped and then settled. "You're right," she admitted, wonder in her voice. "He isn't slimy."

She touched the snake and then pulled away. "Okay. He's not as creepy as I thought, but I don't want to hold him any longer."

Noah laughed. "All right, just put him back with the plants where he belongs."

"Thanks," she said as she set the little guy on the ground.

"For what?"

"For setting me straight about snakes. Now I won't be afraid of them."

That chilled him. Not all snakes were friendly or safe. "Okay, listen, this guy was harmless, but many aren't. Come on."

He didn't have time for this. He really needed to get the entire beet crop weeded before opening the shop, but he also had to keep Monica safe. She was his responsibility as long as she worked on his farm. The thought of someone in his care getting hurt sent him into a panic.

He rushed her into the farmhouse, toeing off his sandals inside the door, with visions of Monica making friends with every snake she encountered. Cripes, what if she picked up a rattlesnake one day?

From one of his overflowing bookshelves, he retrieved a book.

"Noah, I want to get more linens from the attic before I leave today. I really want to show Audrey."

"Hey, great. That's just the kind of stuff she would love."

"That's what I thought."

"But first, come here," he said and sat on the sagging sofa. "I'll show you the snakes you *shouldn't* get close to."

She moved a week's worth of newspapers he hadn't had time to read to the coffee table. "Your place is messy."

"That's because I don't have time to clean. I run a business in town that doesn't bring in oodles of money so I can't hire anyone, which means I work six days a week. Plus, the farming I do doesn't bring in any money because I give all of the produce away to charity, so I can't hire a maid."

"Don't you care about money?" She sounded genuinely curious.

Don't underestimate her.

He set the book in his lap. "I do. I have a healthy respect for what it can do for people. I'm not so naive that I don't understand the value of it in my life and for my future—that's why I work hard. But I can't care so much about it that I won't give to others, or that I'll care more for keeping my house clean than working in service to others."

Monica nodded in understanding and sat down beside Noah. He opened the book to show her snakes she should avoid that were native to Colorado.

"You have a lot of strange ideas, Noah," she said, "but I'm starting to respect what you think."

His pulse lurched. *She respects what I think.* Her opinion shouldn't matter so much. It did.

She picked up the book and thumbed through it.

She'd stunned him with her simple honesty. For once, he was speechless.

MARCIE GREEN RODE into town on a wing and a prayer, last dime spent, belly empty, stomach kissing her backbone, every nerve and pore end-of-the-road gutted and hollowed out. She'd hit rock bottom.

She couldn't help but sigh. *Girl, you're a walking bundle of clichés.*

Yeah, she sure was.

The one and only bus that came through town let her off on Main Street.

That old feeling of being new *and* outside *and* a stranger assaulted her like an old enemy—or friend, perhaps the only one she had these days. At least it was something familiar. There was so little in her life she could think of as familiar these days.

Up and down the street, residents who belonged here strode with purpose, while she stood, just letting it all happen around her. She should have belonged here, too, but she'd been robbed.

And it was past time to right a grievous wrong.

She studied the town like a connoisseur. Sizing up every new town was something she'd become good at. Every town had a unique character.

Accord, Colorado.

She knew next to nothing about it except that, if she had her way, it would become home. Her new home, last home, only home she'd ever need from now on. She'd moved so many times, she barely knew how to spell *home* let alone recognize it when she found it.

She studied her new *maybe* home.

Spruced-up storefronts lined the street. Old-fashioned globe lamps on black cast-iron posts held huge baskets of blue lobelia and white alyssum, along with orange pendulum and pink tuberous begonias.

Pretty.

Donna had been an avid gardener and had indulged her interest in every new town they'd lived in, for as long or as little as they'd stayed. She had taught Marcie a lot.

When she thought of Donna, spasms of betrayal wrenched Marcie's empty belly. Mere seconds after Donna had told her the truth, Marcie had left her in the hospital and hadn't looked back.

For all of her life, she had thought Donna was the one person she could trust. How wrong she'd been.

She rubbed her hand across her stomach. "Settle down."

A man walking by smiled at her. "New haircut. Nice change. It suits you."

People sure were friendly here.

Movement in a window nearby caught Marcie's attention. Just beyond the glass, a man watched her intently. Unlike the friendly guy who'd just said hello to her, this man's eyes were calculating, sizing her up.

Marcie checked the name on the door. John Spade. A lawyer.

If this tall, dark-haired guy standing in the window

was Mr. Spade, he was a good-looking man, even if too spit-shined for Marcie's taste. A lawyer, though. He had to be making a good living.

Conscious that the suit he wore was worth more than everything she owned, which was stuffed in her backpack, she thought *money is everything*. She needed money. Now. Yesterday. For her entire life there hadn't been enough. Soon all of her troubles would be over, maybe even by the end of the day.

She had plans.

The way lawyer-man John Spade studied her, as though he could see into her mind and dissect those plans, sent a chill up her spine.

As she walked away, she felt the man's eyes still on her.

All along Main Street, her thoughts echoed the pace of her footsteps.

I want. I want. I want.

She passed a café with a lineup stretching nearly to the door. A woman with a small girl by her side stepped out with a huge bag in her hand, no doubt full of baked goods, smiled at Marcie then walked on down the street.

The child nibbled on a cookie with yellow icing.

Mind-numbing scents drifted out of the bakery, cinnamon and sugar and vanilla.

Marcie's mouth watered.

If she had her way, she would enter, take a seat and order everything in the display cases—but she didn't have a cent to her name.

Staring in through windows and doors closed to her—this, too, was familiar.

An outsider looking in.

Story of her life. Always on the outside.

Soon, though, that would change.

She wandered through town, getting the lay of the land, passing the impressive and stately old Victorian B-and-B. She read the plaque out front. It used to belong to the founding father, Ian Accord.

She continued on until she found the house owned by the current Accord descendants, Milton Accord and his daughter, Monica. It wasn't quite as impressive as Ian's house, but it could hold its own in any of the dreams she'd had about it.

She approached along a walkway lined with purple and white sweet alyssum. She kind of doubted either Milton or his daughter did the actual planting themselves. They probably had plenty of employees to indulge their every need.

The clomping of her boots echoed on the stately veranda. She shouldn't be wearing boots in June. They made her feet hot. But she had no money to buy sandals. Not yet.

She knocked on the door.

The man who answered was handsome, his face only lightly lined. At a guess, she would put him in his early to mid-sixties. He was aging well, with that patina of gloss Marcie associated with the wealthy.

When he saw her, his eyebrows rose to his perfectly barbered, tastefully graying hairline.

His eyes grew misty.

She hardened herself to the emotions she saw there—love, hope and guilt in equal measure.

As much as she wanted to give in, especially to react to the love, there was no room in her heart for sentimentality. She was on a mission.

When he didn't say anything, just continued to watch her with a mixture of expectation and dread, she took matters into her own hands.

"Hi, Dad. Can I come in?"

CHAPTER SEVEN

MONICA TURNED OFF the alarm clock and rolled over in bed. She stared at the ceiling, thoughtful, musing on how the simple things in life could reap the biggest rewards.

She was really starting to get off on this farming business. The days were flying by, one after another.

She was falling into bed every night dead tired and waking up refreshed and ready to work. When was the last time she'd felt like that?

On the heels of that thought came a more surprising one. She looked forward to going to the farm every morning not only for the fresh air, sunshine and satisfying crunch of honest labor, but also for the chance to see Noah.

She liked learning from him. Every day he taught her something new. Yesterday's lesson about snakes had turned out to be less terrifying and more edifying than she would have ever thought.

Throwing back the covers and bounding out of bed, she splashed water on her face, applied face toner and brushed her teeth. She ate breakfast before calling her dad. She'd tried repeatedly last night, but he hadn't picked up.

Just before heading out, she called him again. No answer. Maybe he was sleeping in.

So after putting in a deeply satisfying two hours

at the farm, she came home and showered then tried him again. Still no answer.

Okay, this was getting really strange. Dad was always available to her. She had nothing earth-shattering to share. She only wanted to tell him about how good working on the farm felt—how much less a punishment and more a learning experience it was turning out to be.

If she couldn't reach him later today, she'd stop by and see him tonight.

At lunchtime, Monica stepped out to pick up something at Tonio's—she needed her Maria-and-Joseph fix today.

"Maria," she called up through the open window of the office.

Maria rushed down to greet her. "You have garlic scapes again? We finally have some in, but had to order them from across the other side of Colorado."

"Actually I brought something to show you. Not food," she explained, taking a couple of embroidered handkerchiefs out of her purse.

"Ooooh. Where did you find these?" Maria handled them with care. "This work is beautiful. My grandmother used to do this kind of thing when I was a little girl back home in Italy."

Monica explained everything.

"Your heritage. It's good to become acquainted with it. How lucky for you it was still in the house."

"It seems that no one wanted to take responsibility for it, so they just left it there."

"I'm happy for you, Monica. I would love to see the rest."

"Yes! Come for coffee the next time we have a day off together."

They burst into laughter. They never had a day off at the same time. It would be even worse now that Monica had all of this community service to put in.

She picked up a sandwich and salad then stopped in to see her former sister-in-law, Audrey, in her floral shop.

She found Audrey alone in the store. They hugged.

"I just have a couple of minutes before I have to head back. I'll eat my lunch in the back room of the gallery."

"Sit down and eat it here. It's been a slow day."

Monica loved the scent of The Last Dance and loved being surrounded by flowers, everything in Audrey's shop fresh and green.

"Love your dress," Monica said. They had such different styles, but she adored Audrey's flamboyance. Today, she wore a red dress with huge white polka dots and a neckline that fell off her shoulders. She had a full figure, so Audrey must have been wearing heavy-duty foundation garments to get away with going strapless.

"I brought something to show you." Monica took out the hankies and Audrey pounced on them.

"Oh, my God, these are genuine, aren't they? Handworked? None of that machine-embroidered crap. Where on earth did you find them?"

Monica explained, and then disclosed, "Noah said I can keep anything I find that belonged to my family."

"Oh, Monica, that's so great." Audrey raced around the counter and enveloped her in a hug. "I'm so happy you've found this part of your history."

Monica felt her eyes water. Audrey understood. "Yes. It's too good to be true." After she'd married Billy, she'd been so happy to find she shared a major life event with his sister—losing a mother too early—and finally had someone to talk to about it. The loss of their mother hadn't seemed to affect Billy as much as it had Audrey. He'd never talked about it. Audrey had, though, and for that Monica would be eternally grateful.

"This was my heritage. Dad should have retrieved it for me years ago. But he said he didn't think to check the attic when he sold."

"Maybe he was too grief-stricken."

Monica nodded, thoughtful, trying to remember. "I was just a newborn, but I think for a little while after her death, just from remarks I've heard over the years, Dad drank too much back then."

"It wouldn't surprise me."

"He's drinking too much again."

"I suspected as much. He's not the strongest man around." Audrey slapped a hand across her lips, as though to catch the words and shove them back into her mouth. "I'm so sorry. I shouldn't have said that."

Monica squeezed her arm. "It's okay. It's the truth. I've come to accept that over the years."

"Given what my own dad is like now, I had no right to say that."

"Another thing we have in common." Monica's smile felt very sad. Even as adults, children still needed their parents. But maybe now was the time to give back, for the happy childhood Monica's dad had given her.

Audrey spread the fine linen handkerchiefs across her counter. "Look at the work on these. It's exquisite. I'd love to see the rest."

"Come over next week. You want to talk exquisite? The bedsitting jackets are to die for."

They made a date for the following week and Monica left the shop.

Noah might not be crazy about her, Olivia remained a tiny bit angry at her, and her dad seemed emotionally unavailable these days, but Monica still had friends in town who cared about her. Sometimes she just needed her fix.

A woman stepped in front of her.

"Oh, excuse me." Monica nearly bumped into her then stopped and stared, and stared more. Monica could have been looking into a mirror. This woman could be *her.* In that second, the air became too thin and the sunshine too bright.

Dizzy, she stumbled but caught herself.

She raised her hand not only to block out the sun, but also the vision of this woman in front of her.

Monica had a strange ominous sense that her world was about to blow apart.

In a moment of unwelcome insight, a lot became clear—her father's evasiveness, his worry, his drinking. A dark cloud had arrived in town, one her father must have known was heading this way. The storm's face was Monica's, albeit with a harder edge and a keen hunger in her eyes.

The hair was short and funky, but the face was Monica's.

The woman spoke and Monica tried to block out the sound of the voice because it, too, was her own.

"We were lied to," this nameless person with Monica's face and voice and body said. "Our parents kept us apart our entire lives."

Our *parents* kept us apart? Not just dad, but our *parents*? But Monica's mom was dead. Wasn't she?

"I'm your twin sister," the woman said, still using the voice she'd stolen from Monica.

"My *what*?" Monica put out her hands to ward off this creature, this lying scumbag alien.

"Your twin."

"No."

"Yes."

"I don't believe you."

"It's true."

Wild with dread, her glance ricocheted around this normal street in ordinary Accord. She was ready to wake up from this nightmare, any minute, any second. *Come on. Wake up.*

But no. This was real. She pinched her arm. She was awake. She hadn't slipped into a parallel galaxy.

Glaring at the woman, Monica leaned her hand on the outside wall of Audrey's shop, brick abrading her palm with the bite of reality. "You're a liar. This is a sick joke."

This couldn't be happening.

Coherent thought eluded her.

This person, this woman with *her* face and *her* body, had to be playing a trick on Monica.

"I'm not a liar," the woman insisted. "But *we* were deceived."

"I don't believe you." Nor did she believe her own eyesight. This wasn't real, was some kind of optical illusion her fevered brain had conjured, except that she wasn't fevered and she wasn't overtired and she was eminently rational.

She squeezed her eyes shut then opened them. The woman, the one who was Monica but not Monica, was still there. "Who are you?"

Her mouth had gone dry. Her blood pounded, roared through her ears as though a freight train thundered down Main Street.

What was wrong with the air today? Why was it so thin? She couldn't breathe. Light-headed, she stumbled to one of the park benches town council had installed along Main Street for beautification and sat heavily, her legs no longer able to support her.

The woman followed her. "I'm Marcie Green.

I used to be Marcie Granger. I should be Marcie Accord, but our dad kept you instead of me."

Our dad. Was that bitterness in the ersatz Monica's tone? Dad kept Monica instead of this woman? Of course he kept her. She was his daughter. This woman wasn't. What kind of nonsense was this woman spewing?

"Are you on drugs? Go away." She tried to yell, but croaked instead. "Why are you lying?"

"Look at me." Voice fervent, the woman touched her own face. "Look at this. We're dead ringers for each other. I'm not lying. We are sisters."

"Don't say that!" Monica slashed her hand toward the woman, not making contact, but desperately wanting to hit her, to annihilate her, to make her go away so Monica could pretend this never happened.

The problem with seeing a thing, though, was that once seen, it could never again be unseen. Once seen, it lingered forever in the recesses of the mind. Even with shock and disbelief, Monica would never be able to lock out the memory of having seen this woman's face.

Still, she fought. "Don't you dare say we're sisters. It isn't true."

"For God's sake, open your eyes," the woman said, leaning forward as though to convince Monica with the force of her personality and her desire. "We are sisters."

"Why are you being so mean to me? I don't even know you."

The woman looked like she was trying to control herself as she drew in a huge breath and held it. When it whooshed out of her, she seemed calmer.

"You're right. I am being hard. I've had a few weeks to get over my shock, but this is new to you. I'm your sister—your twin."

Impossible. Daddy had never lied to her in her life.

A thought occurred to her, one that gave her strength in its existence as a possibility. Why hadn't she realized it from the start? "This is a scam, isn't it? Did you see my photo on Facebook or on the internet somewhere?" She shoved the woman away from her. "Don't stand so close to me. Did you think just because you look a bit like me you could get up close and personal and rip us off? Is that it?"

"I don't look *a bit* like you. Except for our different styles, I look *exactly* like you. I'm telling the truth."

But Monica refused to buy it. "Go to hell."

She ran away, sped away, because she didn't want this woman following her to her father's house, where she planned to get answers once and for all about why her dad had been acting strange lately.

Was it this woman? Was this Marcie Green shaking down her dad for money? But she'd also called herself Marcie Granger. There were Grangers who lived a fair distance outside of Accord, but Monica didn't know them well.

Her head hurt.

How could the woman possibly get money from Dad? There was nothing to blackmail. Dad would know he didn't have another daughter. Mom died giving birth to one child, not two.

Our parents kept us apart.

No. Mom died giving birth to Monica.

Delivering one child. Not two.

NOAH SPOTTED MONICA farther down the block. He should tell her to come to the farm tomorrow despite predicted rainstorms. Farming didn't wait on the weather. Farmers were a lot like postal carriers. What was their motto? Neither rain nor sleet nor… whatever.

Monica's hair wasn't hanging down her back as it usually did. She must have it pinned up somehow.

He picked up his pace to catch up to her.

"Monica," he called. She ignored him.

He hustled. With a hand on her elbow, he turned her around. His breath caught in his chest.

Something was wrong. Off.

This was Monica, but not Monica.

Her hair was gone, not pinned up, but hacked off. Had she really cut off all of that gorgeous hair that shimmered almost white in sunshine?

Over the course of one morning, she'd become funky with spiked hair and out-of-character clothing. Monica was always classy. This woman looked anything but.

Noah might have thought he would want Monica to lighten up, but now that she'd changed, he wanted the old Monica back. The real her.

"What did you do?" he asked, sounding pugnacious. "Why'd you cut off all of your hair?"

The woman touched the back of her head where the short ends met her nape.

"I didn't." Even her voice sounded slightly different, huskier and sexy.

"This isn't funny, Monica. What are you playing at?"

"I'm not Monica." She stuck out her hand. "I'm Marcie."

"This is a sick game."

"Nope. Not a game. I'm Monica's sister. Her twin, actually."

"Monica doesn't have a twin. Is this some kind of scam?"

Monica-not-Monica dropped her hand because Noah hadn't shaken it, and he had no intention of doing so. He didn't like being played for a fool.

"I'm serious," she said quietly, her expression sober. "I'm Monica Accord's twin. I only found out about her a couple of weeks ago."

Noah scratched his beard. "How—? What—?" He couldn't fathom what he should ask first. He knew she was telling the truth because, despite the surface similarities, there was a profound difference between this woman and Monica. This was not Monica. "Stuff like this happens in fiction, not in real life."

"I know. As shocked as you are about this, imagine how I felt discovering I had a sister my parents had kept from me." The smile on her face belied the bitterness of her tone. This woman wasn't happy, no matter how hard she would like him to believe she was.

He backed away from her.

He needed to talk to Monica before she saw this woman. He started down the street toward the gallery before pulling up short.

The woman still stood on Main Street watching him.

"Does Monica know?"

A sad smile tugged at her lips. "As of five minutes ago."

Oh, no. Noah flew to the gallery.

He stared in through the large front window. No Monica. He rushed inside.

"Mom!"

She came out of the back office.

"Where's Monica?"

"How should I know? I don't know what's going on with her these days. She went out for lunch and never came back."

"I'll try to find her."

"When you do, tell her I'm angry enough to fire her."

"Hold off on that thought, Mom. I think she has her reasons. Good reasons."

The expression on her face changed, morphed from anger to curiosity to concern—he guessed that she'd been alerted by the panic that must be showing on his own face.

"What's wrong?"

"I don't know what's going on, but something really strange just happened on Main Street and it affects Monica. She's got to be in shock right now."

He opened the door and said before leaving, "The second I get an explanation, I'll let you know."

He searched every shop and her apartment, but couldn't find her. He surmised she might be at her father's house, in which case it was best to leave them alone. So that's what he did, grudgingly.

But all afternoon and into the evening, while gossip swirled through town, it ate away at him. If he was so bothered by this new person in town, the whole thing must be catastrophic for Monica.

Why should he be worried about her? Sure, he'd had a crush on her for years, but the feeling had not been reciprocated. So why worry about her?

The simple answer stunned him. He cared. He was learning that she was more than she appeared to be and he didn't want to see her hurt.

He cared.

THE SECOND MONICA entered her father's house sorrow wept into her bones.

It no longer felt like home. Her childhood, her life to this point, had been a huge deception. A fraud.

Her mind, already giving in to the suspicions her heart fought so strenuously, shifted when she stepped into the living room and found her father sitting on the sofa, red-faced, his demeanor sloppy.

He'd been drinking. A glass hung precariously from two fingers, about to fall. No matter. It was empty.

When she entered the room, he watched her with a level of insolence she'd never seen in him before. The room reeked of body odor and booze. She flung open curtains and windows.

When he saw her face, his insolence faded and became what she was certain he'd been trying to bolster himself against—his own guilt.

"So you finally know," he said with a resigned sigh.

It was true.

Oh, Daddy.

A sense of betrayal choked her. Her childhood home was now a deep freeze of a tomb—a repository of dead dreams and memories.

A chill that had been only skin-deep now spread through to her core. She rubbed her arms then wrapped them around her waist, but the rawness intensified.

She couldn't begin to process this huge, heinous crime.

"Why?" she whispered, because her voice wasn't working well enough to yell. She wanted to rant and ask more and maybe even hit him for this grave, awful secret. Secrets. Plural. He'd not only never told her she had a sister, but, far worse, he'd also led her to believe her mother was dead. They could have known each other. They could have visited.

Where was she now?

The depth of her heartache couldn't be measured in ordinary words.

"Why?" she blurted on a ragged wail.

The last of her father's defiance faded and he sobered up. He patted the sofa beside him.

"Sit. Please."

She did, but chose an armchair across the room, where she curled herself into a ball. She couldn't touch him right now, couldn't be close to him.

For the first time since entering the room, she allowed herself to really look at him. His bloodshot eyes were caused by more than just drunkenness. He'd been crying.

She crossed her arms, both to protect herself from what was to come and from any flimsy excuses he might offer up. Nothing could excuse this. *Nothing.*

He seemed to take note of her body language and sighed. When he rose to retrieve the Scotch bottle from the sideboard, she shook her head.

"No. Leave it. We talk without it. It's time for honesty because, apparently, there has been *none* in our relationship. First question. Is my mother alive?"

He grimaced, but set down the bottle and returned to the sofa empty-handed.

"No." He rested one elbow on the arm of the sofa and covered his eyes. "I'm sorry."

When she made a sound, a mewl of disappointment, he dropped his hand and regarded her with a damp gaze. "I wish she was. I would give anything for you to have known her."

The temptation to cross the floor and hold him, both to offer comfort and to receive it, softened her too much. She hardened her heart.

"I need answers."

"It's a long story." He scrubbed his fingers through his hair, mussing it even more. "Sometimes it doesn't make sense to me, but your mother and I did what we thought was best."

When she would have interrupted, he raised a staying hand. "I know it won't seem like it to you. Not at first. But hear me out. We were young and scared and had tough decisions to make."

He stared at the coffee table, where rings left by too many drinks had scarred the antique mahogany. When Monica had still lived here, that table had been spotless. The damage was recent.

Sacrilege popped into Monica's mind, her concentration stuck on a minor detail that was out of place in this moment. She quelled the thought. Who cared about furniture right now? All that mattered was the truth.

"We married too young, straight out of high school. We were nineteen, Karen only just turned, but we loved each other." His breath hitched, raising suspicion in Monica.

"Is that completely true?"

"Yes, but it was complicated. We thought we could make it work anyway."

"You've always led me to believe you adored her."

"I did. Deeply. I've never found anyone who could replace her."

His expression crumpled. His face grew older. For long moments, Monica waited for him to speak again without prompting. He'd gone somewhere deep and private.

Then he said, "I loved *her*, at any rate." His voice was weak. "As it turned out, she loved someone else."

Monica's chill grew. In all of Dad's stories he'd never said anything about Mom not loving him. "Not Judge Easton," she said, voice flat. That would be the ultimate betrayal.

"God, no." John barked out a laugh. "She hated the guy. Couldn't stand his arrogant and bullying ways. The man you saw in court? Just an older version of the teenager we went to school with. Gord hasn't changed one iota."

"Then who was it?"

"Her best friend."

"I thought you were her best friend. Why did she marry you if she loved another guy? Who was he?"

"*She* was Donna Granger."

"She?" Monica startled. "Mom was lesbian?"

"Yes. Same-sex marriage was illegal at the time— keep in mind it was nearly forty years ago—and Karen was trying desperately to deny who she really was. She thought she could make herself love me as more than a friend."

Monica reeled, stunned into silence. Her mother had been gay.

"It wasn't as open a time as it is now," her dad continued, while Monica struggled to catch up to this new development.

"Wait. Slow down." She got up to retrieve a throw from the back of the sofa and wrapped it around herself, holding it so tightly her knuckles turned white as she curled into the armchair like a wounded animal.

Dad sat back and gave her a chance to breathe. "This is big stuff, I know."

Could that be any more of an understatement? How about enormous? Huge? Catastrophic? She had a sister she hadn't known about. *Big* couldn't begin to describe the beast devouring her intestines.

When she felt she could see clearly without her thoughts caroming around, she said, "Go on. Tell me everything."

"She was terrified her parents would find out she loved a woman, but after our one time sleeping together on our wedding night, we knew it would never work between us. It's really hard for a guy to stay aroused when a woman is gritting her teeth to get through the sex."

"Too much information, Dad!"

"God. You're right. I'm sorry, Monica." He reached into his pocket to take out his cigarettes then dropped his hand. Monica had been so proud of him when he'd given them up three years ago. Looked like his body still remembered the habit of reaching for a cig in times of stress. "I do want you to know one thing, though. There was true affection between us. We were good friends. Your mother was a warm, physical woman. We held hands and hugged. It was unfortunate there was nothing romantic on her side.

"Anyway," he continued, dropping his hands into his lap, "she was confused. Lost. So was I. She confessed how she felt about Donna. How were we supposed to make our marriage work? How could either of us live the rest of our lives without a physical relationship and without a romantic attachment to each other? We decided our only course of action was divorce." He stood and wandered to the window, staring outside, but his gaze looked unfocused. "Then we found out she was pregnant from that one night."

"With me."

Over his shoulder, he smiled at her sadly. He didn't state the obvious. *With two of you.*

"Were you upset?"

His smile turned sweet. "God, no. I was happy. Overjoyed."

"It complicated things, though?"

He nodded.

"So, what happened?"

"Since she was pregnant, we couldn't divorce."

"Why? It's not like you lived in the Dark Ages. People got divorced, Dad, even when they were expecting."

"I know. The problem was her parents. They were deeply religious. They used to stifle her with their rules and prayers. Personally, I think they were so strict with her because they guessed how close she and Donna were. They would have been horrified. This went so far against their religious beliefs. At one point in adolescence, they actually forbade her to see Donna, so the two met in secret."

He jiggled the change in his pockets and wandered around the room restlessly. "She told me everything after our wedding night. Before you think poorly of her, I need to stress again that she had genuine affection for me. She apologized so often I grew sick of hearing it. Her intentions had been good. She'd been certain she could make it work, until the wedding night when she realized she'd made a catastrophic error in judgment. Too bad I was hurt in the process."

"I'm glad she loved you at least a little. Not just this other woman."

He sat back down and seemed to shrink. It must have hit him hard back then to learn the truth about his wife. If this situation was bad for her, what must it have been like for him?

"Yes, she loved me, too, but not as much as she loved Donna. She loved me as a friend, a buddy. We had been friends since childhood. She knew I would never hurt her, but it was a mess. Foolishly, I hoped I could change her heart, that I could make her love me more. Of course, it didn't work. I understand things better now."

"So what did you do?"

"First, we moved away from Accord. It was too

hard to figure things out with her parents constantly telling her how she should be living her life. We limited our contact with them. We needed time and space to think."

"Where did you go?"

"We moved to a small town in Colorado. We didn't tell her parents we stayed that close. We needed to be away to figure out a way out of our problems, by ourselves, without them breathing down our necks."

"But what about the babies? You must have found out there were two of us."

"Yeah. That was a shocker. We were thrilled and terrified. We were too young to make rational decisions." He stood again, like a jackrabbit, unable to settle.

"Your mom was caught between a rock and a hard place. She couldn't marry the woman she loved. Her parents would have been horrified. They weren't evil. They were afraid of something they didn't understand. They wondered what they had done wrong to make her the way she was." With a rueful twist of his lips, he added, "Even while they denied that she was the way she was."

"So what happened? You devised a diabolical plan?" Her anger might have abated, but only a bit. These people had rolled a pair of dice that had affected her life irreparably.

Brow rising, he responded, "Diabolical? No. We didn't think so." His surprise that she would think it was seemed genuine.

"There must have been something else you could have done," she cried, pounding the arm of her chair.

"Like what?" he demanded. "Tell me, in your great wisdom, what would have been a better course?"

"There's no need for sarcasm. Or yelling."

Dad gripped the hair on the sides of his head, leaving it to stand out like a demented scientist's. "Yes, there is. You don't get to second-guess our decision. We were young, little more than *half* your age now. What would you have had us do?" He gestured toward her and her uptight, resistant body language. "It's easy for you to sit there in judgment like some grand pooh-bah. You didn't have to find solutions. Hindsight is easy, especially at your age in a different, more accepting time. If we had stayed together, we were looking at a lifetime of pain for both of us. And loneliness. We couldn't even sleep together as husband and wife. Do you think either of us wanted that for the rest of our lives?"

She had nothing to say. Maybe he was right. Maybe not.

"Don't you think we questioned our choices over the years? Don't you think I did, especially after—"

The guilt on his face had hairs on the back of her neck rising. "After?"

He rubbed the back of his hand across his mouth. "Never mind."

"No, Dad. No more lies. No more omissions. I need to know everything."

"First I need a coffee." He made a move to stand,

but fell back onto the sofa like a dying fish. "I need a coffee," he repeated, as though focusing on that detail could keep everything at bay.

"I'll get it." She needed a break, too.

When they were settled in with mugs of hot coffee, he said, "Let me finish what happened with the birth before we move on to the rest."

The rest?

There hadn't been enough already? What more could there possibly be?

CHAPTER EIGHT

"IN THE HOSPITAL, everything was fevered. Rushed. We were making decisions too quickly. We had chosen to deliver in Denver instead of locally and didn't tell Karen's parents when she went into labor—we didn't want them showing up. Only Donna was there, with a car trunk full of suitcases.

"Karen was worried but also excited. Her life to that point had been deeply unhappy because she hadn't been able to express who she really was.

"She said she wanted happiness. For once in her life, she wanted to be truly happy." His voice cracked.

Oh, Dad, you poor thing. "Was that hard for you to hear? That she hadn't been truly happy with you?"

He stared out the window and swallowed before answering. "Yes. I had already come to accept it, but to see her so happy to be leaving me, it…"

Monica knew her dad well. "You tried really hard to make her happy, didn't you?" A determined man, Dad wouldn't have gone down without a fight.

"Oh, yes." His smile, sweet with traces of his remembered youth, turned inward, snagged by memories. "I used to bring home these little bouquets of violets. She called them posies. She loved them. Of course, I learned quickly that I couldn't buy her love. She would smile and thank me sweetly, but I might as well have been her brother for all the romantic love she showed."

"That hurt?"

"Yes."

"Did it make you angry?"

"It might have if she'd been a different person. All of that great stuff I told you about her every night before you went to bed?"

She nodded.

"It was all true." He traveled inward again on a private journey that Monica couldn't follow.

She would like to leave him to continue his trip down memory lane as long as he needed, but the here and now pressed in on her. "At the hospital, Dad?"

"You have to understand that we weren't fully mature adults yet. We were trying hard to be, but we weren't strong, and now we were responsible for two young souls.

"As I said, your mom wanted to be happy. She thought that if she returned to Accord with me, to live in close proximity to her parents, she wouldn't be. So she and Donna were running away together."

"With the babies?"

He nodded. "That was the decision she had made and I had truly thought I would be okay with that. You were born first and I made the mistake of holding you. I fell in love. There was a bond. I'd never felt anything like it. I couldn't let my babies go.

"We fought and it wasn't pretty. Donna got involved, accusing me of being selfish. Goddamned right I was being selfish. You were my baby girls, too, not just Karen's."

He jiggled one knee up and down. "We came to a compromise and decided to each keep a baby."

"Dad, that's insane. An absurd decision. Things like this don't happen in real life."

"Want to bet?" he snorted. "Read the papers. Go on the internet. For years I was obsessed with finding real-life stories about twins separated at birth. I read newspapers from the largest cities across America. I searched the internet for lost-twins stories, found tons of them from around the world and was heartened any time they found each other. It happens more often than you would think. Believe it or not."

Dad stared into the cold, empty fireplace.

"You have to remember we lived in a small town, not someplace progressive like New York City. This was forty years ago. I know that doesn't sound so long ago, but it's taken time and years for people's attitudes to change. Personally, I didn't care what people thought. Karen did. Her parents had raised her to worry."

"Were they a good couple?"

"Karen and Donna? Yeah," he admitted. "They really were. They loved each other. Anyway, we both ended up with a daughter. Karen's parents were furious that she had run off with Donna, angrier about that than about one of their grandbabies being taken away. Which really bothered me.

"They disowned Karen and told everyone she had died birthing you. To my eternal regret, I went along with them so they could save face in the community.

And so there I was, living alone in a strange town with you. I decided I wanted you to grow up in Accord. I moved back home. I needed there to be stability in your life, and we have a history here. Also, I moved back here with you so my parents could get to know their grandchild, but they died far too soon."

"Did they know that Mom was still alive?"

"Yes. I told them. I couldn't keep that from my own parents. They didn't agree with the way in which Karen's parents handled things, but your grandparents had always been liberal in their leanings. They accepted a lot."

"My mom's parents died when I was a toddler. Why didn't you contact my mother then so I could meet her, so I could know her over the years?"

He reached his hand into his pocket again for a nonexistent cigarette and withdrew it. "Because, in the most…" He drummed his fist on his thigh hard enough that it looked like it hurt. His jaw tightened. "In the most *perverse* and unfair irony, your mom died only a week after they did, in a hit-and-run."

Monica sucked in a breath that froze in her lungs. So close. She had almost known her mother. Learning that she hadn't died giving birth to her and now realizing she had lived for a few years afterward was like losing her again.

"Why couldn't I have met Marcie? Why didn't you bring us together then?"

"Because Donna disappeared with her after Karen's death."

"Why?"

Bleakly, he said, "Because I told her I wanted to bring Marcie home. The hell with what the town thought of our deceptions. Cripes, every town has its scandals. I wanted you two to be raised together."

"And Donna wouldn't agree to that?"

"No. She was grieving and said she had to keep the only part of Karen she had left. Her daughter. She said I could hire all of the lawyers on earth, and all of the detectives, but they would never find her and Marcie. She was going to raise Marcie as her own." His voice cracked and he took a moment to pull himself together.

"I offered to purchase her a home in town. She said she refused to live like Marcie's aunt or a distant relative. She insisted she was now Marcie's mother. I never heard from her again."

"Then how—?"

"Marcie contacted me two weeks ago. While Donna was in the hospital waiting for surgery, she shared Marcie's history with her in case she didn't make it. Now Donna is the one who's been disowned, by Marcie who is very, very angry about everything."

"No wonder." Monica was angry, too. She wasn't sure how she was going to deal with it. "Where do we go from here? Do we all pretend we're one big happy family?"

Her dad sighed. "I wish I knew."

The gulf between them might as well have been an ocean. Monica had never felt this far away from the only family she knew. It hurt. It was sad. She couldn't let it go. She had no one else, except apparently a sister.

"May I come over there?"

He stared at her with hope. He opened his arms. She crossed the divide that separated them and burrowed into him, tucking her legs under her and tossing the throw over both of them.

She curled against his chest on the sofa, safe within the curve of his arm across her back, like old times, except that these were new, uncertain times.

She rested her head on his shoulder.

"It's just you and me against the world, kid." Dad's old line.

"Things have changed, though, haven't they?"

His sigh rumbled up from deep inside of him. "Yep, they sure have."

"Will she become part of our family?"

"She already is. You two share DNA. You once shared a womb. Your mother is dead. Donna has been rejected by Marcie, who is the only parent she ever knew, but she still has a father here in this house. I assume she'll want to get to know me."

"Do you want to get to know her?"

"What do you think?" By not answering her question directly, she knew he was trying to soften the blow.

"You do."

"She's my daughter."

So simple a truth. So shattering.

They sat in silence for a long, long time, lost in their thoughts.

The doorbell rang, startling both of them.

Monica answered it.

Marcie stood on the veranda.

"Come in," Monica said, coming to realize this stranger had as much right to be in her father's home as Monica did.

She didn't know what to do with this woman—didn't know how to be with her.

It was all too eerie to look into someone else's face and see your own.

Marcie entered the living room. Monica stayed where she was. She heard her father ask, "How are you doing?"

"Okay." Monica heard uncertainty in that voice, so like her own. "People in town are looking at me strangely."

"Of course they are. This is probably the strangest thing to happen in Accord in decades."

Monica stood in the doorway, noting the affection on her father's face as he talked to this other woman, as well as seeing the hope on Marcie's face.

Change was here to stay and Monica didn't know what to do. Tired, exhausted by too many revelations, all she wanted was her bed. She didn't care that it was only four or five in the afternoon, she needed to sleep, to escape all of this unwelcome reality barreling down on her.

"I have to go."

They stared at her.

"Now?" Dad asked. "You can't stay a while to get to know your sister?"

Her sister.

"Later. I need to rest."

Monica left, because this woman was already making inroads into her life, and Monica wasn't ready to make room for her.

When she returned to her apartment, there were phone messages from Maria, Audrey, John Spade and Laura Cameron. She returned none of them. At some point she would have to talk to people. Not yet.

She stripped out of her clothes, dropping everything onto the floor, then crawled into bed. She slept fitfully that evening and into the night, when she slept at all.

Her alarm went off, the radio came on, she rolled onto her back and stared at the ceiling in the gray light of dawn, but no answers about where she went from here magically appeared.

Did she care? Should she care? Not today.

Too many revelations, too much emotion, had left her as deboned and lifeless as the fish she'd caught with Noah.

She brushed her hand across Billy's side of the bed, the fabric soft, but offering scant comfort.

If Billy was here, he would tell her a joke, make her laugh.

"You always said you wanted a brother or sister,"

he would say. "Now you have one. It's not the end of the world."

He would be right. She had always wanted a sibling.

He would also be wrong. It was the end of the world. *Her* world. Her parents had lied to her, egregiously. Egregiously. *Take that, Noah Cameron. Bet you don't think I know a word that big let alone understand it.*

Nothing in her life was true. Her entire childhood had been one big lie.

How was she supposed to get over that?

Her mom and dad had engineered such an extreme solution to an unprecedented problem that they'd left all parties less than whole and hurting.

Was Marcie that thing that had always been missing inside of Monica? That gaping hole that had always needed filling? Was it possible to lose a piece of yourself when the tiny creature with whom you had shared a cozy womb was ripped away and never seen again? Never *seen* again? No, the problem was not the seeing—it was the *feeling.* She had never felt her again.

Double whammy, though, because she'd lost her mother, too. The beautiful nurturing vessel that had been her home for nine months had not been replaced with her mother's warm arms and loving words.

Everything had been taken from her.

And the woman she'd met yesterday, while familiar, didn't match her preconceived idea of a sister. Sisters didn't come to town to take everything away.

She rolled over, ready to go back to sleep. Her eyes were gritty, as though she had the mother of all hangovers, yet she hadn't consumed a drop of alcohol. That was what happened when you cried yourself to sleep.

Why should she get up? Why should she care about anything?

She closed her eyes, but an insistent hammering interrupted her bid for oblivion. It wouldn't let her fall back asleep, wouldn't let her not care about the day.

Someone was knocking on her door. She pulled Billy's pillow over her head. She could no longer smell him. So much loss.

The last thing she wanted was a visitor. But whoever it was at her door wouldn't give up. The pounding went on and on.

Forcing herself out of bed, she answered the knocking.

Noah stood in the hallway, grim determination sobering his handsome face. Strangely, given how volatile their relationship had been, she was glad to see him.

"Noah," she said, her voice as dull as the weather beyond her living room window. "What are you doing here?"

"I came to see if you were okay. I tried to find you yesterday, but couldn't, and then I had to go take care of the farm after closing the shop."

"Why were you looking for me?"

The expression that flitted across his face could only be described as compassionate.

"Oh, God." Her early morning, depression-soaked voice whispered out of her on a guttural sigh. "You know?"

"Yeah. The whole town does. It's the biggest scandal to hit in years. I'm sorry, Monica. I'm not making light of it. It's just the truth." His voice was deep and serious. No, he wasn't joking at her expense. He looked at her with such a deep well of empathy she wondered how she could have ever thought of Noah Cameron as self-righteous and cold. He cared about people—and *people* seemed to include her.

"Nobody knows the whole story or what to think," he continued, "so they're making it up as they go. Some of the rumors floating around are pretty wild. Can I come in? These coffees are hot. I need to set them down somewhere."

For the first time, she noticed the two huge paper tumblers from his sister's bakery. Laura's café made the best coffee.

"How did you get into my building?"

"My natural charm."

She snorted, surprised that he could make her smile when "lower than a doormat" didn't begin to describe her mood. She took one of the coffees and walked away to her small galley kitchen.

As though from a great distance, she heard the front door close. She turned around. Noah was toeing off his sandals in the hallway. His size and big red personality made the space shrink. His thick socks stood up in big puffs around his toes.

He padded in woolen-hushed silence down the hallway.

When she stared at him, he said, "Hazel MacEnright let me into your building on condition I share whatever I learn from you about the new woman in town. Your doppelganger."

"Will you?"

"Will I what?"

"Share what you learn with Hazel?"

"What do you think? My allegiance lies with you, not with her. Hazel's always been a malicious gossip."

He cocked his head to one side. "Any misinformation you'd like me to share with her when I leave? It would give me great pleasure to mess with her head."

He wasn't Billy. He couldn't make her laugh until tears streamed down her cheeks. She'd give him huge kudos, though, that he could make her smile not once but twice at a time like this.

"Tell her the new woman's an alien here to suck the brains out of nosy old bats."

"I like it. Done." He put down his coffee and took a paper bag from under his arm.

"Hope these aren't squished."

"I'm not hungry."

"I have four of Laura's cinnamon buns."

Monica took two plates out of the cupboard. "Maybe I can manage one."

When she turned back around, Noah was smiling, a little sadly, but smiling nonetheless. He'd seen right through her. There wasn't much that would keep her away from Laura's cinnamon buns, not even calorie counting. Not even a brand-new, hitherto unknown twin sister.

She had a twin sister. The pain in her chest caught her off-guard.

She crumpled. Noah caught her, his arms wrapping around her before she hit the floor.

He led her to the sofa. "Have you eaten at all since yesterday?"

She shook her head.

He helped her sit down. "Seriously, Monica? White leather?"

She stared at him, bewildered, before realizing he was speaking with such disdain about her sofa. "Oh. Billy liked it. He wanted it."

Noah didn't look convinced. She shrugged. "Believe me or don't. I don't care. I have a sister. A twin. I don't care."

"Yeah, you sure do care." He retrieved her coffee from the kitchen and brought it to her, taking off the lid and placing what looked like a gallon of coffee in her hand. "How could you not care? Of course you care that you now have a sister."

"No, I don't care. I hate her. I hate my dad. I hate my mother who I never met." Her hand shook. Her body shuddered. Coffee dribbled onto her T-shirt.

"Give me," he said. "Let me."

He put one hand on the back of her head, his long fingers so good, solid and real, unlike her life at the moment. He brought the coffee to her lips. Carefully, she sipped. It went down like a dream.

"That's good."

"I had to guess how much sugar and cream you would want."

"It's perfect." She meant it. She couldn't have doctored it better herself, a shot of strong tasty caffeine and a sweet milky confection all wrapped up in one.

He left her to get the buns and she missed that strong hand cupping her head.

"Noah," she whispered when he came back. "What am I going to do? I don't know what to think. It's all too bizarre."

He wrapped his strong hand around the back of her head again and held her drink for her. Nice. She didn't know whom to trust anymore, but Noah was here helping her, and he seemed to care. The force of her desire for his embrace rocked her.

"Tell me what's going on." He let go of her and placed her drink on the coffee table. He shimmied to the other end of the sofa so he could turn sideways to talk to her, hitching one knee up onto the sofa cushion.

The distance dissipated the heat she'd found so comforting, leaving a cold vacuum. She shivered and Noah got a wool coat from the closet beside the front door. He covered her with it.

She would rather have had his arms to warm her, but the coat would do.

A thought struck. "Why did you come here? We're not even friends."

"I was worried. I thought you might not be all right."

She picked up her cup and stared into its depths before taking a big gulp. Warm again, she said, "I'm not all right. But I think I need to talk about this."

"I'm all ears."

"What about the plants? Don't we need to get out to the farm?"

"I've been up for hours. I did a bunch of hoeing already."

"Which ones?" Why did she care? It wasn't her farm. But every day she saw changes in the plants.

"Potatoes, carrots, onions, turnips."

She smiled. "You left the radishes for me?"

"Yep. And the beets." Humor crinkled his eyes at the corners. "Your favorites."

"The bane of my existence, you mean."

"Enough talk about the plants. They're fine. You're not. Talk to me."

She didn't know if what her dad had told her was confidential, but did it really matter anymore? If the truth didn't come out, who knew what the town would make up? As Noah had already indicated, speculation would be even more bizarre than the very outrageous truth.

She began talking and didn't stop for a good hour.

The detritus of their breakfast sat on the coffee table. Her nerves hummed with caffeine and sugar overload. At some point today she should get real food into herself.

"What do you think, Noah? Could they have done things differently?"

"Sure. Yeah. In hindsight, everything can always be done differently. Things might not have worked out any better, though. All you have right now is the responsibility to move forward. Take what's been dished out and deal with it."

He brushed a strand of hair back from her forehead and tucked it behind her ear, the action innocent, but also exquisitely intimate. Her skin tingled. Her body shivered.

"Do you know what you need today?" he asked.

Yes, she did. She really did, and it was sexy and X-rated, and with Noah, and how strange was that? She stood too abruptly, gathering up their mess for the recycling.

He followed her to the kitchen. When she dropped everything into the blue box, she said, "Look. See? I recycle. I use this all the time. Notice yesterday's bread wrapper. You're not the only one who recycles." Babbling like an idiot, she concentrated on the inconsequential because his calloused fingers on her ear had left a delicious, unsettling quivery thrill.

She wanted to throw him down on her bed and have her way with him—with Noah Cameron, of all people. He reached beyond her to drop the paper bag he held into the box. His muscled shoulder touched hers. She jumped away.

"I should—I need—" She didn't know.

"You need to come out to the farm. Put on some old clothes. We'll work in the rain." Noah grinned. "Do you own anything old?"

"Of course." She was surprised that a day on the farm sounded like a good idea. She pulled up short as disappointment shot through her. "Oh. I can't. I have to work."

"No, you don't. I already talked to my mom."

"You shouldn't have done that, Noah. Not before checking with me."

"Do you really want to work in the gallery today with passersby gawking through the windows to get a glimpse of you? Not everyone will be sensitive about this."

She hadn't thought of how much attention this would focus on her. What a nightmare.

"No," she admitted. "Your mom has been coming down hard on me lately, though. I don't want to give her an excuse to fire me. Contrary to what most of the town thinks, I support myself. I don't go to my dad every month for my rent money."

Given the hint of red in his cheeks, Noah had probably assumed exactly that. Honest to God, the people in Accord needed to get a life instead of constantly speculating about hers.

"When we talked this morning, my mom was the one who suggested I talk you into taking today off."

"What about you and the shop?"

"There's a Closed sign in the window. If someone wants something badly enough they know they can call me at the farm."

"This is very kind of you, Noah."

He shrugged off her praise, but looked pleased. "I need to pick up groceries for our lunch."

"And I have to shower and get dressed."

"Okay. I'll be back in about…twenty minutes?"

"Sounds good."

He looked surprised.

"You sure? Don't you need more time than that, for like, makeup and stuff?"

"Noah, I'm going out to work in the rain. Makeup would be a waste of time. Go. I'll leave the door unlocked for you to come back."

IF EVER NOAH needed proof of how imperfect his fit with Monica was, her apartment said it all, like multiple exclamation points after the statement "this woman doesn't belong with you."

He stood in her living room with two bags of food, one in each hand. He hoped she liked what he'd picked up—Tonio's lasagna and a baby-greens salad.

The white leather sofa sat across from a large, clean fireplace. No ash residue here. A large canvas, white paint slashed with red and green and blue, hovered above the glossy white mantel.

Not a single flake of peeling paint. No comfy old-woman-in-a-shoe-with-a-bunch-of-kids-running-around hominess.

Here was the shallow gloss and sophistication he associated with the old Monica, not the one he'd come to know.

This summer's Monica startled, charmed and seduced him with her playfulness and childlike whimsy, but wouldn't that have always been there? Had he spent so much time ignoring her that he hadn't seen the real woman beneath the polished veneer?

Why had he allowed his adolescent prejudices to bleed into adulthood? He had done to Monica the very thing that had often been done to him. He had judged her strictly on appearances and preconceived notions.

Standing in the middle of her picture-perfect apartment, he had to wonder who she really was. This living room came from the pages of a magazine. There was nothing lived-in or real about it.

While she finished whatever prep work she was doing in the bathroom to turn herself into an even more beautiful woman, Noah stole down the hallway to check out her bedroom.

As a teenager, he'd wondered how she slept. Of course, his vivid imagination had insisted *naked*.

He'd also wondered where she slept and had wandered past her house once trying to guess which bedroom was hers. He had wanted to scale the side of her father's house to peek in through whichever window might be hers, but not to catch her naked. Okay, maybe to do that, but mostly to satisfy his curiosity about her.

Who was Monica when she was alone? What went on underneath that perfect facade? When no one was looking, did Monica do normal things? Did she pick her nose? Belch? Fart?

As a boy, he'd doubted it. He still doubted it.

He stepped in through an open doorway and stopped, arrested by the vision of feminine beauty that was her bedroom. Lace coated a four-poster bed. Dripped from it.

What should have been cloying and sweet instead fascinated him with its girly-girly-ness. Images of making love to Monica in the yards of white lace that would float up and cover them like icing sugar while she wrapped her long legs around him robbed him of breath. Her private bower, the absolute antithesis of sexiness, filled him with lust.

Was there anything about Monica that *didn't* fill him with desire? He ticked everything off on imaginary fingers. She was cool and she made him hot. She was hot and she made him hot. She was angry, happy, sad, vulnerable, clever, smarter than he'd ever imagined and it all made him hot.

He had it bad.

The more he got to know her, the more infatuated he became.

And the tears she'd let fall in front of him, the vulnerability he hadn't expected to find, made him want to hold her for much more than just sex. He wanted to protect her.

Gabe said she didn't cry in public, but she'd already done it with him three times. What was that about?

Holding her while she'd cried had been hard. He couldn't walk away, either, not when she needed support. Being friends with her was tough, especially when he wanted more, and she needed only a shoulder to cry on.

He couldn't take much more of his unrequited love without imploding.

He wandered to the far wall, where a row of bookshelves told yet another new, bold story about Monica. The books were classics, everything from *Little Women* to *The Brothers Karamazov*.

Monica? A reader?

What really snagged his attention were the rows and rows of hard-sided binders. He took one out to find it filled with magazines in protective sleeves. He checked another binder. Same thing. Binder after binder held vintage magazines dating as far back as the forties. *Vogue*, both American and European issues. *Vanity Fair*. Even, surprise surprise, *The New Yorker*.

He'd known that she liked fashion and was always dressed beautifully, but this collection of magazines represented something more. Nobody put together this kind of collection without having a passion for the subject.

"Noah?"

He spun around, guilty. He shouldn't have been snooping.

He pointed to the magazines. "This is amazing."

She approached while her light floral scent played around him like happy fingers coaxing melodies from a keyboard. "Do you like old magazines? I love them. Let me show you my favorite *Vogue*. And considering that I love all of them, that's saying a lot."

She took the binder from him and flipped through to one issue. "This is from the mid-sixties." She thumbed through it, showing him photos of Twiggy-esque models with enormous eyes and baby eyelashes painted beneath, and wearing pastel-colored shifts with white go-go boots.

"Look at how creative the photography was."

He didn't go in much for fashion, but even he could appreciate the creativity in the photo spreads.

He had always thought her interest in clothes frivolous, but in her excitement he recognized a deep-seated passion.

He understood passion.

"I've picked up every American and French *Vogue* for the past twenty years. I collect as many vintage copies from the forties, fifties and sixties as I can find. The sixties were amazing."

This animated Monica was a stranger to him. He liked her. "Mod London fashion was dynamite. Mary Quant's miniskirts? Fantabulous. White go-go boots! And those divine models Jean Shrimpton and

Veruschka. I wish I'd lived—" She caught herself and tucked the binder back onto the shelf in its proper slot. "Sorry. I shouldn't be boring you with this."

"I'm not bored." He sniffed. "Cinnamon?"

She lifted the ponytail she'd pulled her hair into. He leaned forward and pressed the tip of his nose against skin still faintly humid from her shower.

He closed his eyes. "Yeah. Cinnamon."

"Yes." Too soon, she stepped away from him.

He headed back to the living room, because standing in her bedroom made him ache physically, but also with a bittersweet longing that would never be requited.

When she stepped into the room ready to go, he asked, "Why do the living room and the bedroom seem so different? Do you have a split personality or something?"

"No." As he watched, she seemed to sag, sadness seeping into her. "The living room is all Billy."

"*Billy*? No *way*."

"I know, unexpected, right? He was such a basic, down-to-earth guy, but he had weird ideas about being married to me. Because of the Accord name and my dad's money, he thought we should have a showcase home. We couldn't afford a house because I wouldn't ask my dad for the down payment, so he thought that at the very least our apartment should be magazine-worthy. He chose all this furniture."

A casual disdainful flip of her hand clued him in to what she really thought of it. "I mean, it's gorgeous and he showed amazing taste for a guy who grew up in a normal, relatively low-income home, but there's no warmth. No personality."

"I have to agree with you."

"And this…" She walked to the mantelpiece and straightened an already perfectly aligned painting. "I hate this painting. Billy was adamant that we needed it. It cost me a fortune. I guess I'm not very smart because I don't get modern art. I like landscapes, like the one in my bedroom."

He hadn't noticed a painting in her bedroom. He strode back down the hallway. On the wall opposite the bed hung a landscape, orange, red and golden fields at sunset. The warmth and beauty of the painting stunned him.

When he joined her in the living room, he said, "It's gorgeous."

"I put my foot down when it came to decorating the bedroom. I wasn't having a repeat of this." She gestured around the living room with her chin. "I wanted to express myself there."

She sure had done that—her bedroom was an unexpected window into her soul, and different from anything he would have expected from Monica.

"Why did you let Billy have his way so much in here? Shouldn't it have been a collaborative undertaking? I mean, come on, Monica, you have a mind of your own."

"I'm not sure how to explain it, except that I was indulging Billy because he'd grown up with so little."

"You felt guilty 'cause you'd had so much more compared to him?"

She nodded.

She looked tired, drained, leaving him feeling protective. He'd been feeling that way since he'd seen that woman, Monica's sister, on the street yesterday.

"Let's go. You need farm therapy."

"Weeding," she said. "Just what the doctor ordered." At least she was trying to smile.

They headed out to the farm, Noah driving because she looked too exhausted to handle such a task.

When they arrived at the farm, he turned off the radio she'd flicked on at the beginning of the drive. Monica Accord, he had learned, did not like silence.

Before she got out of the truck, he stopped her with a hand on her arm. "Do you know what you need to do?"

"No. What?"

It had started to drizzle. The windshield wipers squeaked across the glass because there wasn't enough rain to really lubricate them. He switched off both them and the engine. "You have to redesign your living room to reflect who you are, not who Billy needed you to be."

She watched the rain, sad again. "Oh, Noah. That living room wasn't about who Billy needed *me* to be. It was about who *he* needed to be."

After dropping that insightful bombshell, she got out of the truck and headed to the back of the farmhouse for the rubber boots she kept by the back door.

The more he got to know her, the more he liked her. She was not only sensitive and generous, but also perceptive. So much to learn about this woman.

So much to learn about himself, too.

His mother liked clothes and manicures and spa days. Did he come down on her as harshly as he did Monica? No.

His sister didn't use only organic ingredients in her bakery. He encouraged her to use as much as she could afford, but a lot of it wasn't. Did Noah come down hard on her? No.

An interest in nature and the outdoors didn't make him superior to others, not by a long shot. He knew that and yet he'd used it against Monica more than once.

God, he liked her.

So why did he have to hang on so hard to his negative opinions of her?

To protect yourself, dude. You still want her as badly today as you did twenty years ago, and the two of you live in wildly different worlds. Worse, after wanting her for so many years, how could you handle rejection if you made a move and she said no?

CHAPTER NINE

THROUGHOUT THE DAY, while he handed her a hoe and she raked fledgling weeds from between the radishes, and while they turned the compost heap—that is, Monica turned the bulk of it while he manipulated a shovel with one hand, turning only small clods at a time—and while they ate lunch, he watched her, watched the rain turn her ponytail to a thin stream down her back.

All day, precipitation fell in a steady, warm drizzle. Not once did Monica complain.

He drove her home at dinnertime.

"Noah?" she said quietly, breaking the silence that only his thumb drumming on the steering wheel had pierced to that point.

"Yeah?"

"Today was a really good idea. A chance to spend time away from my problems. I had a lot of time to think things through."

"Good. I'm glad."

"I know we haven't always treated each other well, but what you did today was special. Thank you."

"You're welcome." Her sentiment warmed him. His impulse to rise above the tension between them, and their differences, had been right. "What are you going to do tomorrow?"

"Tomorrow morning I'll go to work. I'll take things a day at a time. But one thing I know for sure is that I don't hate my parents or my sister. I'm still angry, but I'm going to keep an open mind."

"It will be hard to get through this." He drummed his thumb harder. "I know we haven't been friends, but promise me that if you need anything, you'll call me anytime, day or night. Okay?"

"Okay." She smiled and touched his arm. "I will."

He liked how much she conveyed with the simplest of gestures.

In front of her apartment building, she got out of the truck, closed the door and leaned on the open window well. "You're right about my living room. It's time to make it my own, isn't it?"

"Yeah."

"I'll think about it. I don't have the money right now, but I'll definitely do something if circumstances change."

She didn't have the money? Everyone in town knew her dad would give her anything she wanted. Why not just ask him for funds?

"You were a good friend today, Noah. Thank you."

Her statement warmed him, pure and simple, just flat-out warmed his soul that he'd been good to Monica and she'd appreciated it.

"RAG-BAG KID! RAG-BAG KID!"

Marcie ran as fast as her little legs could carry her, the flapping sole of one of her shoes slapping the ground, but she couldn't outrun the name-calling.

She ran to a teacher supervising the schoolyard,

but the woman was busy with a girl who had a badly cut knee.

The teacher told Marcie's bullies to stop, but the second she picked up the girl and carried her into the school, they started in again on Marcie.

"Snitch."

"You're not supposed to tell on people."

"Where do you get your clothes? Salvation Army?" That was followed by mean laughter.

Marcie felt her cheeks get really hot, because yeah, her mom did buy her clothes at the Sally Ann, or wherever they were cheapest. Before she started school, Marcie didn't think there was anything wrong with that. But not now. Now she knew secondhand meant bad. And sad.

She went to the door of the school, but the teacher only peeked out, telling her to ignore those girls.

But how? They kept yelling at her. They kept making fun of her.

"Rag bag. Rag bag."

She bit her lip. She didn't cry anymore. The mean girls liked it too much when she cried, so she'd stopped, but it was hard. She had to hold her breath to hold back the tears...

Marcie awoke with a gasp and then cursed into the darkness. The small clock on the bedside table said ten to twelve. She'd been asleep only an hour.

Her heart pounded.

She'd been dreaming again, and holding her breath

in her sleep. She hated those old dreams, hated how far they had followed her into adulthood.

They still had the power to make her feel inferior.

While there had been some good schools in her travels with Donna, there had always been awful moments.

Even if kids weren't calling her names or bullying her, they stared. The first day in a new school could be nightmarish.

Only as an adult had she realized this was normal behavior for kids. A newcomer was a curiosity, whether or not she wore hand-me-downs.

By the time she had come to understand the dynamics, the damage had already been done. Her adult mind had it all straightened out, but her little girl's mind still lingered in her dreams.

"It's over," she scolded herself. "You have a new life ahead of you."

She snuggled into bedsheets softer than any she'd ever owned. They smelled clean instead of stale. When money was tight, laundry got done sporadically. The mattress hugged her body like a glove.

"Calm down and enjoy. You'll never be that poor again." Her voice echoed off lavender walls and was absorbed by a soft purple duvet. Whoever had decorated this room had done a great job. It was pretty.

She wondered whether that person might have been Monica, her sister. She didn't yet know what to make of her, whether she liked having a sister or not.

This whole situation was too strange for words, like something out of a book instead of real life.

Did she want a relationship with Monica, a woman who appeared to be too cool and collected…and who had grown up with everything Marcie's life had been missing? What on earth did they have in common?

For all intents and purposes, Donna was gone. Yes, by Marcie's choice, but she couldn't find forgiveness in her heart, not when there had been so much hardship while all of this had been waiting in Accord. And, most importantly, not while she could have had a family.

Marcie had no one else in her life now but these people. She had to make the most of it.

She lay in the guest room in her father's house. Quite the grand house. Her dad might not be super wealthy, but he sure never had to worry about where his next meal was coming from.

Or his next drink. She sighed. He seemed to be a bit of a lush.

They'd spent the day together yesterday. She wanted answers and what she'd learned had surprised her.

He hadn't abandoned her, as she had assumed. Donna had hidden her from him. She could have grown up in this house, with all of this beauty, in a community where she could have lived her entire life without all of the moving around she'd done with Donna.

She had the whole picture now. Donna had kept them on the go so her dad wouldn't find her. The woman had, basically, stolen her from her father, and that pissed off Marcie.

She rolled over and curled into a ball. Donna had been the only mother Marcie had ever known. She'd treated Marcie well. She had loved her.

She knew all of that, but now she was stuck in this awful situation, in a town where people looked at her with suspicion, with a man who was crying in his Scotch because he hadn't known her throughout her childhood, and with a woman who clearly didn't want to have a sister.

Marcie's self-protective instincts went into over-drive. She didn't want to be looked down on by some rich snob. All through childhood, she'd had a bellyful of people who'd thought they were better than her.

Marcie hadn't created this situation, but she would make it work. She would fight for acceptance, for what should have been hers all along. Monica would just have to get used to having a twin.

So would Marcie. Sobering thought.

If only she could have come here to find just a father waiting for her. Life would be easier.

Starting tomorrow, she would wage a campaign to be accepted, and to get her fair share of what she was owed, of all of the easy wealth she'd missed out on during her rough-and-tumble childhood.

If Monica couldn't accept her, too bad, because

Marcie would fight her tooth and nail for her future inheritance.

Tomorrow morning, she would confront the sister who hadn't stayed around long enough yesterday to get to know her, and who had ignored her all day today.

She was taking her place in this town that should have been her home all along, with the father and sister who should have been her family.

Besides, Marcie had nowhere else to go.

AFTER BREAKFAST WITH her dad, Marcie headed to Main Street, walking over because it wasn't that far.

Her many bracelets jangled on her wrists. Making them was her passion, but Donna had called it her hobby. Marcie wanted it to be more than that. By hook or crook, one day she would make her living creating beautiful jewelry.

Main Street sported all kinds of nice, quaint details…those old-fashioned lampposts she'd noticed the other day. Black wrought-iron benches sat on the sidewalks every thirty or so yards.

Her *dad*—boy it was hard to get used to that word—had told her all about Accord and the upgrades the shops had made a few years ago to bring in tourists. Apparently, it had worked. Storefronts were bright and pretty, and some were really interesting.

She wanted to check out the gallery where Monica

worked. Art held an attraction for her that she couldn't resist.

Marcie had lived in everything from large cities to small towns. She'd learned to be adaptable.

This place, though, was magical. A lump settled in her throat, something akin to nostalgia, which was insane. She didn't do nostalgia. Sentimentality was for schmucks. She was no fool. She didn't fall for that stuff.

Even so, she imagined this street at Christmastime covered with snow and all the shops boasting twinkling lights. Even someone as hardened as she was could melt at the sight of that.

I want.

She shook herself out of her daydream. Time to move on with her life.

The guy she'd met the other day, the one who'd thought she was Monica, loped toward her.

"Hey," he said, stopping in front of her.

"Hey, yourself. You ready to meet properly today? I'm Marcie Green. Or, more accurately, Accord." She stuck her hand out to shake his, refusing to be ignored or put off this time. She might not be the town's royalty like her sister was, but she was just as deserving of respect.

He shook her hand. "Noah Cameron. I'm sorry about how I treated you the other day. I'm not usually like that. I was in shock."

"I understand. Everyone in this town wants to protect my sister. I get that." How would it feel to have that kind of loyalty? The lack of it left her lonely and blue. Donna, in her odd way, had been loyal, but her decisions had been self-serving. It would have been kinder to have brought Marcie home after her mother died.

She stepped away from thoughts of Donna, trying to shake off her anger.

"Small towns are like that," Noah said. "We tend to watch out for each other."

She liked this guy right away, liked his offbeat clothes and red ponytail.

"I hope to be a member of this town for a while. It wasn't my fault that I never was." The tiniest note of self-pity crept into her voice. Darn. She never allowed herself that emotion, let alone shared it with someone else. It was a sign of how these huge changes were affecting her.

His expression softened. "Yeah. I heard the whole story."

He did? Through rumors? From her sister? What exactly did he know?

"I'm sorry things were handled the way they were." Sunlight made the red of his hair pop like fire. She should find beads that color to use for a bracelet or, even better, a necklace.

"I'm not sure I would've taken that approach to the problem," he went on, "but I can't judge."

Neither did she, but she wasn't ready to let anyone completely off the hook yet, not when her parents' decision had given her a nomadic, hand-to-mouth existence of which she was sick to death. The anger she felt was toxic. She was working hard to let it go, but in her fallible humanness, she clung to her wrath because she had nothing to replace it with yet.

She changed the subject. "What happened to your arm?"

"It, um…"

He looked troubled by her question, uneasy. She wondered what that was about.

"I'm sure I'll see you around town." Without answering, he brushed past her and unlocked the door of the army surplus store.

She could go for this guy. Tall, hard and lean, and attractive in an offbeat hippie way.

He had good bones, too, and she wasn't talking about how handsome he was despite the beard that hid half of his face. She could tell the guy was an open book, with a strong sense of decency and morality.

She liked the weird vibe she got from him, the dichotomy of intensity and friendliness. Intelligence was super sexy and, boy, the guy had that in spades.

I want.

She was drawn to him. Maybe this town would work out for her on a few levels.

Continuing down the street until she reached the shop called The Palette, where Monica worked, she stepped inside.

A bell over the door chimed. The air inside the gallery was cool. Colorful paintings adorned neutral walls. Gorgeous, sensual sculptures filled the space. Nice.

She liked art. Why wouldn't she? She considered herself an artist.

Monica stepped out of the office dressed in a linen shift finer than anything Marcie had ever owned. That it wasn't Marcie's style didn't matter. That it cost a fortune did.

Marcie wanted.

"We need to talk," she said without preamble.

"I'm working."

"Doesn't matter. You weren't working yesterday. I know because I came here to see you. You were avoiding me."

Another woman, also expensively dressed, stepped out of the office, glanced at Marcie and then turned her attention to Monica.

"It's okay. Go. Grab a coffee with your sister."

"Olivia, I already took yesterday off. I don't want to shirk my duties."

The woman touched Monica's arm. "These are unusual circumstances. I can make allowances. Go."

Monica didn't look happy, but she stepped back into the office and returned, hitching a purse over her shoulder.

"Come on," she said, her voice toneless as she led Marcie out of the gallery.

In the coffee shop, Marcie chose a cinnamon bun at Monica's urging because, apparently, they were the best on earth. Yeah, right. Small-town provincialism. She also got a coffee to go.

For herself, Monica ordered just a coffee. "My treat." She paid for everything.

Damn straight she should. She'd had it easy all her life. On the heels of that thought, Marcie relented. If Donna hadn't stolen her away, she would have grown up the same way.

They sat on a bench on Main Street, Marcie checking out her sister from the corner of her eye, this strange person to whom she was related. Had she ever wished for a sister, she would have chosen someone more hip, more cool, not this uptight, conservative disappointment.

At the same time, Monica was checking her out, but was pretty blatant about it.

"I don't know what to think of you," she said, surprising Marcie with her honesty. She hadn't thought the woman would be so frank. "I haven't a clue how to deal with this situation."

"Me, either," she replied. "We need to come to terms with things. I'm not going away. For better or worse, we're now family."

She bit into the cinnamon bun. Flavor exploded in her mouth. Okay, so maybe they were good. Beyond good.

"I thought you were exaggerating. These are incredible."

Monica's small, tight smile bothered her. She wanted to break through the woman's control, but she didn't know why. Monica had as much right to be who she was as Marcie did to be who she was.

"Everything Laura makes is exceptional." Monica sipped her coffee.

Marcie gulped hers.

"Did you really not know about me when you were growing up?" Monica sounded wistful, surprising in a woman who looked all-business.

"Really."

"What was our mother like?"

"She died when I was really little. I don't remember her. I pretty much grew up thinking Donna was my mother."

"What was she like?"

There was that wistfulness again. What was she? Mother-fixated?

"She was a good woman, even if she did hide the truth from me and keep me away from this town." That now-familiar ball of mixed and confusing, even contradictory, emotions bounced around her tummy.

Movement in a nearby window caught Marcie's attention. The lawyer, watching everything. Watching her.

"Have you met many people in town?" Monica didn't seem to notice she was being watched.

Marcie wasn't sure what her question was about. Did Monica want to know if Marcie had been spreading around their story? Or did she consider it her social duty to introduce Marcie to the town?

"I've met that big tall redhead. Noah? He's a sexy sip of cool water, isn't he?"

Monica stiffened. Why? Her sister leaned forward to sip her coffee so her hair fell in a screen, hiding her face. Oh, wait. Did she like him? *Like* like him?

They couldn't possibly have the same taste in men, could they?

Strange thing about being a twin... Marcie didn't want anything from her sister other than her rightful place in the family and the money she deserved, and yet she felt a kinship. Or something. Considering they'd never known each other before, Marcie found that downright eerie.

"Is he your boyfriend?"

"No." Monica answered too quickly.

"Who is?"

"I don't have one."

"You're pretty. You're well off. Aren't the men of this town falling all over themselves for you?"

"I've grown up with them." Again with that tight little lift of her lips. "Maybe they'll find you more exotic."

Marcie stiffened at the implied insult. "What's that supposed to mean?"

Monica frowned. "I didn't mean to offend you. My intention was to say that I'm too familiar to them and you're new."

Marcie relaxed. "Oh. I see. Maybe."

"This is awkward." Monica stared into her coffee cup.

"It sure is. I don't know how to change that."

"Me, either."

"Everything all right, Monica?" The voice startled both of them. It belonged to the lawyer. Now he stood on the sidewalk in front of them, even better-looking up close, but aiming a hard-edged stare at Marcie.

The way he placed a hand on Monica's shoulder was anything but hard. It looked tender. Interesting.

What Marcie wouldn't give for someone to touch her with that much respect.

Monica flattened her other hand against her chest. "John, you scared me."

He squeezed her elbow. "Sorry, Monica. You didn't look happy and I wondered if I could be of assistance."

"I'm fine." When he didn't look convinced, she said, "Really."

"Introduce me to your sister."

"The whole town knows?" Monica asked.

"Everyone's speculating. It's natural, considering how much you look like each other."

Marcie watched the interplay. Unless she missed her guess, there was nothing romantic going on here. The dude might like Monica, but he didn't want her. He might respect her, but he didn't desire her.

Too bad. Graying hair at his temples gave him a distinguished air, but his dark eyes were sexy as hell.

Today was a day for meeting complex men apparently. He might look distinguished and conservative, but there was fire in this guy's belly.

She didn't doubt for a second he'd come outside to rescue Monica. What she couldn't figure was what he got out of the relationship. Exposure to the mighty Accords?

His expensive suit said he had plenty of funds, so it wasn't money. Influence, maybe? Political power?

When she glanced back up at his face, she found him watching her, gaze perceptive. Her first thought was...*he sees me.*

He really sees me. He knows how much I want things.

She panicked at being so exposed before realizing she had to be imagining things. No one was that insightful.

Shaken, she crossed her arms to ward off his knowing look. A good girl with exquisite manners, Monica made introductions.

"I have to get back to work." Monica dropped her cup into a nearby recycling receptacle. To Marcie, she said, "We'll talk more," but she sounded as uncertain as Marcie felt.

Monica's careful neutrality presented a challenge to Marcie. Considering how wary Marcie had learned to be with strangers, her personality and Monica's didn't bode well for a quick friendship.

How many times in her life had Marcie lived with

uncertainty? Here it was again. The stakes, though, had never been this high.

"Would you join me in my office?" John Spade might have phrased it as a question, but Marcie knew a command when she heard one. She didn't respond well to demands.

She was, however, curious.

She followed him inside, waiting while he closed his office door and sat behind his impressive desk. He gestured toward a chair to indicate where she should sit.

Leaning back in his desk chair, comfortable in his skin, he swiveled gently, watching her like a hawk eyeing a delectable little mouse.

"What are you doing here?" he asked, presenting her with the problem of deciding how much of the truth she wanted to share with this dangerous, too-perceptive man.

Marcie opted to keep most of her cards close to her chest. She didn't know him. No need for him to know about things like, well, deep-seated need and desperation.

"I've come to meet my father and my sister."

"Meet them? The word on the street that you and Monica were separated at birth is true, then? The story of Karen's death giving birth to Monica was false?"

When she didn't respond, he said, "Care to tell me the rest of the story?"

"Why? What's it to you?"

"I care about Monica. But you… I don't think you're anything like her, are you, Marcie?"

"I hate that name," she blurted. Geez. Where had that come from? She had never shared that with another soul.

"What's wrong with it?" John Spade asked.

"It's hopelessly old-fashioned." She hated herself for how lame she sounded, as though his opinion of her name mattered.

He shrugged. "It's a name." His eyes took her in, lazily. "There are a lot of other things a man can call a woman without using a name of which neither is fond."

He watched her with hooded eyes, as though she were prey. She swallowed. "Like what?"

"Endearments like *honey, darling, sweetheart*. And those are just the nice things."

"And the not so nice?" She shouldn't encourage him. As charged as it was with sexual innuendo, this conversation was inappropriate on so many levels. She shouldn't let him draw her into this kind of game.

"You want to hear the rest? Come out to dinner with me."

What? "Why?"

"Because I don't use those words in my office."

Whew. Okay, was this conversation really happening? The air in the office was too hot. She had to put an end to this.

"Did you ever use any of those words with my sister, lawyer man?"

The lazy smile faltered. "No. Not with sweet Monica."

"So Monica is first-class while I'm…what? Not worthy of respect?"

One mocking eyebrow rose. "It depends. Why are you here? Why do I detect a calculating gleam in your eye when you look at Monica? You're not a nice person, are you?"

"Not always." Most emphatically not. She'd had to fight for every scrap in her life.

"I like that in a woman." White teeth flashed in a face that was too perfectly tanned, probably from time spent in a tanning bed.

His nails were buffed, his hands perfect. The man probably got manicures. What woman wanted pampered hands touching her?

She did. Oh, sweet god, she did.

Even as buffed and polished as he was, there wasn't an effeminate bone in the man's body. Only one word came to mind. Powerful.

She wanted those hands on her skin, all over her.

Her glance shifted to his face. He watched her with a crooked grin. He saw into her mind, into her heart. He knew what she wanted and that was dangerous.

She might want him in her bed, but she wouldn't take him.

"Let's get something straight. I'm every bit as deserving of respect as Monica. She might have come by hers easily because of her birth, but I've fought tooth and nail for everything I have. I expect respect."

She stood, the backs of her legs pushing the chair to bang against the wall, the sound explosive in the still air.

"Do you know why the gleam in my eye is calculating when I look at Monica? Because I can guess to the penny how much everything she is wearing costs, and that includes makeup and the creams she uses to pamper her skin. I can also calculate how many meals I could have bought with all of that excess."

Her voice was every bit as explosive in temper as the banging chair had been.

John Spade nodded. "Okay. Maybe I've misjudged you. I do, however, have one last question. Do you plan to hurt Monica?" He leaned back in his chair and idly twirled a pencil between his fingers, but Marcie knew his question was anything but idle.

"I grew up with nothing while Monica had everything. Is that fair?"

"It isn't, but none of that is Monica's fault. You should also know that she's had her share of grief."

She hadn't heard that. Genuinely curious about that cool woman, she asked, "Like what?"

"Losing her mother in childbirth. Or so she'd been raised to believe. Growing up in that big house alone."

"Poor little rich girl?"

The playful smile fell and John's mouth became a hard slash across his face.

"Her husband, the man she dated since her early teens, the love of her life, died in Afghanistan. Yes, she has my sympathy."

Okay, that must have been hard.

"That apartment is probably paid for with widow's benefits. Which do you think Monica would rather have—the money the army pays her, or her husband back?"

Compelled by decency to be honest, Marcie said, "You're right. That must have been hard. I hadn't heard that."

John relaxed. "Monica would never knowingly hurt a soul. She might not be the most exciting person around, but she is unendingly kind. That's worth a lot."

"I guess. This is all new to me. It's still in shock."

"I can see that it would be. The only advice I have is to be careful. Monica's respected in this town and you are an unknown entity."

"But I don't want to be. I want to belong." The words were out, her deepest desire hanging in the air like dirty laundry, before she could reel them back in. She didn't share herself with others. Why on earth would she open up to this stranger?

This man had her standing on shaky ground and she didn't like it one bit. He must be dangerous in the courtroom.

Expression neutral, he said, "My door is always open."

What did that mean?

She'd met a lot of men in her life, but this man rattled her.

She left his office unsure of herself. What had just happened? His door was always open? For advice? For dinner? For sex? For what?

CHAPTER TEN

Noah gave Monica the space she needed to grieve, or recover from shock, or whatever it was that she had to do. He could empathize, but this situation was so far beyond anything he'd ever experienced, he couldn't fully comprehend what kind of havoc this would wreak in a person's life.

Day after day on the farm, he watched her grow a little stronger, become more herself again.

A week later, she came to him one morning to talk, standing amid the soft drizzle of another rainy day.

"Remember I mentioned the idea of fund-raising? Of putting on some kind of benefit?"

"How could I forget? You were criticizing me for not doing enough for people." He infused his tone with a smile so she would know he was joking. He'd long gotten over how miffed he'd been when she'd first taken him to task.

The flush that spread across the top of her chest and into her throat fascinated him.

"I'm sorry. I shouldn't have been so harsh. I should have found a better way to offer criticism or advice."

"You were right, though. I need to find a way to do more." Funny how hard it would have been for him to have said that to Monica a couple of short weeks ago. Now, it seemed easy, natural.

Every day she spent on his farm, she became more a part of his team. He knew she wasn't sleeping well because of the dark circles under her eyes, and yet still she showed up early every morning.

After that day he'd delivered coffee and cinnamon buns to her apartment and then brought her out here to farm in the rain, Monica hadn't wanted to talk about Marcie. And Noah let it go. It wasn't his place to interfere.

"What ideas have you come up with about fund-raising?"

"I've been thinking the best thing would be to hold a really fun different kind of charity bash this August in Denver. I've put out feelers to the women my dad used to work with and they're very excited." He followed her to the storage shed.

"Who are these women?"

"Some are the wives of corporate giants. Some *are* corporate successes, women who've broken through the glass ceiling. One thing they have in common is a willingness to give back."

She handed him a couple of tools, grabbed some for herself and closed the shed door. She took a pair of gloves from her back pocket and slipped them on.

"Imagine how incredible it would be if you had the cash to hire local students, or anyone who needed work, to harvest your crops and take them into Denver to the food bank and churches for distribution?"

She grasped his good arm. The electricity of her excitement shot through him. "Imagine if you could hire people to help plant in the spring? With employees, you could plant even more fields, make more use of your acreage."

His dream. The level of her enthusiasm rubbed off on him. "Let's rush through chores then sit with a coffee. We need to discuss details."

Later, seated at his kitchen table, he said, "You've obviously been thinking hard about this. Share."

"Originally I thought we should do a big gala dinner, but now I'm thinking something more rustic. Still posh, because we need to attract people with money. That's the bottom line, Noah—you need money. And these women will help me set up the right guest list. But I'm also thinking we should do something different, something fun, that will raise awareness."

She leaned forward, cheeks pink with fire. That her passion was inflamed for his project was sexy as hell.

"What's your idea?"

"How about a barbecue?"

Deflated, he sat against the back of the kitchen chair. "That's it? A barbecue?"

Unfazed, she replied, "I realize it doesn't sound like much, but have faith, Noah. I know what I'm doing." She plunked her elbows onto the table and rested her jaw on her fists. "We could purchase a couple of cows from Robert Keil. Or is it steers? Bulls? Whatever. Anyway, we could give Robert an exceptional price. Our local butcher, Hiram, could slaughter and prepare the meat for us. We could ask Tonio's to cater. And we could hire all of the local men and women who rely on our food to help Tonio's prepare and transport *their* food and then cook it on location. We could hire a bunch of our local high school kids to serve and clean up afterward."

He sat stunned, not because of the grand breadth of her ideas, and not because of her boundless enthusiasm, but because of something she had inadvertently let slip. *Our.* She had called the food he grew on the farm *our* food. He didn't know what it signified, but it stunned him.

He reached across the table, cradled her face in the palm of his good hand and laid a big smacker on her lips. He'd meant to make it quick and fast, an impulse innocently gotten out of hand by desire for this woman and her passion for *his* passion.

Once he began, though, the kiss became a different creature. He couldn't make it fast, or quick, not when he'd wanted Monica for so long—not when he'd craved this for an eternity. So instead, he savored. He luxuriated in the warmth and moisture of her lips. And she let him!

She opened to him slowly, almost shyly. Just another way for her to charm him.

His tongue explored the textures of her mouth.

He pulled away by increments and stared into the surprise in her blue eyes. Sunny skies had nothing on Monica's pretty eyes. The skin of her cheeks was the softest fleece between his fingers. The flavor of her lips sweetened his. Lordy, lordy, lordy, he was a goner.

"Sorry," he whispered, dropping his arms. They were both standing up. When had that happened? "I couldn't help myself."

She smiled, and again he sensed shyness. "May I take this to mean you like my ideas?"

"I *love* your ideas. Let's do it. Tell me what you need from me."

"At the moment, not much." She sounded breathless. Had she been as affected as he'd been? "Once I talk to my dad I know he'll help out for sure. It's the kind of thing he enjoys doing. All I need you to do is keep doing the great stuff you do here."

She headed for the door, too quickly. "I'd better hustle or I'll be late for work. Did you notice how good the beets are looking? They're really coming along. The radishes, too. Maybe I didn't kill too many of them."

She was babbling.

Noah followed her outside. The heat of Monica's pretty body suffused his senses. Curiosity burned inside of him. He'd smelled her perfume on her wrist before, but there had been that time on the ladder leading up to the attic when he could have sworn she'd sprayed her legs.

The rainy day he'd taken her to the farm after learning about Marcie, her perfume had emanated from every part of her.

Did she spray it on different parts of her body? If

he didn't find out where she had sprayed her perfume today, he would perish.

He'd sensed it as an aura around her while he'd been kissing her. Where was it?

With that rash but perfect kiss, everything had shifted. Now he wanted to know everything about her.

Trying to appear nonchalant, he shuffled close to stand beside the goddess and drink in her heavenly aroma—God, when had he become so lame?

On the front veranda, when she turned to him, her direct gaze dared him to pretend he hadn't been trying to get close to her. She knew!

Sheepish in his honesty, he declared, "Okay, I give up."

"Give up about what, Noah?"

She was going to make him spell it out. He told her about the ladder, about how he suspected that she changed where she put her perfume each day.

He spread his hands and must have looked enough like a poor bumbling fool for her pity, because she smiled, too sweetly to be a siren's smile. And he knew that her perfume would draw him onto a whole host of rocky shoals and destroy the equilibrium he'd nurtured since the first time he'd ever laid eyes on Monica. Despite his best intentions, he asked, "Where did you spray it today?"

She didn't move and he wondered if he'd been too forward, but hell, he'd just kissed her and she hadn't complained.

She held out her arm. Her wrist? A bit pedestrian and done before, but hey, whatever.

Then she surprised him by pulling up the long sleeve of her flowered blouse. Okay, not her wrist. She raised it higher. Aaah. The inside of her elbow. Ni-i-ice. But no. She pushed it even higher, to her underarm, then held out her arm and caressed the inside of her biceps, opposite her left breast.

"Here," she whispered. In that quiet, husky voice was the siren. To the horror of his crumbling equilibrium, Noah leaned in. Heaven. Ancient freaking womanly goddess. His discipline completely disappeared when his cheek touched her breast.

He didn't smell her arm. He licked it, with one long, languorous swipe of his tongue and she shivered. Her skin tasted like spring water and bluebells. Bluebells? Cripes, his brain was turning to mush. He didn't care. He could rhapsodize about sirens and sipping from flowers all day.

He broke. Grasping her by the back of her head, he kissed her deeply, ravenously slaking his thirst thoroughly this time. That kiss in the kitchen? An appetizer. An amuse-bouche. He wanted more. The whole enchilada. But nope. There would be no quenching here, because the longer he kissed her, the more he wanted. He could only try to quench, and then still crave.

When at last he pulled away, he whispered, "Oranges."

She smiled and the clouds literally parted and the

sun came out. Coincidence? He thought not. "Yes, Noah. I added just a hint of orange essential oil. Does it work?"

He didn't answer the question, caught by an observation. "You say my name a lot. Why?"

She wouldn't meet his eyes, shy again. Had Kayla Keil been right when she'd said that she'd sensed shyness in Monica all of those years ago? Today, it certainly seemed that way.

"I like your name." With her nail, she scraped a piece of peeling paint from one of the porch's support posts. "It's a good, strong name."

She liked his name? *He* liked the rosiness of her lips plumped by his kiss. Monica flummoxed him—she was calmly confident one minute and quietly bashful the next, but always reserved and cool.

One day, he planned to break through that reserve. Sure he'd seen her cry, and she was passionate about her hobbies, but what would the cool princess be like in bed? Was she cool through and through?

MONICA WALKED TO her father's house at lunchtime. It had been a long day, starting with those kisses from Noah this morning.

She'd spent the rest of the morning trying to forget about them, which was about as easy as forgetting she had ten fingers and toes.

What was she to make of his kisses, other than loving them?

She touched her lips, imagining him doing it again.

Like a giddy teenager, she'd been distracted for hours. A couple of times, she'd caught Olivia watching her strangely, only to realize the woman had spoken to her a number of times and she had neither heard nor responded. How embarrassing.

Billy had been a big, sloppy kisser. Wet and enthusiastic. While Noah was passionate, he kissed with finesse. Wow, did he ever, as though concentrating all of his *über*-intensity in his lips. And fingers. And his one good arm. How could one arm hold her so tightly?

She wanted more, but how to get it? She'd never been sexy. She didn't know how to attract men.

He seemed to like her perfume. She needed to ramp that up. Not that she had a goal. Not that she necessarily wanted Noah in her bed…

Then why did just the thought of making love with Noah send her pulse skittering like fireflies trapped in a jar, and why did her knees turn to jelly when she imagined his long fingers on her bare skin?

She stepped into her father's house and called out to him. "Hey, Dad, are you home?" She hoped like crazy that he was alone.

"In here."

She didn't realize she'd been cringing, worried that he was drinking again. When she entered the living room, she found him in his favorite armchair reading the day's paper. He looked more like himself, relaxed, happier. Well-groomed. Maybe things were working out with Marcie.

The twinge of jealousy that cramped her stomach was beneath her so she ignored it.

"Dad, I need to talk to you about something."

He set aside the paper. "Sit. Talk."

These men. Did they not know how to speak in full sentences?

She told him about Noah's need to feed the hungry, to keep food in the food bank and the food kitchens in Denver full. Then she outlined her plan for a gala barbecue.

"You used to do these things all the time. What do you think? Could it work?"

"Definitely. It's a great idea, Monica."

"Could I count on you to be a supporter? Our first sponsor?"

"Of course. I'll hook you up with my network. What you really need are corporate sponsors. Let me talk to some of my buddies in Denver."

"You would do that, Dad?"

A shaft of sunlight slanted through the window and across her father. Some of the tiredness that marred his face of late had abated, thank goodness. His eyes were clear. He hadn't been drinking today.

"Why would you think I wouldn't help you?"

Dare she express her concerns out loud? Would she be opening a Pandora's box to not only acknowledge her feelings, but to also share them with her father? He watched her without blinking.

"I thought that maybe now that Marcie was here,

she might, sort of…" Why was this so hard? "I thought she might be replacing me in your affections."

The newspaper fell from his limp fingers to the floor. "How could you possibly think that? My heart isn't that small. There's room for both of you."

"I know. It's just that you used to call me every day. You said you liked to touch base. You haven't in more than a week."

"Haven't I?" The question was disingenuous. He wouldn't meet her eyes.

"No, not since before Marcie arrived."

"He's been spending time with me." Marcie's voice came from behind Monica, in the hall doorway. Monica turned around. How long had she been standing there?

"That's nice, Marcie."

"Yes, it is. I missed out on all of the years of his affection that you had." A trace of bitterness tinged her voice. "Is it okay with you that he's spending time with me?"

"I need to clear the air. You seem to mistakenly believe that I don't expect you to get to know your own father." She approached Marcie. "You deserve every bit of attention and affection you missed as a child."

Monica worked hard to be as honest as possible. If she wasn't, then the future would be bleak. She'd had time to think and had come to the conclusion that she didn't want to live with this tension for years to come.

"I'll admit that I'm having trouble accepting your existence. Until a little while ago, I was an only child.

Let's get this straight, though. Despite a natural and understandable reluctance, I *do* want to get to know you."

Marcie looked like she released a breath she'd been holding.

"O-kay. In that case, I will try to, um… I'm not sure how I'm supposed to deal with this," Marcie said.

"Me, either." Monica smiled, perhaps not as broadly as she should, but she was trying. Turning to her dad, she said, "Dad, thanks for your help. I have to get back to work."

That evening in her own apartment, Monica started making phone calls. Olivia was on board with a small sponsorship. Maria loved the idea both of catering the barbecue and of hiring locals to help her cook and serve.

On her lunch tomorrow, she'd call around Denver to get a license to hold an event in one of their parks. If that didn't work out, maybe a corporate sponsor would let her use a parking lot. One way or another, she was getting this done.

Late in the evening, Dad phoned, wanting to know when he could organize a dinner at the house for just the three of them, calling it a "family" dinner. *Family*. So strange. Begging off for a weeknight, saying she was too tired after work most days, she booked it for the following weekend. She needed time to build her defenses. She might have always dreamed about having a sibling, but the reality of one showing up out of the blue in adulthood was still too weird.

"Marcie happened to overhear the stuff about your charity event," her dad mentioned. "She'd like to be involved."

Oh. Did Monica want to get that close to her sister that quickly? Dad sounded hopeful, though.

"Sure," Monica said too brightly. "Maybe she would be willing to donate one or two of those fabulous pieces of silver jewelry she wears."

"I was thinking of a more substantial role than that." Monica knew her dad well. Even across the phone lines, she could sense his frown.

"Dad, this is *my* project that I'm doing for Noah."

"She's your sister."

"I know that, but why should she be involved in this?"

"Because it would be good for her. She can get to know people in town. You can introduce her around."

"I can do that just as easily without having to deal with her along with all of the other millions of details of the benefit."

"See? You could use her help with some of those details."

"No, Dad. I could use the help of someone experienced."

"Do it, Monica. Find her a role."

Monica sighed. Dad wasn't going to let it go, but neither was Monica going to give in. Hoping to put him off, she said, "I'll think about it, Dad."

"Good. Get back to me on that."

After she hung up, Monica threw the idea of Marcie helping out into the metaphorical trash can at the back of her mind. No way was she letting Marcie anywhere near the barbecue.

MONICA JUMPED OUT of bed.

Noah had kissed her yesterday, and they had been the most delicious, skilled kisses.

Could she make it happen again?

He'd been curious about where she sprayed her perfume. Would he wonder today?

Just in case...where should she put it?

She ran through the list of spots he'd already detected. She didn't want to become *too* risqué. After all, Noah wasn't her boyfriend, or anything.

Humming, she picked up her vintage Chanel atomizer and studied herself in the mirror. An inspired thought struck. She would put it on the back of one of her knees.

She'd once told Billy how sensitive she was there, how she loved it when he kissed her there, how she craved the abrasion of his beard when it had grown out a bit during the day.

Unfortunately, Billy was a main-event kind of guy and never afforded the kind of attention to all the bits and pieces that made Monica a sensual creature.

Not like Noah. He seemed to revel in those bits. The rasp of his tongue on the inside of her arm yesterday had sent her senses into the stratosphere.

Dressed and about to leave the room to have breakfast then brush her teeth, she halted and looked back at the bed.

For a couple of years after Billy's death, her bed had become both a comfort and a trap. Day after day after day, she'd lain in it for hours, feeling sorry for herself, missing her dead husband.

Those feelings had eased, had morphed into a kind of low-grade malaise that had dogged her days. Noah would probably wonder how she knew a word like *malaise*.

He underestimated her. Funny. She should be angered by that, but instead found real pleasure in setting him straight. She loved those moments of surprise on his face when he realized she was so much more than she appeared to be, or that he assumed she would be.

The challenge of finding new ways to surprise him had started to urge her out of bed lately.

This morning she was actually eager to start her day, eager to get to the farm and have Noah come close enough to find her perfume. Oh, that amazing feeling of his breath on her skin and the heat of his nearness washing over her body.

And the joy of discovering his nose was as sensitive as hers! And he could name her ingredients!

He had the greatest olfactory organ. He probably wouldn't think she would know that word, either. She knew the word *proboscis*, too, but would never use it to describe Noah's nose. His nose wasn't too long or too pronounced.

Noah's nose was perfect, the right length, with the lightest smattering of freckles.

What she hadn't known was that a nose, the most mundane and least glamorous part of a body, could be so sexy. But Noah made it so.

She made the bed, smoothed her hand over the white eyelet quilt she'd made before she and Billy had gotten married, and smiled. Giggled.

Today she would stump Noah with her latest ingredients. She was sure of it.

All of the base ingredients were still in the same fragrance family, but she had added one new fragrance note.

She touched the bed one last time. This piece of furniture had become many things to her. Today, it was just a bed, a place to catch up on sleep so she could get on with the act of living.

Today, not only had she wanted to get out of bed, but she also cared. She cared about the world and her place in it.

She cared about Noah.

He raced through his indoor morning chores then rushed outdoors only to draw up short.

No BMW waited for him in the driveway. Where was Monica? Not that he was waiting for her. He just needed to move forward with the day, get things done. His arm was in a cast. She had to do stuff for him. That was all.

Ah, but those kisses yesterday. Not only had she yielded to him, but she'd also been aggressive in taking—and he liked that.

He walked his fields. Tomatoes were coming along well, and there were no pests. Good thing he planted a row of marigolds along one side to repel hornworms, and a row of nasturtiums along the other to repel aphids.

He found his mind only half on his plants and the other half on the woman who should have been here by now. He checked his watch. Okay, he was wrong. She still had another five minutes.

But then he straightened and listened as he heard the sound of a car approaching. She was here!

With long strides, he left the field and swung around the corner of the house.

Eyes drawn to a pair of long, bare legs getting out of the car, he missed what she said.

His gaze flew to hers. "Pardon?"

"I brought us muffins to have after we finish our work. I assumed you would have some coffee or tea to go with them?"

"Yeah. I have stuff to drink." Stuff to drink. Cripes. Where was his brain? Still preoccupied with those mile-long legs and trim ankles.

"I'll put these inside." She mounted the porch steps but stopped at the top to watch him over her shoulder. "Noah?"

"Yeah?"

"The back of my left knee." Her look, so cute and saucy, made him laugh. This playful side surprised him, caught him unaware. Made him breathless for more.

From the bottom step, he leaned forward. "May I?"

"Ummm…" Her back still to him, she watched him over her shoulder, then playfully touched one finger to her chin and pretended to think it over. "Yes. Tell me what you think."

I think I'm in love.

Whoa, where had *that* come from? This was infatuation, nothing else. Absurd that he would call this love. But, hey, infatuation could be a lot of fun.

He pressed forward until his face nearly touched her leg and took a delicate sniff.

"Pepper," he murmured.

She gasped. "How do you do that?"

He'd heard that women were sensitive behind their knees. He wanted to test that theory. He ran two fingers along her skin. She shivered.

"What else?" She sounded breathless.

He touched his fingers to his nose. "Traces of all-spice." He licked them and placed them against her sun-warmed skin.

She shivered again. She'd been doing that a lot around him lately.

Goose bumps rose on her flesh. Warm skin, but shivery reaction. God, he loved this game.

Slowly, she stepped away from his wet fingers and entered the house.

"I'll just put these inside." She sounded calm, but breathless.

She was affected every bit as much as he was, he surmised.

The day had only just begun and already he was looking forward to the next one. Where on Monica's body would he find her perfume tomorrow, and would she let him touch her again?

But curiously enough…he was in no rush. If this wasn't the craziest, most fun foreplay he'd ever experienced, he thought anything more erotic would kill him.

And yeah, this *was* foreplay. He'd come to a firm decision after kissing her yesterday.

One way or another, Monica Accord, you will be mine.

MONICA SET DOWN the muffins on the counter and leaned both palms hard against the edge, trying to calm her breathing.

Her heart pounded. What kind of game was she playing? Tomorrow she wanted to find a more intimate spot on her body to spray her perfume. She wanted him to touch her, closer and closer to her core.

She wasn't used to sexual games. There had been nothing subtle about her big puppy-dog husband. Billy knew what he wanted and jumped in with both feet.

She'd lost her virginity to him. It had hurt because he hadn't prepared her for it first. Billy tended to dive into ponds first and check for rocks later. At first she may not have been satisfied, but he had. For a long time, that had been enough.

Later, though, she'd asked for more and he'd been happy to accommodate.

This, though? This…this…*thing* with Noah was driving her nuts. She'd never known long, slow foreplay. And she'd certainly never initiated it.

Her own playfulness, her own sense of control, left her empowered and joyful. It felt good. Better than good. Wonderful!

She wanted to keep this going. She liked leading Noah along.

Then an odd thought occurred to her. Someday soon she would have to lead him right into her bed, not only because she wasn't teasing him, only to walk away, but also because she was hornier than she'd ever been in her life. While this flirtation seemed to burst from nowhere between them, it felt so right. Perfect. Oh, Lord, she wanted the man with a desperation she'd never known before.

There! She'd said it. She was horny.

She touched her breast where her nipple peaked. Oh, so tender. It needed a man's hand. Specifically, Noah's.

Her smile felt Mona Lisa-inspired in the supreme knowledge that she was turning Noah on and he was enjoying it as much as she was.

She sure wasn't ready to give in yet, though. Foreplay had been precious and rare in her marriage, but not here with Noah. He seemed to like it, too. She wanted him with an ache, but she also wanted to play, to build tension, to nurture and appreciate the ache.

She'd never felt sexy before. Now, with Noah, she felt sexy-y-y and wow, it was amazing.

Noah, sweetheart, welcome to my playground.

THE FOLLOWING DAY, she thought of her best idea yet.

Noah, wait until you get a load of this, she thought as she dabbed perfume on her waist, just above the waistband of her jeans.

She buttoned up her sleeveless shirt, but didn't tuck it in, instead tying the long ends into a knot at the front. An old-fashioned style, but it allowed access to the perfume.

She drove out to the farm strangely breathless and a little dizzy by the time she arrived. If this was what foreplay with Noah did to her body, she wasn't sure she would survive going all the way with him.

He stood in the yard, waiting for her.

Without a word, she stepped out of the car, walked around to the front and leaned back on the hood in a sexy pose. Or what she hoped was sexy. She didn't have a clue.

His intense gaze followed her every move, touched every part of her body.

He stalked toward her like a hungry cat and said one word. "Where?" Maybe she did look sexy after all.

"Here." She lifted the knot of her blouse an inch baring her midriff.

Noah's eyes widened.

He leaned forward. No, to put it accurately, he *yearned* forward, his desire a shimmering heat that pebbled her skin.

He bent, breathed on her skin, raising goose bumps, and licked her. Good heavens. This man and his magical tongue, with his propensity for licking her, was going to give her an orgasm this minute, right here in the wide-open outdoors.

He straightened. No smiles today. No cocky grins. No clever thoughts.

"We need to get to work."

He stalked away, turned back, scrubbed his hands over his face and growled, "Soon, Monica. Soon."

She couldn't answer. She was still trying to suck all of the air of which he had robbed her back into her lungs.

Dizzy with hunger for Noah's body, stars danced before her eyes.

Could she survive foreplay?

CHAPTER ELEVEN

MONICA APPROACHED HER father again, this time catching him at the bar without Marcie in attendance.

She ordered her usual bagel with light cream cheese and a black coffee, forgoing all the lovely cream she liked.

Before he could raise the topic of giving Marcie a role in organizing the charity, she said, "Dad, I've been having this weird idea and I'd like your feedback."

She'd been developing this dream, this hope that maybe she could be a businesswoman. She finally had an idea she thought not only held merit, but also fueled her passion.

"What is it?" He was drinking coffee today—not Scotch, thank goodness—and bit into a turkey BLT.

"I want to open a shop-and-gallery combo, here in Accord."

He put down his sandwich, clearly surprised. "What kind of shop?"

"Olivia has the art scene covered, but I'd love to sell items from local artisans, like jewelry and fabric work. For many people who study clothing design, jobs are few and far between when they leave college, especially if they want to stay in the state instead of heading to New York or California. What if they could design *and* sell original clothing here? Stuff that differs from any other clothing sold locally."

He mulled it over. She *thought* he looked approving. "And the gallery part? Wouldn't it compete with Olivia?"

"No, that's the beauty of my plan. I would love to comb local attics and basements to find the treasures that women and men created years ago, then put them on display."

She bit into her bagel then swallowed before continuing. "For example, I would show off all of the amazing embroidery of the women in my family."

"I like it."

"You do? And do you think I could do it? Make a success of a shop like that?"

"If anyone could, it would be you. Ever since you were little you've been fascinated by fashion and fabric."

"I still have to see whether the bank will lend me the money for this kind of start-up—"

"I'll do it. I'll lend it to you. You'd never get it from the bank. You have no track record and no collateral. I'll bankroll you."

Exactly what she'd been hoping. Maybe she should try to stand on her own two feet with this, but Dad's assessment was right. "Thank you, Dad."

Through the rest of her lunch, she felt almost teary. Monica's dad had faith in her and it felt wonderful.

After work that evening, Monica stood outside of Tonio's with Maria.

"It's a good idea, Monica. You must do it."

"I'm scared, Maria. What if I fail? What if I lose my dad's money?"

Maria answered with a philosophical shrug. "It's only money."

"That's easy to say when it isn't my money. I would feel less worried if I were gambling with my own, but I don't have any to gamble."

"It will all be yours one day anyway."

Not true. Not anymore. "Half of it will be mine. I assume Dad will share his inheritance between the two of us equally."

Maria's frown took in the entire town before settling in the vague direction of her father's house. "So much has changed for you. Are you okay?"

Monica's smile felt gentle and grateful, but also sad. "In all of my dreams of having a sister, when I had my little imaginary friend, I never, ever anticipated it would come true. Now that it has, I don't know what to think. I'm trying hard to adjust."

The grocery bag was cutting into her palm, so she shifted it from one hand to the other. "It's so small of me, but I find I'm having trouble sharing my dad."

"Of course. You've had your father's love all to yourself until now." Maria touched her arm. "This I will tell you is the truth about parents and children— there is always enough love to go around. Hearts don't have boundaries. They grow as much as they need to."

"Thank you, Maria. That helps."

"Hey," Maria said. "Here comes Noah. He's a store

owner and businessman. He can help you figure out the shop."

"Shop?" Noah asked turning his attention to Monica. "What shop?"

"It's nothing, Noah." But in saying so she could see she'd hurt his feelings. Saying it out loud, discussing the project, made it too real, too prone to failure. It scared her. If she didn't act on it, then it couldn't fail, could it?

Still, a frown lingered on his intelligent brow.

"Noah, I'm thinking about opening a shop, to sell the kinds of things I love."

"A shop? Really? On Main?"

"Alphonse is closing down his cigar shop. Things worked fine for years, but people aren't smoking like they used to."

"Yeah, Alphonse did well for a while. And he loved his shop because he loved cigars. I love mine because I believe that reduce, reuse and recycle will save our planet. And you, Maria?"

"I love food. I love my products. I love turning people on to good recipes."

Noah redirected his attention back to Monica. "If you love your product and it shows in your marketing, you'll do well." He cocked his head slightly. "What will you sell?"

"I would collect and sell vintage items, but it won't be an antique shop. I would specialize in fabrics and embroidery. And I'd hire local clothing designers to create beautiful clothes that I could sell. The same with local jewelers."

She hesitated to tell the rest, certain that Noah would be as skeptical as Maria. "In the back, I'd set aside space for a gallery of women's fashions from years ago. It wouldn't bring in money, though."

As expected, Noah frowned. "Do you think that's wise? You'll have rent to pay."

"I'll try it out, see if the store can carry it."

She should share the rest. See what he thought. "I want to sell my own line of perfumes, too."

Maria butted in, shoving her arm into Noah's face. "Smell this."

He sniffed her wrist and broke into a wide grin. "It suits you perfectly."

"It does, doesn't it? Not too sweet. Not too pretty. Plenty spicy."

Noah's glance toward Monica was filled with an admiration that warmed her to her bones.

"You should do it, Monica."

"I'm afraid to tell your mom. She'll be angry with me for leaving the gallery."

"She'll support this idea," he said softly.

"Will you—*would* you mind looking at the space with me?"

"Sure."

They headed over together. Monica already had the key with her. She'd picked it up from Bram Weinstein, Accord's resident real estate agent.

Once inside the empty shop, they stood and tried to imagine something other than the contents that had been there all of their lives.

Dust motes floated in sunlight that streamed through the front windows.

"How long ago did Al open the cigar store?"

"My dad thinks close to fifty years ago."

"No wonder he's ready to retire."

"It will be hard on him, though. What will he do with his time? His wife died ten years ago. His children have scattered to the four corners of the earth."

When Noah didn't respond, she glanced his way.

He watched her with a quiet, arrested sort of expression.

"What is it?" she asked.

"You are truly a kind person, aren't you?"

"I try to be. I don't know why you always thought I was cold."

He stepped toward her, then moved closer, the room so quiet Monica swore she could hear dust motes hit the floor.

"You never talked to me."

When she'd been trying to avoid him? She wouldn't have thought that would matter to him. Just to be certain they were on the same page, she asked, "When?"

"In high school."

He'd surprised her. That long ago? That wasn't the answer she'd expected. "High school? I was mean to you in high school?"

"God, no. Mean would have been an improvement."

There was something worse than mean? "I don't understand."

"You didn't see me. I didn't exist for you."

So untrue. "Oh, I saw you, but I was intimidated by you. You were too smart." She twisted her fingers together. "And I wasn't."

"You know that's not true. You do understand how smart you are, right?"

She shook her head. "Maybe now, but back then you had such strong opinions about everything, and I didn't know how to have an opinion. I was—"

She bit her lip. God. She'd almost said it out loud. She'd almost shared her nightmare.

He stepped closer still, until she could feel heat radiating from him and could practically count the gold streaks in his green eyes. "Tell me."

She shook her head.

He pressed against her, compelling her to share. "Please." So gently spoken, so unlike his normal take-charge personality. He looked like the same man, smelled like him, but something had shifted with that soft plea. "Please."

"I was empty." There. It was out in the open.

"What do you mean?"

"There was a huge gaping hole inside of me." Like one of those zero-gravity spaces, the room held them still and aloft, drawing things out of her easily. "There was something missing. That's why Billy was so special to me. He filled all of my empty spaces with his personality."

"Yeah, Billy sure filled a room." No sarcasm. Affection.

"He banished the silence from my life."

"Poor Monica."

She tried to point at his face, but he stood too close to her. "If you say 'poor little rich girl,' I'll clock you."

"No. That wasn't what I meant. It's awful that you felt alone. Bravo for Billy. If I'd known I would have seen you differently."

Cinnamon. If I developed cologne for Noah, I would add cinnamon. It would enhance his natural scent. He'd liked it on her. She would like it on him.

"And now?" he asked.

"Now I feel better. I spent much of my time alone while growing up, even though my dad was the furthest thing from a neglectful father. And I'm learning to be on my own now in a different way—to be content with my solitude."

He nodded, as though he already knew that. "I've seen a change in you this summer."

"For a long time, I've been looking for something to fill the void inside of myself, without relying on someone else to do it. One thing I've always wanted is to own my own business, but I couldn't find a direction. I finally have. I love these ideas, Noah. I want to make them work."

His eyes filled with admiration, like hot sun bathing a beach, and she basked in it. "You'll make it work, Monica."

He came to within an inch of her and she held her breath. He was going to kiss her. She closed her eyes. She felt his breath on her ear.

"Where is it?"

She understood what he wanted and turned around, undid the top two buttons of her blouse and slid it down her shoulders.

She felt his nose on her right shoulder and smiled. Close, but no cigar. He trailed his lips, moist and hot, across the top of her back until he reached her left shoulder. Bingo.

He kissed her there, leaving his lips to burn into her like a brand. She leaned her head back against him.

"Noah," she breathed.

His good hand came to her shoulder and the fingers of his broken wrist grazed her arm. He pressed her away from him. "Not here. Not now."

Not *no*. Another time and another place. Yes. Soon.

They stepped out of the empty storefront together, Monica trying her hardest to be neutral when all she wanted was to throw him on the ground and have her way with him.

When she tried to lock the door, the key wouldn't fit properly. Her hands were shaking. Noah took it from her and managed to lock the door even though his hands weren't much more steady than hers…and that was gratifying.

They walked down Main Street without touching, he to his truck to drive to the farm and Monica to walk to her apartment. She had a huge smile on her face.

Where on earth should she spray her perfume in the morning?

MARCIE WANDERED INTO the bar and found an empty table near the back of the room. Midweek, it wasn't hard to do.

All she wanted was a place to nurse a cold beer and think. Coming here, to this town, while the right thing to do, wasn't turning out as she'd thought. Her dad was a good man, especially since he'd stopped drinking.

She liked their conversations. But her relationship with her sister puzzled her. She couldn't break through the woman's shell.

An hour ago, their father had dropped a bombshell on her. He was going to bankroll a business for Monica. Marcie wanted the same relationship with her father that Monica had, but how could that be? She hadn't grown up with him as her daddy.

She waited for the waitress to make her way over, feeling more than a little lonely in this bar, this town, where she didn't fit in.

"May I join you?" That refined, melodious, *masculine* voice stroked her spine. Without turning, she knew who it was. John Spade.

"I'd prefer to be alone."

He sat down anyway, across from her. She suspected the man did whatever he wanted in life. That his was the only company she could tolerate tonight didn't matter. He peeved her off just because everything in her life seemed to be going wrong, and she didn't know how to fix it.

In each hand, he carried a Corona with a wedge of lime in the neck. "I took the liberty of ordering you a drink."

She liked it. She didn't tell him so, and he chuckled, fully aware that she was holding back.

He clinked his bottle against hers and took a long swig. "So?"

"So what?"

"Are you going to tell me what's wrong?"

"No."

"Why not? Sometimes it helps to talk things out."

While she might need to confide in someone, she didn't want it to be with this man who unsettled her so.

"Talk," he said.

Her urge to tell overcame her reticence. So she told him about her father bankrolling Monica's business.

"I heard about that."

"How do you know already? My impression was it was only just decided today at lunch."

"True, but Monica stopped in to mention it to me. She'll probably need my services soon."

"What kind of services?"

"Lawyerly services that are none of your busi-

ness. She's a client." He snagged a waitress and ordered a couple of plates of fries with curried mayo
dip. "What's your problem with it? It sounds like a
good idea for a shop."

"*That's* none of your business."

He studied her for a long time before he said, "It's
the money, isn't it? You feel slighted. You want your
share."

"What if the shop fails? All of that money will go
down the drain. There won't be much left when our
father dies." That sounded so cold she could have bit-
ten off her tongue for saying it. She needed to keep
that kind of stuff to herself. What was it about him?

She felt alone in this town. Maybe all she needed
was a friend, but John?

The fries came and they ate in silence. The curried
mayo was good. She might like it better than ketchup.

"You need to understand that Monica isn't going
away just because you have a new stake in this
game." He shoved his second empty bottle of beer
aside. "You missed out on a lot of advantages growing up, and I'm betting your dad is feeling guilty
right now. But don't try to take advantage of that."

Anger spurted inside of her. "As if I would."

"I would if I were you."

He paid the bill and gestured for her to precede
him out the door. She buttoned her sweater even
though the evening was balmy. John touched the
small of her back and sent a chill up her body.

"Don't envy Monica. Your dad is pleased as punch

that you're home. There is enough love and money for both of you. Let your relationship with her grow naturally. Give Monica time. This is as big a change for her as it is for you."

She didn't like that he understood her so well. He saw into her too deeply and read her insecurities so clearly.

He kissed her, quick and hard, using his tongue to breach the sealed seam of her lips.

She gave in too easily, drinking in every last drop of the kiss.

He pulled back. His breath fanned her face.

"Things will work out, Marcie. Trust me." He walked away, his parting glance too knowing. "See you around."

She grasped the two sides of her sweater and held them tightly, still battling the delicious chill he'd set in her.

She didn't jump into bed with a man just because he was a good kisser. Okay, a great kisser.

She walked home, still puzzling what to do about John Spade.

MONICA DRESSED WITH care and, in a surprising move, sprayed her perfume on the farthest spot on her body from her core.

Somehow it seemed fitting today. Whatever was going to happen between her and Noah would happen sooner rather than later, but she wanted him to work for it.

Anticipation was making her hornier than she'd ever been in her life. *Horny* was a word she'd never used to describe herself before, and she liked it.

She drove out to the farm.

Noah stood in the yard, angry and potent and dark.

"Where is it today?" Not a nice request, but a demand.

She sauntered past him to the veranda, reveling in the intensity she brought out in him.

On the top step she turned around and slowly slipped off one of the backless sandals she wore. She wrapped her fingers around the newel post for balance then held her bare foot a few inches away from her body, toward Noah, beckoning him.

She'd sprayed the inside of her ankle, but Noah misunderstood. He grasped her foot, his thumb on the inside of her arch, teasing her with the hard rasp of a callus.

He bent forward, eyes watching her with passion and possession, just before he closed them and licked her arch. His propensity for licking would be the death of her. It just about sent her off her feet. She locked the leg that was holding her up and gripped the newel post. Another of the shivers that only Noah seemed to engender in her wracked her body.

These days, all she seemed to do around Noah was shiver. She should write a novel. *The Summer of Shivery Passions. To Shiver or Not to—*

Oh. He did it again before straightening. She launched herself at him. Unprepared, he caught her with his good arm, but fell back onto the dirt of the yard with her on top of him.

For a silent, pregnant pause they stared at each other before Monica took his mouth with her own. He wanted to do passion? Take that, mister. He wanted to do possession? Yeah, she could do that.

She ravaged his mouth. He opened to her and she feasted with her tongue. He tasted like coffee and toast and…tofu? Whatever. He tasted great. She could drink from his cup of passion all the livelong day.

His long-fingered hand, and those rough, callused thumbs, grasped her waist, rose to caress her, the thumb of his unbroken arm grazing the side of her breast before resting in her bare armpit.

Armpit. Such an unsexy word, but when Noah touched her there, she moaned. *More.*

He rolled her onto her back, thrusting his tongue into her mouth. They sparred for control, by turns taking and ceding. Noah's long muscled thigh slid between her legs, pressing hard against Monica's pubis, setting up a bittersweet pain that built every time she pressed back against him.

Delicious. Delectable. Thrilling.

She ripped off the elastic that held his ponytail and shoved her fingers through his hair. A man shouldn't have hair so soft, so sensual and full.

Every part of him appealed to her—his character, his honesty and integrity, and that gorgeous body doing strange things to hers, especially his thigh.

He ground against her. Who knew a thigh could be so sexy, could elicit such a pull, an attraction, such an...orgasm?

It built with an unstoppable power of its own, bursting over her like falling stars. Sweet sexy manna from heaven.

She breathed heavily, came down slowly.

The world, life, sanity, returned.

A breeze ruffled leaves in the oak nearby. Her avian friends who lived in the tree sang their melodies. Noah chuckled low in his chest.

He hadn't even put his hands on her and she had come.

Embarrassed, she fought to get out of his grasp, but he was strong, even with only one functioning arm.

"Hey." He used a soothing voice, but it still rang with amusement. "Stop fighting me. I want to savor this. You were awesome."

Awesome? "I made a fool of myself."

"Look at me." All amusement had fled.

When she refused, he cradled her chin in his palm and gently raised it until she had no choice but to meet his eye.

"That was beautiful."

When he knew she didn't believe him, he went on, "I'm serious. Having Monica Accord fall apart so sweetly in my arms was the sexiest thing I've ever experienced."

She felt him hard against her thigh. "You were turned on, too?"

He nudged her gently with his erection. "Oh, yeah. I want to experience more of you. If that's what happens when we're both fully clothed, I don't think I can survive you with our clothes off. I would die a happy man, though."

He sighed and she laughed. He'd managed to ease her embarrassment. She snuggled against him. She wanted more, too.

Someone clearing a throat nearby shocked Monica. She felt Noah jump, too. They turned at the sound.

Marcie stood behind them, in front of their dad's car. In the midst of their passion, when the world had receded, they hadn't heard her drive up. A low groan issued from Monica. How much had Marcie seen?

Monica peeked at her. Marcie looked chagrined.

"I'm sorry. I thought you came here to farm. To work off some kind of community service sentence."

Noah stiffened in her arms then stood, helping Monica to her feet with a restrained anger she could feel through his palm.

"What are you doing here?" He sounded like a god tossing thunderbolts to earth.

"Our dad sent me to find Monica." She spoke to Monica. "He wants to see both of us. I checked at the gallery first but was told you weren't working today. I thought I might find you here."

Monica pulled herself together, brushing dirt from her pants. "Give me a minute. I'll see you back in town."

"I can wait."

"No need," she said, a hint of steel in her voice. "I know where my father lives."

"I'll wait," Marcie spoke stubbornly.

Noah bent close and spoke to her low and fiercely. "Tonight. Here. I'll make dinner. Seven o'clock?"

Monica nodded, understanding the full implication. They needed to finish what they'd started this morning.

She went to her car and drove away. She checked her rearview mirror. Marcie's car was on the road behind her.

She couldn't possibly be more disconcerted about Marcie catching her rolling around in the dirt with Noah.

MARCIE FOLLOWED MONICA back into town, trying to wash the images of Noah and Monica from her mind. She'd caught them lying on the ground in each other's arms, smiling and talking intimately.

Who knows why they were outside instead of inside in bed, but it was obvious they'd been fooling around.

If Marcie had been low before, now she was downright sick with envy.

Monica had so much. She'd been raised with money in a town that respected her family. The house she'd grown up in was gorgeous. Her bedroom was beautiful.

Marcie had gone snooping in Monica's bedroom. There was still a lot of her sister's stuff stored there from high school, things that Marcie had missed out on like cheerleading costumes and a prom dress—one that Marcie would never have been able to afford.

Sure, Marcie was creative, but it was hard to make a homemade gown look like a one-of-a-kind designer dress.

Monica had lived the ideal childhood in the ideal house in a perfect town. She had everything and now she also had a man who adored her, judging by the way Noah looked at her.

It made Marcie's chest hurt. She wanted someone special in her life, a great guy, someone good-looking like Noah to whom everyone in town gave respect.

John Spade didn't count. He just wanted sex.

Noah desired Monica, but he also cared for her. It had been written all over his face. With one fierce, repressive look, he'd all but dared Marcie to spread dirty gossip about what she'd seen. *As if.*

Yep. No doubt whatsoever—that man was crazy about Monica.

Marcie had nothing but a father who treated her like gold only because he felt guilty. She had no permanence, no official standing in this town outside of being the rag-mag story of the week. There wasn't one person alive who loved her for who she was.

Marcie wanted everything Monica had.

At her father's house, she found her sister already ensconced on the sofa while their dad sat in his favorite armchair.

He gestured for Marcie to join Monica on the sofa. "Would either of you like coffee or tea?"

"No, thank you." Monica sounded composed.

Marcie shook her head to the offer of a drink.

"Let's get down to it." Her dad was a handsome man. No wonder their mother had fallen for him. But then, she hadn't, had she? She'd been in love with Donna.

Marcie could only think Donna must have been a better person, less bitter and happier, before Karen died.

She steered her mind away from bad memories.

"I've been talking to my lawyer. As you can guess, Marcie's arrival changes everything in the family dynamic. Monica, I'm sure you must know that I would have wanted Marcie here all along. Marcie knows that I tried to find her."

He stopped and cleared his throat. He sounded on the verge of becoming emotional. It had been like this often since she'd arrived in to town, often triggering emotion in her, too.

If only she could believe that he loved her and didn't just feel guilty.

"I've changed my will. Monica, you will no longer be my sole heir. Everything will be split fifty-fifty between the two of you."

Marcie sensed Monica nodding beside her.

"I expected as much, Dad."

Saint Monica. Did the woman never have a negative, faulty, *un*saintly thought? She made Marcie feel inadequate and too…too *less than*.

Marcie was getting money. Someday she'd be so well-off that she would never have to worry about security, or where her next meal was coming from again. So why did she feel hollow? Where was the elation she'd expected?

Why, at this moment, did she miss Donna, the only mother she'd ever known? Why, at this moment, when her father was giving her so much, did she wonder if he loved her?

Her father raised one finger. "I have one condition."

Okay, here they come, all of the hoops he wanted her to jump through to earn the right to the money. Marcie waited like an insect suspended in amber. This had all been too good to be true. She should have known it couldn't be true. Story of her life.

I want.

"This house isn't to be sold. It's been in the family for generations and I want it to stay in the family." His glance took in the crown moldings and leaded-glass windows. "My great-great-grandfather built Accord House, but my great-grandfather wanted a place of his own and built this. I love it. I want it handed down in the family."

He waggled one finger. It should have looked silly. It didn't. He was serious and severe. "I don't want any fighting about this. I want the two of you working out who will live here equitably."

I will. With a fierce stroke of desire that knocked her senseless, Marcie wanted this house and everything in it.

Monica stood. "We'll work it out, Dad. I promise."

How? Was Monica going to hand it over to Marcie without a whimper? Or did Monica think that she would automatically live here just because she'd grown up here?

The thought made Marcie crazy.

I want.

Monica kissed her dad on the cheek then left the room.

NOAH RACED THROUGH cooking dinner. He was making spaghetti. Monica would probably have made something gourmet, but he just wasn't that kind of cook. He didn't know how to do anything fancy.

Anyway, the food wasn't the point. What he was certain would come later was the *entire* point of the night.

The food was secondary. It—

He heard a noise at the front door and stepped from the kitchen into the hallway.

Monica stood in the open doorway. She was here. She looked good. He liked her flowery dress.

Now that the moment had come, he felt gauche, like that young boy who had adored Monica from afar for years.

This morning, rolling around in the dirt, he could have made love to her without worry, but now he'd had the day to anticipate it. It all seemed too planned, too different from this morning's spontaneous combustion.

"You're early," he blurted. He'd wanted the house to be perfect for her. He scrambled to straighten the magazines scattered across the battered coffee table.

For the first time in his life, he wished he had a nicer place to offer her.

"You're beautiful," he breathed. "Do you want to start with wine?"

"No."

"Okay, just with dinner?"

"I'm not hungry, Noah. Not for food."

Slowly, giving her time to pull away if she wanted to, but hoping like heck she wouldn't, he pressed his lips against hers. Softly. They parted with the sweetness of a bud opening to the sun.

He fell into the nectar of her kiss. Into the tenderness and unexpected vulnerability of Monica.

When he pulled away and looked into her eyes, he whispered, "You make me wish I was a poet."

She smiled and wrapped her long, cool fingers around the back of his neck, bringing him closer and opening his lips with her tongue. She tasted like chocolate and cinnamon and a touch of pepper. She smelled like citrus.

When she finished having her way with him, he whispered, "Orange."

"Tangerine."

Ah. He'd gotten the bouquet wrong. No wonder.

The woman confounded his senses even as everything around him—the air that cooled his lungs, the heat of sunlight through the doorway and the solidness of the wall—became hyper-real, puissant and sharp.

He didn't even realize he'd fallen against the wall for support and had taken her with him.

Her soft body melded against his. Her long legs fit perfectly between his thick thighs. The long evening rays of the sun turned her hair to gold. Her lips traveled his neck, his collarbone, leaving a damp trail. She murmured sweetly, humming low in her throat.

All of these years later, after falling into hopeless infatuation with her more than twenty years ago, she still left him speechless.

She pulled away, leaning back against his arm around her slim waist. The fingers of his broken arm feathered her hip through the cotton of her dress. "How could you get tangerine wrong? I depend on you to know these things." Her smile, a thing of playfulness and joy, warmed him through and through.

He touched his nose to hers. "Close enough."

What pure pleasure to find this childlike quality of wanting to have fun inside sophisticated Monica. Yet again, she delighted him.

"Come to bed with me." Air hissed between his teeth. He wanted her more than ever. "Upstairs. Before dinner."

Her eyes changed, became more intense and focused. "Yes."

She strode to the kitchen, flicked off the burners under the pots and rushed back to him.

The delight of knowing she was as anxious as he was, as attracted to him as he was to her, lifted him onto another plane. A laugh burst out of him, loud and boisterous.

As horny as a teenager, but grown-up now and sure of the outcome, he pulled her up the stairs, but stopped on the landing.

Her laugh was swallowed in his devouring kiss. God, if only he could take her inside of him. If only he could make her a part of him.

He kissed her until he was dizzy with lust. She returned his aggression drop for drop.

When he stopped, his heavy breathing fanning the hair around her face, he promised, "I'm going to love the ever-living daylights out of you. If we're not careful, I'll do it here on the floor."

She took his hand and headed for toward the bedroom. "Bed, Noah. Now."

Just inside the door, she came to an abrupt halt and turned to him with a beatific smile. This was the essence of Monica, sexy and sweet at the same time.

"You made the bed." Her breathy voice turned the room from a simple place for sleep into a cathedral. A place to worship her body. "For me?"

"Yeah. For you."

She opened the tiny purse she'd carried in with her and dumped the contents onto the freshly made bed. The only things that fell out were foil packages.

"Condoms." He looked at her admiringly. "Smart woman. Um, I don't think we'll need a dozen of them."

"I'm an optimist."

Her eyes burned brightly while her fingers undid the buttons of her dress. For the first time, he noticed that she'd left the power dressing behind. Her body was draped in swirling fabric that covered her to mid-calf in tiny flowers. She wore small tasteful jewelry.

When she finished the long series of buttons, the fabric whispered from her shoulders to the floor.

Noah swallowed because, hell's freaking bells, she wore nothing else.

Perfection had always been an ideal to which he aspired, but here she stood in the flesh, gilded by the setting sun streaming through the window. Thank God they weren't starting this in the dark. She would look amazing lit by candlelight, but the sun paid loving homage to the goddess.

"Noah?" She giggled.

"Yeah?"

"You're wearing too much clothing."

The slow blossoming of his smile sent a visible shiver through her. He *adored* Monica's shivers, loved that he had the power to extract them from her.

As he shed his clothes without finesse, ripping a couple of buttons from his shirt in his haste, she lay back on the bed and watched. "I like the way you do that, Noah."

Momentarily slowed down by his zipper because

he was already hard for her, his pants took longer to take off than his shirt.

Her glance took him in. "I like that, too. I want it." She beckoned with her fingers.

Earthiness? From Monica? A slow smile built, not just on his face, but also in his heart. She just kept getting better.

Naked, he climbed into bed and loomed over her, one knee on the mattress and the other leg between hers, opening her to him.

She grasped him. Sweet...radishes! There were no words for the pure, pleasure-filled pain of icy, collected Monica embracing him with heat and ardor.

She splayed her fingers over him like cool water rushing down a riverbed, but it was hot instead of cooling, and riling instead of calming.

He kissed her long and hard then grasped her hand because she was playing him almost to the exquisite point of no return.

He took his turn adoring her.

His lips devoured everything they touched—God, her nipples! Lavender-dusky, pebbly hard, beauteously erect. Her stomach, the dimple of her navel where the tip of his tongue fit perfectly, her soft perfect lips that opened to him when she spread her legs.

She tasted like a savory picnic on a warm day—like lightness and darkness, earthy and divine. He sucked, licked and prodded, inflamed by her sexy murmurs and dirty epithets. She came with a joyful cry.

He lunged up to hold her, to become part of the shivers wracking her body. She nestled against him until she settled.

He lifted his head. "Where is it?" he murmured.

She understood him without question and rolled over in his arms.

Tracing her spine with his mouth, and her curves with his fingers, he found it near the base of her spine. She'd dabbed her perfume onto the two dimples just above her cheeks.

"Bergamot, tangerine, lemon balm," he whispered. "Sage."

"You sure know how to talk dirty, Noah," Monica murmured, voice shaky with renewed desire. Using the f-word, she urged him to make love to her. The naughtiness of the word broke him. He'd meant to go real slow their first time together, but he had her on her back and was inside of her silky, sopping wet heat before she could utter another syllable.

He'd imagined so much, everything, time and again, but Monica's reality was stellar, outstripping even his active imagination—fragrant, dripping, noisy, hot. Wild and beautiful.

He loved her hard and fast, and she rose to meet him with more gusto than he'd thought Monica possessed. They made made love, both of them quivering, sound receding, reality a mere backdrop to nirvana.

When he came, he pressed his finger against her sweet clitoris so they came together.

For a long, long time, he lay with her, heart pounding, body sweaty.

He'd known it would be good. He hadn't known it would be the most beautiful thing that had ever happened to him.

He'd obsessed about her beauty and her body for so many years, he'd thought only about having sex with Monica—but this had been lovemaking with a capital *L*.

With the added depth of emotion that had built in him all summer, the act had been a holy thing. Lying in the sweaty, aromatic aftermath of their lovemaking, Noah could admit that while it had been earthy and real and lusty, it had been exalted, too, ennobled by the dignifying glory of love.

That was new, unique. In his life to this point, he had been merely infatuated with women. Nothing could have prepared him for this.

For love.

Against his chest, her heart beat in response to his, the hippie and the socialite united by a profound need. "Who would've ever thought we'd fit so well together."

She stirred in his arms, her lithe body stretching while she all but purred. "That was so good. So perfect."

"Yeah, it was perfect, wasn't it?" It had been worth waiting for, worth all of the magnificent foreplay. "You're pretty spectacular, Monica Accord."

She ran her hand over his chest, his collarbone, his

shoulders. "So are you, Noah Cameron. I like your body. I like your face." She grasped a small handful of his beard and shook his head, gently. "What I can see of it." She softened the rebuke with a smile.

"I like this." She grasped him again, limp now, but not for long if she kept touching him. "I want to do more. Can we shower together?"

She wanted to do more. Thank you, God or Yahweh or Buddha or whoever had created this woman.

He jumped out of bed, grasping her about the waist with his one good, strong arm and lifting her onto her feet.

She squealed. "I love how strong you are, Noah. Strong, but gentle, too."

"I'm learning that you're a pretty awesome mix of contradictions, yourself." He cocked his head to one side. "You surprise me. You like to talk dirty."

"A little. It turns me on."

"Me, too. Let's go get clean together and come back here and get dirty again."

"You're on." She ran from the room in a delightful streak of jiggles.

Man, he loved women's bodies. This one's in particular.

Their shower took longer than he expected because Monica wouldn't let him touch her. She soaped her hands and washed him thoroughly.

"I've wanted to touch you for a long time, Noah. I won't be shortchanged. Lean back against the shower wall. Yes, just like that. No, don't touch me. Keep your hands to yourself. Let me do my thing. Enjoy."

And so he did. If he enjoyed it any more, he'd die of ecstasy.

She was thorough, he'd give the woman that, stroking and petting him until he was blind with need, his fist clenched until his nails dug into his palm.

In the end, they didn't make it back to the bedroom, but made love against the shower wall.

Wrapped in a pair of towels, they ate dinner by candlelight. He'd been right in that the glow of the flames did amazing things for her skin.

They sat side by side, talking quietly, murmuring, whispering secrets both profound and mundane until they finished dinner and Monica excused herself.

She came back moments later, saying, "I brought my perfume with me. I put it on again."

"Where?"

"You have to find it."

Noah spread a couple of thick quilts on the living room floor, lay down with Monica and went treasure hunting.

CHAPTER TWELVE

THEY LAY IN the sultry aftermath of another bout of lovemaking, this time back in his bed, with a soft breeze streaming through Noah's open window and drying the beads of sweat that dotted their naked bodies.

Monica ran her hand down Noah's beard.

"Noah, will you do something for me?"

"Anything. Climb a mountain to bring back a sprig of edelweiss? Dive to the bottom of the ocean for the world's largest pearl? What, my sweet?"

She laughed, the feminine sound so rare in his home he was charmed by her yet again.

"Don't agree too readily. It's a big favor. For the charity benefit, will you cut your hair and shave your beard?"

Startled, he lifted onto an elbow to look down at her in the meager moonlight peeking through the window.

"You don't like it?" Her opinion of how he looked shouldn't matter, but it did.

"I like it, Noah, but it might serve our purposes to have you clean-shaven for the gala. Would that work for you?"

This—*this*—had been his biggest fear with Monica, her lifestyle. He wanted to be part of her, but not necessarily of her world.

Why wasn't he good enough the way he was? But

then the admiration in her eyes had him rethinking his insecurities.

Maybe her concern was practical.

"Do you think it will bring in more money?"

"I think the people I'm inviting to the benefit will take you more seriously so, yeah, it might make a difference to how much they donate."

"Then I'll do it." He rolled over onto his back. "*Do* you like my beard?"

She snuggled against him. "I like *you*. Your passion, your generosity, your personal social conscience all appeal to me and leave me breathless." She hid her face against his shoulder. "And feeling inadequate."

What? "No. God, no. Anything but that. I think you're amazing. For years I didn't want to give you credit for anything because I felt inadequate compared to *you*. I thought you would never give a geeky guy like me a second look."

"You intimidated me. You were so smart. I had to fight to bring in good marks, but you knew so much. You were so *you* so early. It feels like it's taken me years to become me."

"I like who you are, Monica. I really do."

Monica fell asleep in his arms. He liked having her in his home, in his bed and his arms.

He touched his beard. It had been part of him for so long, he couldn't imagine life without it.

What the hell was he worrying about? It was only hair. It would grow back quickly.

Even so, a frisson of unease unsettled him.

IN THE MORNING, Monica rolled over, but Noah wasn't there.

She rubbed her hand across the spot where he'd slept, but she didn't feel the emptiness that dogged her every morning. Full of joy and hope, she jumped out of bed, more fired up than she had felt in years—more so even than when she'd been anticipating those mornings of flirtation. The only thought swirling through her mind was *Noah, Noah, Noah*.

She showered then put on her dress.

Downstairs, the scent of coffee drifted from the kitchen. She made herself a cup, sipped half of it, set down the mug then went outside to find him.

He was tending to his fields, his short red hair a fire in the morning sunlight. Short?

Where was his ponytail?

He'd cut his hair already?

He sensed her movement and looked up. His beard was gone!

Dropping the hoe, he strode toward her, his steps eating up great swaths of distance until he stood in front of her, tall and handsome, and all traces of amusement gone. No easygoing hippie this morning, his intensity flared and her stomach cramped with longing.

"Look at you. You're beautiful." She touched his skin, which was smooth from his fresh shave.

His smile was small and sheepish. He watched her steadily, as though gauging the depth of her response.

"I figured I'd better shave soon so the bottom half of my face can tan to match the top half."

"I didn't expect you to really do it, let alone so soon."

"Come here," he said, taking her hand to lead her away, but she stood her ground.

"Noah, wait. This is big." He'd done what she'd asked even though she'd known it wouldn't be a small concession to make. "Thank you."

He shrugged off her thanks. He seemed uneasy about the change.

She let it go and allowed him to lead her around to the lawn at the back of the house.

There in the sunlight lay a couple of flowered quilts with an enticing breakfast spread—croissants he must have picked up yesterday, and tiny jars of different jams and a bowl of what looked like sweetened whipped cream.

"Oh, Noah," she breathed. "You beautiful, romantic man."

She kneeled and prepared two plates, then handed him one. They ate in the gentle heat of the warming day. When they finished Noah laid her down and unbuttoned her dress, taking his time spreading it open.

He draped her body across his legs like a shawl and took a dot of whipped cream onto his finger. When he spread it onto one of her nipples, her body tingled. He touched her with his lips.

"Heavens, Noah. You're going to kill me. I love your mouth."

He took her breast into that full-lipped mouth and sucked. Her body arched.

"Noah, let's do everything imaginable here in the sun. Let's feast on each other all day today. Let's do all of the things men and women can do with their bodies. Teach me things I don't know."

Noah grinned. "Anything, Monica. Everything." He laid her onto the quilt, slid between her legs, slipped his arms beneath her knees, spreading her wide to lust and nature, and entered her.

Her sigh echoed his.

REALITY INTRUDED, EVENTUALLY, but not until Monica made sure they had their day in the sun.

"Tomorrow I'm making a big push to get most of the details for the benefit wrapped up."

"I've been too distracted by you and your insanely sexy perfume to ask how it's been going."

"I got a corporate sponsor to donate their grounds for the barbecue. They'll rent tents in case it rains, too. The lawns at the back of their building are absolutely gorgeous. I remember being there once for one of my dad's fund-raisers."

"Hey, that's awesome."

"That's not all. They've agreed to let us use their parking lot at the side of the building for another barbecue."

Noah perked up. "A second barbecue?"

"Yeah, I had this idea that we could open it up to the public, so the big donors would have their posh barbecue in the back, but anyone else who wanted to attend and offer a donation, any size, could get a meal, too."

"That's a great idea."

"There's more." Monica was proud of everything she'd come up with. "We can also feed the needy. I've been talking to a couple of organizations in Denver. They're putting the word out that if people can somehow get themselves over to the event, but can't afford to make a donation, they'll still get a meal—for free."

Noah's shimmering smile, his obvious approval, warmed her to her core.

The best was yet to come, the part she thought Noah would particularly appreciate. "Want to know the best part?"

"Yeah, I really do."

"We're going to serve sliders at the posh part of the benefit."

"Sliders? Isn't that a little lowbrow for you rich folk?"

She smacked his arm playfully. "Everyone loves sliders. We'll get Maria and Joseph to supply amazing condiments. Have you ever tried their pickled eggplant? Incredible."

"Okay. Sounds good, but there's a lot of high quality steak that will be wasted if it's all going to be ground up."

"It isn't." She couldn't hold back a mischievous giggle. "We're also going to have steaks, *but* we'll be serving them in the parking lot to the so-called hoi polloi and the homeless."

The spread of Noah's white smile was the morning's sunrise, healing and benevolent after a long darkness. She basked in it, because all that glorious heat was aimed her way.

"Brilliant," he whispered. "Absolutely brilliant."

MARCIE STEPPED INTO the art gallery.

She needed to make friends with her sister, with *someone*, at any rate. Since coming to town the only person she'd spent significant time with was her father.

And it was good, better than good. Getting to know her father was turning out to be more rewarding than she could have anticipated. But she could spend only so much time with him.

Monica spotted her and approached.

"Hi," she said. "What can I do for you?"

Something had changed. The woman positively glowed. What had happened?

It struck her hard. Monica and Noah were getting it on.

Envy—stupid, stupid envy—burned through Marcie.

I want.

She bit the inside of her cheek so she wouldn't say something nasty, something beneath her. She'd come to the woman for help. The last thing she should do was alienate Monica.

But she wanted to. She wanted to rant and rave and break through the bonds of unfairness and inequality in which life had bound her.

She didn't make a peep. Instead, she swallowed her anger and said, "Will you come out to lunch with me? My treat."

Her father had given her an allowance. He was setting up a room for her jewelry-making and had let her order supplies online using his credit card.

This was her chance to get ahead, to start making money from her craft, more than a few odd dollars here and there. She could start a website. She could sell across the country. She could do what her heart desired—to design gorgeous pieces all day long and make a living from her passion.

But first, she had to get through today's lunch, to swallow her pride and ask for her sister's help.

Her sister. That was still so hard to come to terms with.

"I'd love to have lunch with you," Monica answered, perky and friendly, no trace of that small, tight, condescending smile in evidence, thank God.

Marcie disliked that controlled smile, but the reason it had been banished bothered her even more.

Monica, who had started life with so much more than Marcie, who had really had the perfect life, just kept getting more and more thrown her way.

Monica gathered her purse and they went to the café-bakery again.

"They make an amazing BLT with added avocado," Monica said. "That's what I'm ordering. I adore avocado."

So did Marcie. Okay, so her twin liked avocado as much as she did. No biggie.

When they were seated at a table, lunch in front of them, Monica asked, "What's up? What do you want?"

When Marcie stared at her, surprised that the woman was more perceptive than she'd given her credit for, Monica laughed.

"Oh, come on. We haven't exactly hit it off. I assume you need something or you would never buy me lunch."

Marcie finished chewing and laid her sandwich on her plate, giving herself time to swallow her pride along with the avocado.

"I need you to take me around town and introduce me to people." She wiped her fingers on her serviette. "I'll be honest, I hate asking you for help."

"I'm sure it took a lot of courage." She seemed to reach a decision quickly. "I want to help. Our lives have been lopsided. I'll do everything I can. What do you need? How's it been going so far? Have people not been friendly?"

"They've been okay. I mean no one's been mean, but the way they look at me leaves me cold." Before Monica could misunderstand, she rushed on. "They aren't *being* cold, but I'm an interloper while you're a solid part of their world."

She picked up a piece of lettuce from her plate and

tucked it back into her sandwich. "I've put a lot of effort into coming here to make a new life."

Here came the hard part—admitting her deepest wishes. "I came to find a home, but I'm still what I've always been. An outsider."

Monica's look was sympathetic. No pity, thank goodness. "Marcie, I'll let you in on a secret about small-town life. Unless you were born in town, it will take years to become a true part of it."

Marcie's disappointment must have shown because Monica said, "You have a secret weapon, though."

"What's that?"

"Me." Monica finished her sandwich and wiped her lips delicately. "And the scandal that has embroiled our family. Believe it or not, that can work in your favor."

Marcie cocked her head to study this woman who looked so deceptively benign, but who had an awesome head on her shoulders. "How?"

"People are thirsty for something different, even while they distrust anything new. And though you are different and also new, you'll have the benefit of my patronage."

"Patronage? Geez, what century are we living in?"

Monica laughed again, the radiance of her happiness casting Marcie further into gloom.

"It may be an old-fashioned concept, but it carries a lot of weight in this town. Dad and I will give you validity."

That raised Marcie's hackles. She was good and

fine on her own, thank you very much. "I'm valid as I am without the mighty Accords behind me."

"True. Dad and I are just giving you a shortcut into acceptance by this town. Isn't that what you want?"

She had a point there. So they made plans to hang out on Monica's next day off.

As they left the café, several people stopped them. Marcie watched while Monica worked her cool, aristocratic charm, including Marcie in every conversation until people started looking at her differently, and even smiling at her.

When they parted at the gallery, Monica winked. "See? It worked, didn't it?"

It did. So why did Marcie still feel so disconnected?

IN THE FOLLOWING week, Monica threw herself into the organization of the benefit, feeling more alive than she had in years.

She spent her mornings on the farm, her days at work and her evenings on the phone pulling everything together.

A couple of days she hung out with her sister and, to her utter shock, enjoyed it. She took her to Tonio's and The Last Dance to introduce her to Maria and Audrey.

Marcie seemed to thaw by small increments.

Monica crossed her metaphorical fingers. Maybe a relationship with her sister was possible.

Her nights were Noah's, nirvana and heaven and

paradise rolled into one because she spent them with him, the master of sweet lovemaking.

But soon the time came for dinner at her father's.

"Noah, come with me. Please. I want to introduce you to my dad."

A startled laugh burst out of him. "Your dad? Monica, I've known Ian my whole life."

"I know, but not as my boyfriend."

His self-satisfied smile made her respond in kind. "When you put it that way, okay."

She walked the rows of potatoes with Noah looking for pests.

"I've been thinking about the situation with Marcie and the conclusion I've come to is that I like getting to know my sister. We had a rocky start, but I'm trying really hard to change that. I spent too much time alone growing up. My dad will be gone someday. Not for a while yet, I hope. But it would be amazing to have a close sibling when that time comes. To have someone else in life besides just me."

"I get that," Noah said. "I love Laura and adore my niece. If they have more kids, I'll spend the rest of my life showering them with love. I feel like I'll never be alone because they are all my family."

"I'd like to have that, too. If I don't put in a strong effort with Marcie, if I don't find some way to make her a true part of the family, I will someday be alone."

Monica would have loved for Noah to protest, to say, "I will always be here for you," but their relationship was far too new for undying, forever declarations of love. She understood that, but she wanted to hear them anyway.

Back to the problem at hand, she asked, "What do you think of Marcie?"

"I think she's so consumed by envy that she's going to cheat herself out of her family if she isn't careful."

"Noah! She's not that bad, is she?"

"Bad? No, but she has a hole that needs filling, and you and your dad might not be enough."

"I can't worry about that, Noah. I can only do my best to befriend her."

"Yeah, that's about it. And maybe the solution to all of this is to kill her with kindness. To show her what a family can really be by showering her with warmth and affection. We both know how kind you are at heart."

She liked when he said good things about her.

Noah took her hand and held it while they inspected the crops. "I've seen Marcie around town. There are times when she looks lost to me. If she catches me watching her, she toughens up and becomes a bit of a hard-ass."

"I've seen that behavior, too, but I don't know what to do about it."

"There's nothing you can do. It's self-protection on her part. I don't know how you break through that."

"It sounds like she had a difficult childhood, moving around constantly."

Noah swiped sweat from the back of his neck. The

atmosphere had become hot and heavy with impending bad weather. "That could sure make a person develop a hard shell."

"Yes. She has that. For sure."

Noah pointed to the ominous clouds gathering on the horizon. "There's a severe storm coming in. Head on to your father's and I'll get there when I can. Don't hold dinner for me. There are things I still need to do here."

He kissed her, hard and fast, and she wanted more—couldn't get enough of Noah—but she had to pick up groceries and then rush to her dad's to start on dinner. Not only was she a guest in her father's house tonight, but Dad had also asked her to cook the risotto he loved so much.

She spent the first couple of hours at her dad's house cooking and fuming while clouds gathered and darkened the day, bringing with them an unnaturally early twilight. Rain started coming down hard.

While *she* coated a leg of lamb with olive oil and rosemary and put it in the oven to roast, and while *she* prepared a salad and put it in the fridge to chill, and while *she* made an apple pie to put into the oven to bake while they ate dinner, and while *she* chopped vegetables and grated Parmesan cheese for the risotto, her father and twin sat in the living room bonding.

No wonder she was fuming. Neither had offered to do a thing to help.

The fourth time she heard a burst of laughter from

both of them, she stormed into the living room and said, "I could use some help in the kitchen."

Her father stared at her. "I thought you liked cooking."

"I do. I just don't like being treated like a slave." She stared at Marcie. "Are your fingers broken? Can you not chop a few vegetables?"

Marcie glared back. "Yes, I can, and I will, but it wouldn't hurt to ask nicely."

Her father laughed. Monica rounded on him. "Why is this funny?"

"Because the two of you are fighting like real sisters."

Monica looked from one to the other before bursting into laughter herself. "Marcie, dearest sister, will you please help me in the kitchen?" she asked with exaggerated decency.

"Of course, darling twin," Marcie responded in kind. "Lead the way."

Their father followed them into the kitchen and sat at the table while they worked. "Is there anything I can do?"

"In a minute you can make that great Thai salad dressing I like so much." Monica handed him a small cutting board, a paring knife and a hunk of fresh ginger.

"You got it."

She took the lamb out of the oven to rest, put the pie in and then served the salad in the dining room as a separate first course, watching the street through the front windows for Noah's arrival. He'd become such a strong part of her life in the past few weeks.

Rain pelted down, harder now.

Drive safely, Noah.

"Monica, I like the addition of peanuts to the salad." Dad had opened a bottle of wine and poured each of them a glass of chilled white.

She cleared the salad bowls then returned with the leg of lamb, still watching the storm through the window.

"Dad, can you carve, please? Noah's late, but the risotto won't wait. He told us to start without him."

"He's fine, Monica." Dad must have heard the worry in her voice. "He's capable. He'll get here safely."

The wind howled around the house. Good thing the apple pie was close to done. She had a bad feeling they might lose power.

She dished up the risotto. She should have been in the kitchen stirring it until the last minute, but such is life when you are both chef and guest. She'd had to let it sit for a few minutes, but added a touch of hot broth to make it creamy again, then finished with the Parmesan.

Dad reached for his fork. "What kind of risotto is this?"

"Broccoli."

"No asparagus?" Dad's favorite.

"Sorry, Dad. It's too late in the season."

He tasted it. "It's incredible, anyway. Thank you, honey bun. Excellent as always."

Monica happened to be looking at Marcie when Dad called her *honey bun*. She looked miserable. Monica made a mental note to have Dad come up with something special for Marcie.

Funny how Monica's relationship with Noah had opened her heart in other areas. She wanted her sister to be happy, too.

"This is delicious," Marcie said. "Is there anything you can't do?"

The question could have been sarcastic. Monica wasn't completely sure it wasn't, but took it at face value.

"Yes," Monica responded. She wondered how it felt to come into a family in which one daughter was already well-loved, while the other had no relationship at all with her father. *Kill her with kindness.*

Monica continued, "I can't make exquisite silver jewelry."

Mouth open, Marcie froze with her fork almost to her mouth and a small dollop of risotto fell back onto her plate.

"You do make all of the fantastic jewelry you wear, don't you?" Monica chewed lamb while she watched Marcie struggle with the compliment. Her jewelry really was exquisite. Monica would love a few pieces.

"What? I mean, pardon?"

"You make your own jewelry, don't you?"

"How did you know?"

"Because every time I've seen you you've been wearing different pieces, but all of it with a strong signature. And judging by the way you dress, that signature is yours."

Monica watched Marcie try to parse the statements, maybe wondering if there was an insult in there somewhere. There wasn't. Monica loved her jewelry.

"You have talent."

Marcie put down her fork and clapped. "Impressive deductive reasoning, Sherlock."

One corner of Monica's mouth kicked up ever so slightly.

"Thank you." She bent her head regally, all in jest, and it felt amazing to have fun with her sister. Might this all work out, after all? "I would love to own some of your jewelry. Will you show me the complete collection some time?"

Just then Noah arrived, bursting through the front door then slamming it shut against the wind.

"You made it." Monica rushed to greet him and kissed him on the cheek. "I was so worried."

"It's wild out there. There was hail out on the farm. I'm hoping all of the plants are far enough along to survive."

"Come in," Monica said. "Sit down. I'll make you a plate of food. The risotto should just barely be okay. The lamb is still warm."

"I could eat a whole lamb by myself. I'm starving." He toed off his shoes and hung his raincoat by the front door, then came in and sat at the table across from Marcie.

Monica noticed a look on Marcie's face that she found odd. Unless she was mistaken, Marcie might be a little too *in like* with Noah. Would that cause problems?

"I hauled out tarps and covered the herbs. They're the most delicate crop."

With a burst of wind, hard bits of ice pounded the windows. Monica handed him a full plate of food and said, "You brought the hail into town with you."

When they were all settled in, her dad asked, "What's happening with the benefit?"

They'd been having such a nice dinner. Monica had actually been enjoying herself, but her tension returned in spades at her dad's question. Monica might be trying to be nice to her sister, but she still didn't want her working on the benefit. It was Monica's baby. She'd never taken on this kind of challenge before and had a lot to prove—to herself, to her father and to the town.

Maybe there was a part of her that wanted to show off for Noah, to prove to him that she was useful, that she was so much more than she appeared.

In a flash of insight, she understood that she still felt she *had* to prove herself to him.

No. She didn't want to share this particular spotlight with Marcie.

With more insight, she realized that she would share her father with Marcie, but there were limits.

Marcie couldn't have a piece of every part of Monica's life, especially where it intersected with Noah.

A flash of lightning lit the skies, followed too soon by a clap of thunder that sounded like it hit the roof.

The lights went out.

Galvanized into action, Monica felt her way along the walls to the kitchen to retrieve candles from the pantry. Dad followed and pulled a flashlight and small lantern from one of the drawers.

"Grab the matches, Dad."

Her father turned on the flashlight and led them back to the dining room by its narrow beam.

"We can finish eating by candlelight." Monica snagged a couple of brass holders from the sideboard, slotted tapers into them and lit the candles. "The oven will stay warm for a while, so I think the pie will cook through."

They finished eating their dinner with the wind still howling around the house and the town beyond the windows in darkness, all talk of the benefit forgotten and replaced by worry about the weather.

Monica thanked whichever gods had caused the blackout and distracted Marcie and Dad.

After dinner, she got the ice cream out of the freezer quickly. Who knew how long they would be without power? The pie was cooked through and Monica dished out ice cream onto each slice.

They ate in silence, the atmosphere surprisingly cozy and chummy, maybe because of how unusual the situation was.

"We'll have to leave the dishes for the morning. No water," Monica said.

"Just for the record," Marcie said, "I was going to offer to do them before you could order us to."

In the darkness, sitting in a small intimate circle of candlelight, Monica replied, "I believe you."

Noah and Marcie carried the dishes to the kitchen and stacked them neatly to be dealt with in the morning.

"I don't think anyone should go home tonight," Dad warned. "This storm doesn't seem to be abating. I'm worried about flooding. Monica, you can sleep in your room. Marcie, you have your room in the guest bedroom. Noah, there's a small room Monica used to use for sewing. It has a single bed in it. You can sleep there."

"Thanks. I appreciate it. But if you don't mind, I'll sit up for a while. I'm worried about the farm. I don't think I could sleep."

"That's fine. I'll leave the lantern down here for you. Girls, I'll take you up with the flashlight."

"I filled the Brita to the brim earlier in case of a blackout." Monica picked up a candle and retrieved the water from the fridge. "I'll bring it upstairs. We can take turns brushing our teeth."

"Good thinking," Marcie said.

Everyone seemed subdued by the unusual turn of events.

Monica approached Noah while Marcie and Dad stood at the bottom of the stairs waiting. She kissed him, explained where the sewing room was and then went to bed.

She tried to sleep, tossing and turning for a couple of hours. In time, she gave up trying and crept down the hallway to the sewing room.

Empty. Noah wasn't there.

Curious, she tiptoed downstairs in the darkness to the living room.

Outside, the gale had stopped its furious pounding against the windows. Rain fell in soft patters, released from its earlier frenzy by the dying wind.

Only the glow of the small battery-powered lamp on the corner table illuminated the living room. She stepped close.

For a couple of years an unfinished jigsaw puzzle had sat on that table. Every so often Monica and her dad would do a bit of it and then leave it again for months on end. They hadn't done anything with it since last Christmas.

The puzzle lay complete on the tabletop, finished by Noah as a strange gift to her, she was certain, like a cat dragging home a dead mouse for its owner.

Earlier in the evening after dinner, she'd complained that it had sat there too long, which bothered her, so he must have finished it. How had he done it so quickly? The man was brilliant.

It was as pretty as she'd thought it would be.

She heard the soft exhalation of a breath and spun around. Noah lay on the sofa fast asleep, his broken arm grasped by his right fingers. Foolish man. Why hadn't he gone to the guest bedroom as instructed?

Quietly, she left the room, returning momentarily with a blanket. She covered him and tucked it around him.

She turned to go, but a hand snagged her wrist. She gasped.

His eyes were open. Gaze unwavering, he raised her hand to his mouth and placed his lips inside of her cupped palm. His damp breath warmed her skin while his tongue traced her life line.

Then he let go, closed his eyes with a smile and settled in under the blanket.

She was left to hold that bit of sexy sweetness inside her fist and to wander back to bed unsettled and hyper-alert.

By morning, the power was back on.

True to her word, Marcie did last night's dinner dishes, with Noah's help.

Monica heard them murmuring in the kitchen and wondered what they were discussing.

She sat in the living room with her dad and told him about all of the work she'd been doing on the farm.

"Dad, Judge Easton might have thought he was getting revenge on you in making your daughter work on Mom's farm, but he did me a huge favor. I love the work."

"Really?" She didn't blame him for his skepticism. Who would have thought?

"I seem to have an aptitude for it. Not at first, of course, but Noah has taught me so much. I love watching the plants grow. It's wonderful to nurture them to maturity. And of course, as a cook, I love using the produce."

She told him about that amazing evening teaching kids how to cook fish *en papillote*.

In his smile, she thought she detected pride in her. She sure felt proud of herself.

The growth she'd experienced this summer had been nothing short of life-changing. Who would have thought, when her summer had started so disastrously, that it would turn out so well?

"And Noah?" Dad asked quietly.

"Noah is a great man. The work he does is inspiring."

"About the benefit—"

"Done," Noah shouted from the kitchen. "The last dish is washed. What's for breakfast?"

Saved yet again, Monica bounced up from the sofa like a jack-in-the-box. "I'll make it." Anything to get away from her dad's questions, which she knew were heading toward how to include Marcie.

She made bacon and eggs, because the power hadn't been off long enough to ruin anything in the fridge.

They sat down to breakfast.

"Noah, I don't honestly know what your farm is about. You don't eat or sell any of the food?" Marcie studied him as though he was a rare insect. "You give it all away?"

"That's right. I'm a registered charity, so I can't sell the food. I support myself through my store."

After he finished telling her about his farm, Marcie said, "Sounds like a great idea, Noah. I'd love to help out."

Monica's heart sank. As hard as she tried to communicate telepathically that she didn't want Marcie anywhere near her and Noah on the farm, he didn't seem to catch her reluctance.

This was another area she wanted to keep as hers and hers alone. She was learning rapidly how many boundaries she had in sharing her life with Marcie.

"That would be great. Right, Monica?"

She stared at her plate. She might be helping Marcie to become accepted in town, but Monica still wanted the separate life she'd always enjoyed. The confusion she'd first felt when Marcie arrived in town was returning.

"You should also give her a role in the gala barbecue." Dad finally got it out. Spirits sinking, Monica knew she could no longer avoid this conversation.

"I would like you to donate some of your jewelry for the silent auction I'm setting up," she told Marcie.

Would that be enough?

"Come on, Monica, you can do better than that," Dad urged.

Obviously, far from enough.

"Dad, I know what I'm doing. This is my project. Why can't you let it go?"

"Because I want both of my daughters involved."

"But this has nothing to do with Marcie."

"Why can't you open your heart to her and show generosity of spirit?"

"In the past couple of weeks, I've shown my generosity by taking her around town. I've opened many doors for her."

"You can do more. You can include her in this."

"I repeat, this is *my* project."

"It's mine, too," her dad said.

"How is it yours?"

"I was your first sponsor. I put you in touch with other corporate sponsors."

"You don't have faith that I could have done this on my own, do you?" To her horror, her voice cracked.

"Monica, you've never done anything like this before."

"Wasn't there that one event," she began quietly, "that you did on your own for the first time?"

"Yes, but—"

"Did you expect others, your parents and friends, to have faith and support you?"

"Yes, with good reason."

Monica's blood ran cold. "Why should your parents have been sure of your success, but you aren't sure of mine?"

"Because you have no experience with anything."

"With anything? You think I'm useless?"

"No, but I…this isn't coming out right."

"Monica," Noah said, "why not just let Marcie help?"

Noah's siding with her father felt like betrayal. "Don't you trust me? Why would you think I would need Marcie's help when I've told you all of my amazing ideas and how much work I've already done?"

"I didn't mean that you would need her help, per se, but an extra pair of hands would be useful." His expression seemed to be pleading with her to give an inch.

"Because Marcie knows so much about fund-raising, right? *Right?* This woman who's had no exposure to it should help me—me, who you don't seem to think is capable despite the exposure I've had." Through with shredding Noah, she returned her attention to her father. "Throughout my childhood, I watched you in action and I learned, and yet you think I can't do this on my own. Marcie has had no exposure, none whatsoever, yet you think she should be given an active role. You don't see anything wrong with this scenario?"

"She deserves a chance to learn, too. Do it, Monica," her dad ordered.

"So I'm to make up for your mistakes. I pay the price for the poor decisions you and my mother made."

"Monica!" her father barked.

"Thanks for the offer, Marcie," Monica said to her

twin. Dad and Noah were crazy, and she wasn't budging one inch. "But I should be just fine on my own."

"Monica." Dad's voice hit a warning note. "Don't do this."

"Why am I even talking? None of you are listening. I am a capable person. I will organize the benefit just fine on my own."

With an uncharacteristic action, her father pointed his fork at her. "You will include your sister in this or you can forget any contribution I was going to make."

Monica stood slowly, trying to rein in her anger, but it didn't work. "How dare you, Dad? You're using blackmail to force her help down my throat?"

"She is your sister!" he shouted.

"And I am your daughter! The same one I was before she came to town. You go ahead and accept her, with my blessing, but do not, *do not*, shove her down my throat."

"How dare *you*?" he countered. "We will be a harmonious family and one of the ways in which this will happen is if we involve each other in our lives. Is that clear?"

"I'll say it again, do not force her down my throat. Why are you forcing this issue?"

"Marcie asked to be involved."

"So now we get down to the truth. Marcie wants this so you are giving in to her. Have you been giving her everything she asks for?"

"I did with you," he growled. "I spoiled you."

That hurt. Despite all that she had inherited,

Monica had never taken a speck of it for granted.
She treated others kindly, never lording her father's
riches, or their standing in society, over anyone.

"This is my project," she said. "I will run it in
whichever way I see fit."

"Not if I have my way about it. What if I tell the
women to stop cooperating with you? What if I call
the CEO and ask him to cancel your use of his fa-
cilities?"

Her heart was a leaden object falling through her
body to the floor. Who was this man? "You would
do that?" she whispered.

"I *will*. You involve your sister in the project, or
consider it done, as of today. And another thing, I'll
pull the plug on your business, too. No money."

Was it possible to hear a heart shatter like the most
fragile crystal tinkling into narrow shards? Where
had the man she'd known all of her life gone? This
stranger was not her father. "Why?" she asked, struggling to understand what had broken in him.

"Shut up and sit down."

Unheard of. He'd never told her to shut up. They
didn't speak to each other this way.

This was neither conversation nor constructive
debate.

"Easy," Noah murmured. Monica didn't know
whether he referred to her or her dad.

"And you, Noah? Where do you stand?"

"I don't agree with your dad's methods, Monica, but I get where he's coming from. He's trying

to make Marcie part of the family. What's wrong with that?"

"What's wrong is that he's doing it at my expense. Why don't you see that?"

Monica turned to her father. "I will never forgive you for this." She glared at her sister. "And you! What have you been doing to my dad that he would behave so out of character? What have you been plotting? One day you're going to realize what a mistake you made in tearing our lives apart."

"Monica!" The neighbors probably heard Dad's shout, but Monica kept her attention on Marcie, whose mouth had gone white at the corners. She was furious. So was Monica.

"You are manipulative and mean-spirited."

Her father shot to his feet. "Apologize this instant!"

"No, Dad. You win. The charity benefit is off." To Noah, she said, "I will show up at the farm every morning on weekdays to finish my mandated hours, but that's it. You want help with anything else, ask her, or him."

She threw her napkin onto the table and stormed to the hallway. At the door, she said, "You men are a pair of fools. You'll learn too late how stupid you've been in being conned by her."

"She's my daughter." Her father stood at the head of the table, red-faced, but she no longer considered him the head of the family. She had no family. "You may not talk about Marcie like that."

"I can. I will. I did."

"Then don't bother coming back to this house until you've learned to behave."

Her heart breaking became a keening cry. Dear good God, how had it come to this? She had to leave before she broke down.

She heard Noah suck in a breath. "Hey. This is all going too far. Everyone calm down."

"You and Mom made a huge mistake years ago and now I'm paying the price." Her voice broke.

"And why not?" Marcie shouted and Monica saw real pain in the depths of her eyes. "For years, I paid the price. Now it's your turn. Fair is fair."

"You don't want *just* your fair share. You want it all. You want everything I have. In fact, you want to annihilate me. We could have made this work if you had come here with different goals, but I no longer trust you. It's too late now. Go to hell." She met the hostile gazes of all three people at the table. "All of you go to hell."

She left the house, walking with long strides to put distance between herself and that ugly scene... and those people. She'd lost her life.

Even before she heard footsteps behind her, she knew Noah would come after her.

He grasped her elbow to spin her around. "Don't you think you were being harsh back there?"

He looked at her as though the whole incident had been her fault. "No, Noah, I don't. I thought you were there to support me. How was it your business to invite Marcie to help me?"

He spread his hands, clearly lost. "In the kitchen, she offered. I thought it was a good idea to get past everything. I thought she was sincere."

"Why? Did you think I'm too stupid to figure out what's right for my family and what isn't? What will work for me and what won't? Do you think only *you* can determine how to get past everything? Do you, with your mighty brain, believe you know what's right for everyone? Even me? Or *especially* me?"

"No, but…"

"But?"

"I guess I did it for Marcie. She missed out on a lot in her childhood."

She crossed her arms hard against her body, preserving what little warmth she had left. "Since when have you become such good friends with her?"

"I'm not, but I see the real inequity in the situation."

"Your prejudice is showing. You have always resented what I grew up with, Noah. You think that because Marcie grew up with less than me that she deserves *more* than me. Well, guess what? You're wrong."

That he had sided with her sister saddened her to no end. "Here's the thing, Noah. She's here to take as much as she can get, but she's also here for revenge. She wants to take me down because, in her eyes, I was the chosen sister."

The sun's morning rays turned his hair to flames as they always did. She'd grown to love the color.

This morning all of that beauty hurt her eyes. "I think you're exaggerating," he said.

"Of course you do, because despite how much we've come to mean to each other, you still think I'm not as smart as you. You think you know better about everything than I do. You know what, Noah? There are all kinds of ways to be smart. There are different kinds of intelligence. I'm not exaggerating about Marcie and I'm not wrong about her. You'll see. She wants everything that I have and she'll get it in any way she can. She wants to destroy me."

"That's outlandish. She's not the evil stepsister from a fairy tale."

"No, she isn't evil, but she is desperate. She wants too much and she will use Dad, and even you, to get it. She knows what's between you and me, and it's eating her alive. She wants it for herself. She wants everything that I have. *Everything.*"

"You're behaving like a jealous shrew."

All affection for him fled. She turned to walk away. "This conversation is over."

"Wait. Is…" He looked shell-shocked. "Is *it* over? Or is there something still between us?"

"There was, Noah. There isn't anymore."

"But—"

"Goodbye, Noah. I'll be at the farm bright and early every day to do my two hours and then I'll be gone. I'll pay my dues like a good repentant girl, but only the minimum. For all of the rest, you're on your own."

"Monica, please. Let's rethink the things that were said here."

"Goodbye." He must have heard the finality in her voice because he let her go.

CHAPTER THIRTEEN

Monica marched straight to John Spade's office.

"John, I need your help. I need a friend." She didn't care that both his receptionist and Kayla witnessed her asking John Spade for friendship.

After one look at her face, he said, "Come into the office." He closed the door behind them. "Sit. Explain."

She told him what had just happened at her father's house and what her dad was prepared to do to scuttle the benefit. She also shared all of her concerns about Marcie.

"If you tell me you're on her side, or if you tell me I'm just being jealous and should accept my sister the way she is, I will go buy a gun and shoot you, John. I've had it with people not trusting my intuition."

"I trust you, Monica." He smiled grimly. "I trust your intuition. Your sister is needy. She wants a lot of things. Understandably so."

She shot out of her chair.

"Relax," he said. "I'm on your side."

Monica moved to stand in front of the window, staring unseeing into a small alley between two buildings. It connected to the alleyway that ran along the back of the shops on Main Street. Her vision blurred. She didn't want John to see how close she was to losing control.

What was happening to her that she couldn't keep

her emotions locked inside where they belonged? She'd never had trouble in the past. She'd done most of her grieving for Billy privately. Maybe that had been the wrong thing to do. Maybe all of the emotions she kept in close check needed to come out.

"So you believe me that she's pushing herself too far into my life?" she asked.

"Yes," he said from right behind her. She hadn't heard him stand and approach. His hands rested on her shoulders, their weight reassuring. "For the record, I do like her, but she definitely wants what you've always had."

Curious, Monica asked, "How do you know?"

"I've had a couple of conversations with her. I like both of you. I like how different you two are. You know how much I respect you, Monica, and your instincts are good here, but maybe you should consider giving her a role in the benefit."

She threw off his hands and paced to the other side of the room. "What's wrong with you damned men? She tries to take everything from me and you all *love* her." He raised one brow when she swore. "I've been the good little girl all of my life and all of you treat me like dirt."

"Let's get something straight." His voice had hardened, all traces of amusement gone. "I don't treat you like dirt. I hold you in the highest esteem." He sat behind his desk again. "You can come in here and criticize your sister and I will not think less of you.

I appreciate your honesty. One thing I won't accept, though, is you telling me I treat you badly."

She fell into the chair and covered her face with one hand, unable to stare down his disappointment in her. "True. You've always been wonderful to me."

"Also, while I might like your sister's devious mind, would I trust her if I were you? Not by a long shot. As I said, she is needy, and that neediness will motivate her to do things she shouldn't."

He twirled a pen in his fingers, lost in thought. "Okay, let's talk about how we're going to get your father to cooperate where the benefit is concerned."

"It no longer matters. I've washed my hands of it. Noah was there and didn't support me, either. He was encouraging me to take help from Marcie. If you see her so clearly, you must see that would be disastrous."

"Difficult, yes. Disastrous, no."

"I wanted her to make jewelry for the auction. Dad wasn't happy with that. He wants her to have an *equal* role in organizing the event. She has no background in this at all. Zero."

"Your father is misguided in this." He leaned back in his chair. "As far as Noah goes, he's being an idiot."

Her laugh sounded bitter. "I think so, too." It was mean-spirited and she shouldn't like it, but she did.

"He has you. Why on earth would he destroy whatever it is that's building between you?"

"How do you know there's anything happening between us?"

"In this town? Everyone knows everything, Monica. You know that. Nothing can be hidden."

"You're right. Of course everyone knows. But to get back to the important point, Noah is being an idiot. He's getting what he deserves."

"On the other hand, Monica, he does need this benefit. The second I heard about the benefit for his charity I knew it was the right thing to do. There are families hurting in Colorado and people like Noah make a difference."

"I didn't realize you were an altruist."

"I'm not, but neither am I blind. I see what happens to families like the Keils, and it isn't because they aren't hard workers. Sometimes people need a helping hand. The good ones, at any rate. Given that, the people who will really suffer from this fund-raiser not happening will be those who would have benefited by this charity, not Noah."

He had a point, damn him. "If I do decide to go ahead with this, what can I do? Sue my father? That seems extreme."

"You don't have to do a thing. Your father brought me his business when I first opened here nearly twenty years ago. We've been doing business ever since. I'll reason with him."

Monica wondered what form John's *reasoning* would take. "Knowing how cutthroat you are, I'm sure he'll listen."

"I prefer to think of myself as persuasive." His smile, though, was pure pirate.

"What do I do about Marcie?"

"Give her something safe to do."

"I truly did want her to donate jewelry for the silent auction. I was sincere about that. Her work is fantastic."

"Persuade her to do that and then augment it with a job that won't interfere with your control of the project."

"Okay." A weight had been lifted from her shoulders. She stood and he followed suit. "Thank you. You've been wonderful. I've taken your valuable time. Please bill me for it, okay?"

His quelling look chastised her. "I will not. My door is always open for you, Monica."

On impulse, she leaned across the desk and kissed him, sweetly, because she felt no romantic attraction to him, but she did appreciate him.

He kissed her back, just as sweetly. "It's too bad things couldn't have worked out between us."

"It is, but I'm not your type, John." At the door she halted with her hand on the knob, struck by a truth. "Marcie is, isn't she?"

He took his time responding as he stared down at the desk, before raising his intense dark gaze to hers. "She is."

"Another man I've lost to her."

"No. I will always be your friend."

"At the moment, John, that is of far more value to me than sex or romantic love." They shared a moment of mutually reflected admiration and then she left.

Out in John's waiting room, Kayla approached her.

"I know we aren't close friends, Monica, but if you need anything from me, will you please let me know?"

"Do you know what I would like from you, Kayla?"

Kayla shook her head.

"To *be* close friends. Let's go out for coffee one day soon."

"I would like that a lot, Monica."

Monica smiled and left.

Bad timing. Noah walked down the street heading to his store.

She tried to deke around him, but he wouldn't let her pass.

"Monica, I've been thinking."

"Exercising that massive brain of yours?"

He smiled ruefully. "Yeah. It wasn't working too well at breakfast, was it? You invited me over to lend you support and I failed you." He shuffled his feet. "I know I let you down. I apologize."

"Okay. Thanks. I appreciate it."

He looked at her skeptically. "I'm being sincere here, Monica."

"So am I. I appreciate the apology. I would have appreciated support against my father and Marcie even more. The damage has already been done."

A brief pained expression flitted across his face. "Is it irreversible?"

She studied him, cataloguing all of the features

of his face that had become dear to her. "I don't know," she answered quietly. "I honestly don't know. I thought we were developing a friendship."

"So did I." He reached a tentative hand to her shoulder. "I—I don't have the words to make it right."

"Let it go. I'm too tired to deal with this anymore right now. I need to go home and get dressed for work."

He stepped away, clearly dissatisfied, but he would just have to deal with it. She had enough of her own stuff to take care of.

So John would get the charity back on track, but what would she do about the business? She couldn't compel her father to give her that money. There would be no shop. She had only just found her dream and already it was over.

She and Noah parted ways, each walking away in their own directions, and Monica had never felt so separate from the world and the people around her.

"AUDREY, I DON'T know how to fix this." Noah couldn't sit still. He wandered around the flower shop like a caged panther.

"You could always apologize."

He jammed his hands into his pockets. "Already did. She didn't accept it."

Audrey whistled. "She's really mad. Why wouldn't she be? You didn't support her when she needed it most."

"I was trying to get her to be reasonable."

Audrey's look of horror was almost comical. "You didn't *say* that to her, did you?"

"No. I was trying to defuse the situation. It was pretty damn tense in the Accord house this morning."

"But why try to defuse it by getting Monica to change her stance? Why not Marcie?"

He stared at her.

"Why was it so important to you to shape what Monica thought? To change her? Because she was the rich one all of her life and Marcie the poor one? Is that why you sided with Marcie? Why didn't you get Marcie to change what she wanted? You always side with the poor and feel disdain for the rich. Monica doesn't deserve that."

"My God." Noah continued to stare. "It's scary how perceptive you are, Audrey. I mean, it's like you know me better than I know myself."

"You know all of this, Noah. You just won't admit it to yourself because you think you're so fair. You try, I know you do, but you are as capable of bias as the rest of us."

Noah raised his hands to scrub his beard before remembering it was no longer there.

"About that, Noah." Audrey pointed to his face. "Why did you shave and cut off your ponytail?"

"Monica thinks it will help us make more money at the fund-raiser. And I thought I should get some sun on my skin first."

"You've had a beard since you were a teenager. How do you feel about it being gone?"

"Honestly?"

She watched him with her enormous eyes. "Of course."

"I want it back. I feel naked."

"It's a big part of who you are. That was quite a concession to make."

He rubbed his face. "Yeah. I guess that's what relationships are all about. Compromise. I need to make it up to Monica for not supporting her today."

Audrey came around the counter and hugged him. "Go home and think some more about this, but tomorrow, grovel."

THE FOLLOWING MORNING Monica put in her two hours at the farm before work, as promised, but she operated by rote, half of her dead and the other half still in shock.

She avoided Noah, actively walked away every time he approached.

How had everything gone so wrong?

Was she just jealous? Yes, to a certain extent, she was jealous—jealous that he had taken her sister's side. But that wasn't all of it. Why couldn't he see that Marcie was driven and frantic?

At lunchtime, she stepped out of the gallery to head to the café and ran smack-dab into Noah. For God's sake, was the man everywhere?

"Hi," he said. "I missed you this morning."

She frowned. "I was there. I know you saw me."

"No, I mean I missed *you*. I know you were there

physically, but I've grown used to—" He glanced away. Noah, shy? That didn't seem possible. "I like how we flirt. I like to know where you've put your perfume. I like our lovemaking."

"Me, too. It's the most fun I've had since Billy died."

His brows shot up and he smiled, slowly. "Yeah?"

"Yeah." How could the man do this to her, make her like him even when she was angry with him? "But, and this is a big but, I feel betrayed by you."

"Aw, don't say that. I hate that I did that to you."

"What changed your mind?"

"I told Audrey everything. She set me straight. Boy, did she set me straight. She said I needed to have more faith in you and your abilities. She said I should respect your evaluation of the situation, and of your sister. She was right."

Monica only nodded. She wasn't sure she was ready to forgive him. She would share a bit, though. "I haven't given up on the charity bash. I've been talking to John Spade and he's going to try to reason with my dad."

Noah stepped closer and touched her jawline. "You would still work on it even after I've been such a fool?"

"Yes, Noah, I'll still work on it, if things can be worked out with Dad."

"I'll talk to him, too."

"Okay, but do me a favor."

"Anything."

"Talk to him when Marcie isn't around. She has a strange hold on him. It's his guilt—she seems to be able to use it against him."

"Do you honestly think she's that bad?"

"Not bad, no. I don't believe she's evil, but I do think she feels so aggrieved that she's prepared to do anything to get what she wants."

That finger still rested on her jawline and she liked it too much. "I'm sorry I doubted you, Monica. I'll be careful how I approach your dad. Will you be at the farm tomorrow morning?"

"Yes."

"Can we go back to how things were? I've really come to like having you on my farm."

"I really like being there, Noah. I'll see what I can do."

She brushed past him and walked away, but he called out, "Where was it today?"

She answered, "You'll find out tomorrow," and walked on, bathing in the luxury of his laugh.

SHE DROVE TO the farm the following morning, lost in thought. Noah was one of the best things that had happened to her in years. He'd given back to her the happiness she'd lost with Billy's death.

Now that her temper had cooled, she realized that Marcie had succeeded in driving a wedge between her and Noah. Maybe not intentionally, but it had happened nonetheless. Marcie had managed to destroy something valuable in Monica's life and

Monica had let her. The heck with that. She wanted Noah back.

Noah had shown poor judgment, but he'd also apologized.

In hopes of catching him before he got out into the fields, she was super early this morning. It was still a bit dark.

One light shone in the living room.

Shoving open his front door, she barreled in, hell-bent on taking what she wanted in life.

He was in the living room, standing in front of his armchair with a book in his hand, intelligent brow furrowed in concentration, red hair warmed by the yellow glow of a table lamp. When he saw who had barged into his home, he relaxed, until he saw the determination on her face.

"Monica!" His frown turned to a smile and then to a look of consternation. "Monica?"

She strode across the aging carpet until she stood six inches away from the big brainy hunk, tender-ness for him running through her veins like sap. No way was she letting her sister ruin this.

"What are you doing here so early?"

"This."

She took his face in her hands and planted her lips on his mouth, pressing her body against him. Oh, sweet heaven, he felt incredible, hot and lean, his stringy muscles hard beneath her hands. She'd missed him. It had only been two days yet she had missed his body, his mouth and his arms.

She kissed him for all she was worth.

He opened his lips and her tongue poked through, dueling with his, two swords at play, but no wounding. God, no. Only joy.

Joy!

She reveled in the heat that poured from him, both from his body and from his passion. His good arm snapped around her, locking like an iron band across her back.

They stopped kissing. She pulled back far enough to look into his warm green eyes.

"Ah, Noah," she whispered. "You don't do anything halfway, do you?"

He grinned and picked her up.

She squealed.

"It seems that you don't, either."

"Where are you taking me?"

"To bed. Okay?"

"Noah, that is so-o-o-o okay."

THE DAY OF the barbecue arrived.

Noah stood under one of the party tents in a rented tuxedo that fit him perfectly, but left him uncomfortable.

Monica had insisted on the tux, even though the event was starting early, in late afternoon.

Weeks later, he still hadn't gotten used to being clean-shaven. He felt naked, too exposed. He *liked* his hair. He *liked* his beard.

Things had been going well with Monica, beautifully, and he was crazy about her, but standing here left him feeling like a different person, not like himself.

He'd gone through this with women before, women who'd wanted to *clean him up*, to make him *presentable*.

Sure, there was a reason tonight, the fund-raiser, but would his appearance really have been a detriment? Would it *truly* have affected donations?

He watched Monica work the crowd in her soft, flowing dark blue dress with the large matching sun hat, her bare arms strong and tanned. She was happy and looked younger than her thirty-eight years. On her feet were a pair of high-heeled sandals, nothing more than thin strips of leather, probably bad for her spine. He couldn't complain. They made her legs look a mile long.

She was the star here, not him.

"She sure fits in here, doesn't she?"

Noah glanced down. Marcie had joined him.

"Yes," he answered. "She sure does." That fact left him wondering about their future. Were the differences in their backgrounds too massive to be overcome? He certainly didn't fit in here and doubted his ability, or desire, to learn to.

Miserable, and looking for a distraction from his blue funk, he turned his attention to Marcie.

"How did the planning go?"

She shrugged. "Not bad. I hired the students who

are serving today and organized the buses to bring them here and return them home."

"Hey, that's great."

She shrugged. "Yeah, and I liked making the jewelry for the auction. There have been a ton of bids on it. Some of these rich people have even shown interest and have taken business cards. Monica convinced me to have a bunch printed up in time for this shindig."

"That was wise of her."

"Yeah, it was."

Alerted by something in her voice, he asked, "What's going on in that devious brain of yours? Monica facilitated helping you get clients for your business venture. She gave you a role here today."

She snorted. "Yeah, as a glorified sheepherder."

"What do you mean?"

"I'm supposed to be herding the students, making sure they're keeping everyone happy, and that glasses and plates are never empty."

"What's wrong with that?"

"I wanted more."

"You always do."

Her glance sharp and unhappy, she asked, in a tone just as sharp, "What do you mean?"

"I mean that you have a whole world more than you've ever had in your life and you still don't seem happy. At some point, you'll have to accept that enough is enough."

She stared at him, her perfect beautiful face so

like Monica's, but troubled. "Enough? *Is* there such a thing?"

"That's the problem for you, isn't it? Will whatever you are given, or can take, be enough to satisfy you?"

He walked away. Marcie had to find her own happiness in this world.

Uncomfortable in his monkey suit, missing his beard and itchy with a foreboding he couldn't identify, he drifted aimlessly around the party, present but not truly a part of it.

The past kept intruding on the glitzy present. He'd been involved with this kind of affair before and it hadn't ended well.

Stop. This isn't New Orleans and Monica isn't anything like Deirdre.

His thoughts spun. He'd avoided this kind of shindig, as Marcie had called it, for years, because the associations for him were bad.

Only now did he realize that while he'd been enjoying love with Monica, and while he'd been caught up in her excitement organizing this event, anxiety had been building, festering inside of him like a malignant tumor.

Stop! For God's sake, give it a rest. Don't mistake today for the past.

He didn't want to be here, and didn't want to be doing this. It raised too many negative emotions he'd thought he'd buried—obviously not. All he had done was hidden them, or hidden *from* them.

Antsy, he needed to get out of here, to hobnob with normal people.

Did he and Monica have such vastly different lives that they would never find common ground? Were they destined to always miss each other, as the old saying went, like two ships passing in the night?

MONICA WATCHED NOAH from across the room.

Who knew that under all of that hair there was such a handsome face? She still couldn't get used to him looking like this. She liked it, but loved his long hair and beard, too.

Despite how busy she was, Monica's gaze had been drawn to him, time and again.

The past couple of weeks, once they'd kissed and made up, had been blissful. She couldn't remember ever being happier.

The joy of getting up every morning to nurture growing plants, the pleasure of kissing Noah whenever she wanted to, the ecstasy of lovemaking unlike anything she'd ever experienced—how could life possibly get any better?

The event was an unqualified success. Even though it was only four in the afternoon, guests mingled in their tuxes and long gowns, buying meals of sliders and fries at a hundred dollars a pop, and they loved everything.

Marcie had done a good job organizing and transporting a bunch of high school kids from Accord into Denver, and whoever else wanted to make money serving. They were all busy delivering meals and collecting dirty plates.

Kayla Keil passed with a full tray of champagne flutes, jaunty in her black pants and crisp white blouse. "*Awesome* event, Monica," she whispered, then approached a group with the drinks.

Monica caught Noah staring at her. He came over, took her hand and dragged her through the building and to the parking lot, where the *normal* people, as he called them, and the homeless noshed on steak and baked potatoes with all of the trimmings.

Everyone gave what they could afford, and she and Noah watched people donate anywhere from a buck to fifty dollars, many of the attendees coming to Noah to introduce themselves.

"Love the work you do, man."

"This is the best fund-raiser I've ever been to."

"I work at a soup kitchen and we've always appreciated your produce."

Monica couldn't have been more proud of Noah, or so she thought, until a man with rheumy eyes, wearing rags and pulling a ragged old shopping buggy with squeaky wheels, came to stand in front of Noah.

Noah shook his hand as though they were old friends. "Ray, I haven't seen you since last fall. How are you?"

"Not too good. Arthritis and diabetes are bad, but I can't complain. Got myself a girlfriend. She takes care of me real good."

A woman approached, her clothes not much bet-

ter than Ray's rags, but her smile was sweet, if a little vacant.

"This is Ruth," Ray said.

Noah shook her hand then introduced Monica. She
shook their hands, too.

"Is she your girlfriend?" Ray's wink was saucy.
Traces of the young, handsome man he must have
once been lingered in that wink.

Noah looked down at her and held her hand, but
there was something lurking there that Monica
couldn't put her finger on. Her unease cleared up
when he said, "Yes, Ray. Yes, she is."

Ray whistled. "You're some lucky man."

"Ray, you and Ruth find a good spot to sit and
we'll get you a couple of meals. On the house. You
want coffee or soda?"

"Yes."

Noah didn't skip a beat. "Coffee and soda coming
up. Double cream and sugar, right?"

"You got it. Same for Ruthie."

He took Monica over to the line of grills and fixed
up a couple of plates, really loading them, while
Monica put together a plastic tray of hot and cold
drinks.

They left it all with Ray and Ruth, who were childlike in their contentment.

"You're a good man, Noah Cameron." Monica cud-
dled close to his side.

"You're not so bad yourself. You did a stellar job

today." He wrapped his right arm across her shoulders. "Did things work out with your dad?"

"We came to an uneasy alliance. He's here and doing his part, so I'm grateful for that, but his support has been grudging at best. Same with Marcie. We tried to work things out, but…" She spread her hands and shrugged.

Noah glanced away, taking in the entirety of the view before him. "I don't think this event could have been any more successful."

"You might be right. I was really blessed with all of the amazing support. The Denver ladies got all of these people out. The Colantonios did an incredible job. They've even set aside a whole bunch of sliders in a fridge inside for all of the helpers. As soon as this ends at seven, they'll all sit down to eat."

"We'll eat then, too. Okay?"

"Yes. See you in that sweet little gazebo at the back of the property at seven. Okay?"

As it turned out, Monica didn't make it on time because too many of their posh guests lingered after the event, even while the staff finished cleaning around them and then sat down to eat.

It seemed that everyone had had so much fun they didn't want to leave.

After the last guest departed, Monica slipped indoors to a private room in which she'd left a bag with a change of clothes. She couldn't wait to get out of these heels. Her feet were killing her.

She changed into dark jeans, a white cotton shirt

and a pair of red flip-flops, then went looking for Noah. She didn't find him so she sat with a bunch of kids while she ate sliders and excellent coleslaw.

NOAH DEPOSITED THE bag of cash into a drawer in an office that the company president had designated for his use. He hadn't counted it, but knew it had to be thousands and thousands of dollars.

His earlier anxiety had calmed, eased by the success of the event.

He left the empty building, waving to the security guard on the way out. They'd made arrangements with the man earlier that only Noah and Monica were allowed in that office.

The money was safe.

Noah needed to eat. Starving, he grabbed a couple of sliders. His belly was about to kiss his backbone. Now that it was all over and everything had gone off without a hitch, he could relax. His stress had fallen away. Monica had pulled it off.

She was, in short, magnificent.

He needed her in his life permanently. He couldn't imagine life without her. He planned to tell her so tonight.

While he ate, he cruised around among all of the helpers, thanking them. In all, close to a hundred Accord residents had turned out today to help. While Noah had offered to pay them all from tonight's receipts, knowing that many of them could use the money, most had turned it down and were here as volunteers, including the Keils.

He talked to them for a long time. Since Monica had gotten Kayla the two jobs, the young mother had blossomed and had come out of her shell. Both Robert and Kayla were more relaxed and easy with Noah. Monica had been right when she'd made her first visit to the Keil ranch. They hadn't been on an equal footing, but they were now.

He needed to see Monica. He needed to tell her how smart she was.

He checked for her at the gazebo, but he was far too late. He'd missed her when he'd been loading equipment into the vehicles going back to town, and filling a van headed for the food kitchen with left-over food.

After he finished eating he helped to load the last of the stuff going back to Accord and took care of some final details.

At last, with the few remaining buses and cars leaving, he was about to head inside to pick up the money and then find Monica, when he saw her sidle along the building too far away for him to call to her.

What he saw in her hand froze his blood. She moved with stealth, checking to make sure she wasn't being followed, sneaking along the side of the building with the canvas bag of money in her hand.

There was no mistaking the bag and no mistaking the way she moved. Memories he'd thought long buried assailed him...of Deirdre and New Orleans and betrayal.

Not again. God, no, not again. Not Monica. Not when he'd convinced himself she was real and honest and the best woman on earth.

But his eyes hadn't deceived him. He knew what he'd seen was real.

Why? *Why*, Monica?

He ran along the building to catch her, but by the time he got to the front she was gone. Had she had a partner in crime, someone she'd driven off with?

This wasn't supposed to happen again.

He'd given her everything, after years of distrusting women and himself, he had given over all he was, all he had, including his naive heart, to Monica Accord and she had stomped it into the dust.

CHAPTER FOURTEEN

MONICA FINALLY FINISHED loading her car with a couple of items the Colantonios couldn't fit into their vehicle.

Boy, was she tired. She'd had to park far away from the event, on the far side of the school buses Marcie had hired.

She trudged back, sublimely happy. Everything had gone better than she could have ever hoped. She couldn't wait to find out how much money they'd made for Noah.

Back in the office where she'd stored her bag of clothes, she looked high and low, but there was no trace of it. Someone must have picked it up by mistake.

Giving a mental shrug, she left the building, waving good-night to a security guard on the far side of the foyer. The bag had probably made it into someone else's car. It would turn up in Accord sometime tomorrow, she was certain.

Where was Noah? He wouldn't have left without saying goodbye. Or at least without arranging to meet back at the farm to celebrate.

She bumped into him just as he was coming around the corner of the building, thunder on his face.

"There you are," he said. "What did you do with it?"

"With what?"

"With the money. I'm surprised you had the nerve to stick around. Did you think that just because you'd changed your clothes, I wouldn't suspect you? Did you think no one had seen you? I did, Monica."

Something was wrong—very wrong. The way Noah looked at her. The way he spoke to her. He was breaking her heart.

"What's going on, Noah? What's happened?"

Noah stared at her, wide-eyed. "You're going to pretend you didn't do it? I *saw* you, Monica. I saw you take the money and sneak away."

Sneak away? "I *didn't* take the money. Why are you doing this, Noah? I thought you trusted me. I thought you were good and honorable."

"I am!" he shouted. "You're the one who isn't." He scrubbed his hands over his face, a face that had become dear to her, but that she didn't recognize at the moment, as twisted as it was now with fury. And betrayal. "I knew this was all too good to be true. I should have known I couldn't trust you."

Couldn't trust her?

"You stole, Monica. Not from me. This is not about *me*. You stole from people who desperately need help. If this hadn't happened to me before, I would have thought it was impossible, but I know. Oh, do I ever know how dishonest women can be. You're no better than those people who steal charity boxes off the counters in donut shops or convenience stores."

He might as well have slapped her. How could he say these things to her? After all they had been through? After she had opened herself up to him in so many ways?

Trust that had been hard-won was now gone, broken like an old set of toys in a long-forgotten toy box.

Crazy ideas chased one another through her mind. Was he trying to extort money from her? From her father?

And yet... Noah wasn't a dishonest man. She knew in her heart that he was a good man. She knew he wouldn't blackmail her or her father for money. His anger, his sense of betrayal, was real.

She was beginning to understand. A terrible suspicion formed. "You're certain that it was *me* you saw with the money?"

The hurt on his face opened a wound inside of her. Not only was he angry with her, but he was also disappointed. She had done nothing to deserve this, but she was pretty sure she knew who had. God, it was so obvious. Noah should have figured it out right away.

"You're sure it was *me*?"

"Yes." He sounded tired. Then something changed. She saw the doubt. "Oh, shit. Marcie. But, the clothes..."

"What was I wearing?"

"The blue dress you'd been wearing all evening and the sandals and the big floppy hat."

"What time was that?"

"About fifteen minutes ago. I was going to get the money and then look for you."

"Noah, I changed out of that dress close to an hour

ago. I just went back now to get the bag with my clothes that I'd left inside. It's gone. Marcie took it."

"Why would she…?" He trailed off, because he had obviously come to the same conclusion Monica had. "Why would Marcie steal the money?"

"And in my clothes? To make me look bad, of course. To destroy what we have. I don't know why she would do it like this, though, by taking all of that hard-earned money destined for good people."

"I know why." Noah looked more lost than she'd ever seen him. He'd been shaken badly. "Oh, my God, Monica. I should've trusted you. I should have known it was her."

"Yes, you should have. Right away. Why didn't you?" She stepped away from him, angry and hurt, underestimated by him yet again. "What did you mean you know why? Why would she steal *this* money?"

When he looked culpable, her spider sense kicked in. "What's going on here?"

He told Monica a story about his old girlfriend and the work they did when he was in his early twenties, raising money for rebuilding New Orleans.

"I was fired up with zeal. I wanted to save the world."

Deirdre had skipped out on him, with all of the money, with thousands and thousands of dollars. Then he told her how hard it had been to trust again. About how he'd finally done that with her only for her to betray him in exactly the same way. Or so he'd thought.

"Did you tell that story to Marcie?"

He nodded.

"When?"

"When we were washing the dishes at your dad's house the morning after the blackout."

It hurt that he had shared this with Marcie instead of with Monica. That ugly green-eyed monster stirred inside of her.

"You two sure managed to cover a lot of ground in that one conversation."

"Yeah, I guess we did. She just seemed really interested in me."

"And you didn't think it was awfully coincidental that the same thing was happening to you again? I don't believe in coincidences, Noah."

"I guess I wasn't thinking straight." He kicked at a stone. "This evening brought up memories of that time. I didn't realize I was still affected so much by it. I thought I'd put it all behind me."

"Marcie couldn't have found a better way to discredit me in your eyes than to have you think I was stealing from you. That your history was repeating itself."

"I'm such a sucker." He smacked his hand against the wall. "I can't believe I fell for it, but I did, hook, line and sinker."

"You sure did. It was an incredibly knee-jerk

response, too. I'm disappointed, Noah. You should have trusted me."

He looked miserable. "But she must have known you and I would work this out. She can't go back to Accord now. She's lost her family and the chance for a good home and security in her future. She's lost everything. What the hell was she thinking?"

"I can't begin to guess, Noah. But what I do know is that you need that money. How on earth can we prove that she has it? I mean, even you thought I was the thief. How can we prove it was Marcie?"

"I'll handle this. Leave it to me."

"We need to go to the police."

"Let's hold off on that."

"Why, Noah? Compassion?"

"Yes."

"Then you're a better person than me."

"Let me find her and talk to her first, then we'll see how compassionate I am."

Against her better judgment, Monica nodded.

Noah grasped her shoulders, leaning in for a kiss that rivaled anything he'd ever given her before. It was heartfelt and earnest, but she couldn't let it in. She still hurt beyond belief that he'd thought she would steal from him. History be damned, he should have trusted her.

When she didn't respond, he pulled back to stare at her. If he'd looked betrayed a few minutes ago, now he looked heartbroken and she guessed he'd just realized how much he'd lost, and it was a heck of a lot more than just money.

"Go," she said. "Do what you have to do to catch Marcie."

She walked away to her car. At some point, the school buses had all left for Accord. She hadn't even heard them drive away.

Just before getting into her car, she glanced back to where she'd left Noah and found him still watching her. He hadn't moved a muscle.

He might be miserable, and she might be angry, but the thread of love, the attachment between them, hummed with the high voltage of a power line.

Could they get through this? She didn't know.

She drove to her father's house, furious and determined to take control. Too many people were hurting her. It was time to take care of Monica.

Her dad should have listened to her concerns about Marcie. He should have trusted Monica. Just like Noah should have trusted her.

From now on, Monica was living by her rules and no one else's. Even though she had come to it late, she finally knew what she wanted to do with the rest of her life and no one was going to stop her.

The people in her life had underestimated her. No more. From now on, she was taking the world by storm, but first, she needed money.

She was going to her father with her hand out. But, and this was a big *but* in her mind, she wouldn't be taking the money for free. She would pay back every last cent.

He had promised her money to start her business and then had taken that money away. Out of nowhere, he'd placed conditions on her. It wasn't fair.

Tonight, she was correcting that.

Not bothering to temper her actions, she burst through the front door into the darkened house and marched upstairs. She had to keep the anger burning hot and bright, or she wouldn't be able to control the terrible betrayal trying to shatter her heart.

She wasn't strong enough for that right now. Anger was easy, refreshing, burning away all of her doubts and fears. She had a course of action.

When she thrust open her father's bedroom door, it slammed against the wall.

"Christ!" he shouted. "What—?"

Two bodies writhed on the bed in strips of moonlight pouring through the window.

Her dad sat up, pulling the covers to his chest. Someone tried to make herself small and invisible behind him. So. Dad still had a sex life. Whoop-dee-doo.

"Cover up," she said. "We need to talk."

"Can't this wait until morning?" Monica heard the steel behind the question. Dad wanted her out of here. Too bad.

A voice whispered, "I don't like your daughter."

Monica rounded the bed. "Who is that hiding behind you like a sniveling coward?" Great phrase.

Sniveling coward. She needed to use that on Noah one of these days. "I recognize that voice. Lee-Anne Clark. How nice to see you in bed with my father."

"You wouldn't have to," Dad said as he hitched a blanket more securely around Lee-Anne's shoulders, "if you hadn't barged in here. Do you have any concept of the word *discretion*?"

He didn't sound happy. Too bad. "Do *you*, Dad? Do you do anything honestly? Why not date Lee-Anne out in the open instead of skulking around in the darkness?"

"She's married."

"I know. Hence, my question. Do you do anything honestly? We both know the answer to that—no."

"Get out of here."

"Nope."

She saw him startle and why not? He must be shocked that his nice, perfect daughter was fighting back. As a child, she had never disobeyed him. As a teenager, she had toed every line. Maybe this was finally her teenage rebellion. As uncomfortable as she was in here, at this moment, she wasn't leaving until she got what she came for, Dad and Lee-Anne's sordid affair be damned.

"We'll talk tonight. Now."

"You should show a little respect for your father." Lee-Anne sounded angry, too, and maybe a little fearful. Perhaps she thought Monica would betray her to her husband.

She leaned close to Lee-Anne. "I don't give a flying fig what you think I should do, you dishonest, lying sl—" She couldn't say it, couldn't call her such an ugly name, even if Monica was striking out left, right and center, hitting anyone who got in her way.

Lee-Anne gasped. Her hand swung out. She snagged a hank of Monica's hair.

"Ow! Let go!" Monica grabbed the woman's hair in return and the entire thing came away in her hand.

Lee-Anne gasped again, her hands flying to cover her wispy gray hair. "Give that back."

She started to laugh, and couldn't stop. Was all of her life a delusion? Was everything false? Worse, was there no single person in her life who was honest, on whom she could depend?

The simple answer stunned her. She no longer trusted her instincts.

She stared down at Lee-Anne and her father. "Here." She handed back the wig, but the damage had already been done. None of the luscious hair that made the woman so attractive was her own.

"Is your body at least real? For Dad's sake, I hope so."

"That's enough." Dad tried to exert his fatherly authority. He didn't know that ship had already sailed, never to return. Where before he had been angry, now he was cold. "What's wrong with you?"

"I'm me, Dad. I'm finally me. No more *nice girl*. I've lived my life the way you wanted me to. I've been the good girl. I was no intellectual genius, but I busted my butt in school for top grades. I was cheerleader and prom queen. You were always proud of me. But what if I had failed you the way you failed me? I trusted you to be honest, but you lied to me my entire life."

She was burning so hot she felt cold. "Now, it's payback time. I want money. A lot of it. I'm starting my own business and you're going to finance it, just as you promised you would before you unfairly reneged. I'll let you know within the next few days exactly how much I'll need. I will pay you back at a fair interest rate over time, because *I'm* an honest person."

"And if I don't want to help you?"

"How lucky for me that you and Lee-Anne have handed me leverage on a silver platter. If you don't cooperate, if I don't see the money in my account when I need it, I will call Graeme Clark and tell him what I've seen here tonight."

"Don't tell my husband," Lee-Anne whispered. "He'll cut me off."

No one, Monica thought, no one was ever going to be her meal ticket. She *would* make her business work. She *would* be a success. She *would* pay her father back and never lean on him or anyone else again. She never wanted to be in Lee-Anne's position.

"What happened to you this evening?" Dad asked the question quietly, but it screamed through Monica's consciousness like a fighter jet. *I've been betrayed.*

She couldn't answer him without shattering. Better to just leave before exposing her vulnerability to him. She no longer trusted this man.

"I'll have my lawyer call you tomorrow with details." With that parting line, she left the room.

Before she could leave her former home, she heard him on the stairs and turned around.

He'd pulled on a pair of sweatpants. The hair on his chest was going gray. He was growing old. They were losing each other.

"I would have given you any amount of money you wanted," he said when he reached the bottom of the stairs. "You didn't have to threaten either me or Lee-Anne like that. Why?" It was all so quietly, so reasonably spoken when the entire situation was anything but reasonable.

"No, you wouldn't have given me any money I wanted, not without conditions. Remember, Dad? You already promised me this money and then took it away when I refused to let Marcie help with the benefit."

"You should have given her an important role."

"She stole the money."

"What?"

"The money we made today at the benefit? Marcie stole it. Noah witnessed it. There's no mistake. She's guilty."

Stunned, he stood for a long time without speaking. He dropped to sit on a stair and seemed to diminish.

Air seeped out of the balloon of her indignation. They were losing each other, she and her father.

"Why are you sleeping with a married woman?" she asked quietly. "There are lovely single women in town who would jump at the chance to go out with you, Dad. Why choose someone like her?"

He spread his hands. "I—I don't deserve those lovely women. They're too good for a man like me."

"What do you mean a man like you? You've always been great. Until recently. I don't know why you have to drink so much these days. I don't know who you are anymore."

"When Marcie contacted me, when she came back to town, I realized how much I'd screwed up when you two were born." He gripped the newel post. Monica heard movement upstairs and the bathroom door closing. "Your mother and I should have worked out something better. You were right about that. At the very least, I should have told you the truth years ago."

"Yes, you should have. Answer this one question. Honestly. Did you really try to find Marcie after Mom died?"

"Yes. I spent a fortune trying to find her, but Donna was smart and crafty."

"So now you're beating yourself up about it all?"

A sigh gusted out of him. "Yes."

"Stop," she said. "I want my father back, the good guy who did his best raising me. You can be that man again." She gestured toward the upstairs hallway. "First, get her out of here."

With a rigid nod, he conceded, "I'll ask her to leave. I love you, Monica. I don't want to lose you."

"Like I said, I want my father back. Do that for me, Dad. Become good again."

"I can do that."

She left the house and strode down the walkway to the sidewalk, where she came to an abrupt halt.

This was supposed to be a night of triumph and celebration. She was supposed to be spending it with Noah. She didn't know where to go.

Her lonely apartment waited, silent and dark, the place where all of her problems had started on a night in June when her loneliness overwhelmed her.

She drove to that place anyway, because there was nowhere else to go. On Main Street, she passed Tonio's just as Joseph and Maria were locking up.

Monica, on a quick stop, parked and called, "Maria."

Maria grinned. "What a success! What a wonderful night. You must be so happy."

When Monica approached, she passed under a streetlamp.

Maria frowned. "What is it?"

When Monica stood in front of her, Maria opened her arms. "Come here. Tell me what's wrong."

Monica stepped into her embrace, laid her head on her friend's shoulder, felt Joseph's big warm hand rubbing her back and cried.

MARCIE SAT IN the dark alley, back against the wall of the hardware store, surrounded by cardboard. Dampness from the concrete seeped into her buttocks and the backs of her thighs.

So what? She was beyond saving. She'd gone too far tonight. The second she'd driven back into Accord it had registered that she didn't want to lose this place, or her father, or her sister. Too late.

Her envy and need had blinded her. There was no way this would ever work.

A rodent scurried behind the garbage can against the opposite wall.

Her hollow laugh bounced from the walls. This was where she belonged. With the rats.

She swiped her damp cheeks. She didn't cry often, but she cried now, for the loss of her humanity—she was subdued and battered by her need for more.

She'd just pulled the most stupid stunt of her life. Noah had been right. She didn't deserve a sister like Monica.

In her lap sat the bag of money, mocking her, reinforcing what she'd learned about herself since she'd entered this small town—that she needed to grow and become a better person. That she needed to learn to accept. That there really was a point when a person realizes *I have enough*.

How ironic to learn this too late, after one heinous, irredeemable, impulsive act.

Beside her, the ridiculous little purse she'd stolen from her twin sat on the damp cement. She opened it. Monica's cell phone sat amid a small jumble of lipstick, a twenty-dollar bill and a bunch of change.

Lo and behold, it also held a condom.

No doubt her sister had planned to celebrate her success with Noah. Those plans were shot now, courtesy of Marcie.

Marcie took out the cell phone. Only one person in this town would help her now. Only one person liked her the way she was, ugly warts and all.

She called him.

Ten minutes later, John Spade strode down the alleyway, dressed in jeans and a white T-shirt that clung to his chest. A black leather jacket swung from his left hand. Black leather and John Spade. If she didn't find it so hot, she would think it an oxymoron. Sure, the man might pamper himself, but he also worked out. Ob-vi-ous-ly.

She'd never seen him dressed down. She liked this version of him.

His glance took in the dress he must have recognized as Monica's. He noted the sun hat tossed into a puddle nearby.

"What have you done?" That it was merely a question, that there was no accusation in his tone, said a lot about either him or her. She wasn't sure which. He expected that she'd done something bad and was prepared to deal with it. Because he was a lawyer and had seen the worst in mankind? Or because he expected the worst in her and accepted it?

The answers didn't matter, she was so crazy happy to see him.

She picked up the bag of money and handed it to him.

In the dim lighting cast by a security light over a door six feet away, he unzipped it then whistled.

"When you go bad, you do it in a big way. The money raised at tonight's dinner?"

She nodded.

"Why take it? Are you that hard up?"

Why did people always think the only thing that motivated her was money? She threw Monica's stupid little bag against the far wall.

"It's not about money, okay?" she shouted.

He held out a calming hand, just as she imagined he would in a courtroom, but she didn't need a lawyer—well, yeah she would eventually. What she really needed at this screwed-up, broken moment was a friend to fill the empty chasm of her soul.

"Be my friend for one night, okay? Just for a little while." To her horror, her voice broke.

He sat down beside her.

"Aren't you afraid of getting your designer jeans dirty?" The bitterness of her tone cut like acid through the night.

"You've got me all figured out, haven't you?"

"You bet." Why did he always have to sound so calm and reasonable? Why couldn't she ever catch him in a weak moment, like he seemed to always do with her?

Her hard edges threatened to send this man running, yet she couldn't stop herself. Fear and her conscience, the sure knowledge that she'd hurt a couple of truly good people in Noah and Monica, sent up her defensive walls.

"Just once, I'd like to break through that damned serene wall of your grand lawyerly facade."

He lunged close and grasped her by the waist. The world spun. Next thing she knew she was lying across his lap, her jaw cradled in his determined hand, his strong body enwrapping her in warmth.

"You don't know a goddamn thing about me."

"I do so. I—"

"Shut up." When he kissed her, he came down hard, his body thrumming with passion. She felt it everywhere he touched her—in his arms, his chest, in the hard thighs beneath hers. She hummed with an equal passion, part lust and part need, lightning striking in every part of her.

This man. This man could undo her like no one she'd ever known. Undo her and then put her back together in a better way, as a stronger her. He made her more *her*.

By the time he came up for air, she was a pile of pliable jelly in his lap. She would have done anything for him, gone anywhere with him.

Her knee-jerk response kicked in. She gave nothing to *no* man.

When he felt her stiffen in his arms, he laughed. The smugness in that chuckle sent her hackles rising up her back like spreading wings, razor-sharp and ready to whip.

She rose up onto her knees to run, but he stopped her.

"Don't." He snagged her wrist, his fingers a manacle. "Stop running. Stay and deal with the problem you've made."

He was right, damn him. "I don't know how."

"I'll help."

She wasn't in the habit of trusting people. "Why would you help me?"

"Because I like you."

So simple. So direct. "That's it?"

"That isn't enough?"

There it was again. That word. *Enough.* "Yeah. It is."

"Okay. Come home with me and we'll sort this out."

"What about the money?"

"Bring it with you and we'll figure out how to manage this so you don't go to prison for years." He curled his fingers through hers and picked up Monica's little purse.

Prison. She'd screwed herself so badly.

She tottered on her sister's high heels beside John.

He stopped beside a parked car. A Porsche. Surprise, surprise. She made a sound of derision that might have been a snort. "You people and your ridiculous amounts of disposable income."

He smiled. "The bank still owns half of this car."

"Doesn't that worry you?"

"Nope. I have my affairs in order."

Once they were both seated, John put the car into gear and took off. He pointed to the bag of money in her lap. "You do understand the repercussions will be serious."

"Yeah." She turned to face him. "I know I will be arrested. I know I will probably go to prison, but you know what I'm learning?" Her voice sounded thick with tears.

"What?"

"That incarceration and a criminal record aren't the worst that could happen."

"What is?"

"Losing my family."

In the dim light from the dashboard she detected the hint of a smile on his face. "Bingo. I'm glad you've come to your senses."

On the short drive into and through town, and on down the road to John's mansion in the countryside, Marcie contemplated her future. It looked bleak.

Inside his house, she barely noticed her surroundings, only that her hand was wrapped warmly in his as he dropped the bag onto a table and led her upstairs, stopping finally in a dark bedroom.

"What are we doing here?"

"I'm not sending you to jail before we've had a chance to make love. I don't fancy conjugal visits in prison. Let's start our relationship here."

"Conjugal? But doesn't that mean… We don't even know each other."

"I know my own mind. Do you know yours?"

"I don't know," she whispered. "I'm so confused."

"Do you want to spend the night in the spare bedroom?"

This man scared her with his self-possession and sophistication, but she wanted him more than she'd ever wanted another man. Spare bedroom? *No way!*

"Let's make love," she said.

He answered her with a deep, low, satisfied laugh.

THEY SAT IN the living room on opposite sofas. They had showered since making love.

Marcie had never been so thoroughly loved in her life. She hoped John felt the same way.

She wore a plush white bathrobe, the sleeves rolled up. She'd never worn anything more sinfully decadent in her life. She might has well have been wrapped in the arms of a couple of dozen angora rabbits.

John wore jeans and a shirt.

"Down to business." John cradled a snifter of brandy.

Marcie sipped from a cup of hot cocoa, sorry that her brief divine interlude was over. The second John had taken her into his arms in the bedroom reality had disappeared. Now it was back with a vengeance.

He placed the bag of money on the coffee table.

"You should never have taken it."

"No, I shouldn't have. I don't know what happened. I didn't plan it."

"If I thought you had, we wouldn't be here right now."

"I saw how successful Monica was, how much everyone admired her, and how much Noah loved her, and I snapped. I saw where she put her clothes in one office. I saw where Noah put the money in another. I knew the security guard would think I was Monica. I grabbed the opportunity to make her pay." She sighed. "For something she'd never done. *She* hadn't hurt me. Our parents had."

She curled her knees up to her chest and wrapped her arms around her legs, holding on as though for her life. She dropped her head to her knees and cried, hot, heart-wrenching sobs she hadn't known she'd had in her.

John, in his great wisdom, let her cry herself out. Long minutes later, he said, "Feeling better?"

She lifted her head and there in front of her face hovered a box of tissues. She took it from his hand and cleaned herself up.

The bag of money still mocked her from the coffee table.

She should not have taken it. Monica had never been responsible for the way Marcie's life had turned out. And Noah... God, the guy had done nothing to her.

Picking up the bag, she stared at it. What now?

She sensed John walk behind her before hard hands fell onto her shoulders.

"You need to come with me." With a light pressure on one shoulder he urged her to stand.

"Where to?"

His hand at the small of her back, he directed her down the hallway and into an office.

"Sit," he said.

He opened the top drawer of a beautiful oak desk and pulled out one sheet of paper and a silver pen.

"You're going to write a letter of apology to Noah and Monica. One will do. I imagine they're both at his place this morning, which is where we'll go next."

She wrote the letter, pouring her heart into it, they got dressed and then they drove out to Noah's farm, but Monica wasn't there.

At first, Noah didn't give an inch, but eventually he agreed to read her letter.

She'd never written anything more genuine or important in her life.

The three of them sat and talked for an hour until Noah became convinced of Marcie's remorse and that she would never do anything like this again.

When they stood to leave, John put his hands on her shoulders, his support priceless.

"Noah, the money's been returned," John said. "Marcie's sincerely sorry for her actions. Is there any way we can keep this out of the courts? Is it enough that the money is here now?"

Noah stared at Marcie for long, long moments until

she said, "Remember last night when you asked me if I understood the concept of having enough?"

"Yes."

"Today, I understand. I'll make it up to you and my father and Monica. I will never pull this kind of trick again in my life."

He studied her with a pensive frown and nodded. "I believe you."

He hugged her and shook John's hand. "No charges. As long as Monica agrees."

As they were leaving, Noah said, "Good luck getting Monica to listen to you, even to an apology. She won't talk to me."

CHAPTER FIFTEEN

MARCIE FOUND MONICA in her apartment, wary, angry and hurt. Marcie knew where she lived because she'd researched everything about her sister.

Yesterday, or the day before, or her first day in town, she would have been curious to have a look around Monica's home, but not today. Today, nothing mattered but making things right.

"Can we talk?"

"I don't want to hear anything you have to say to me. I don't trust a word that comes out of your mouth."

"I don't blame you, but please let me say my piece and then I'll leave."

She swallowed. This was more difficult than anything she'd ever done. She had so many amends to make.

"I know you don't want to hear this, but I am truly sorry for everything I've done to you."

Monica didn't respond. It was like she had a force field around her, repelling Marcie's words.

"I came to this town bitter and more alone than I've ever been in my life. At first I wanted to get as much money out of our father as I could. But he was more generous than I could have possibly hoped he would be. Then I met you and saw everything that you have and all of the things I'd missed out on while growing up. I became consumed by envy."

Marcie could almost hear her words bouncing back from the shield Monica had erected against her.

"The more I saw of you, the more I wanted everything you had. Actually, I guess I wanted to *be* you. I'm not good and kind like you are. If we'd grown up in the same house, you would have been the good daughter and I would have been the rebel. I don't know how to change or if I can."

Marcie perched on the edge of the sofa and gripped one hand inside of the other.

"I heard you returned the money to Noah," Monica said. Marcie couldn't determine her mood from her flat tone. "He called me. He also said that he's willing to not lay charges, as long as I'm okay with that." Monica turned from the window to look at Marcie for the first time since she'd entered the room. Her expression shifted. Yeah, Marcie knew *she* looked like hell, but Monica looked more like the ice goddess than ever. "I told him that I'm fine with you not getting charged. There's only one thing I want from you now."

"Anything," Marcie whispered fervently.

"Where is our mother buried?"

"I can tell you that. It'll take you about eight hours to drive there."

"Eight hours. She was so close all along…"

"Yes." Marcie paused. "I know I have no right to ask, but there's something I want from you, too."

"What?" The chill emanating from Monica was downright regal.

"I know that I threw away my best chance of ever having a family, but I would like to find a way to start over." She gathered her courage around her, because rejection was the one thing that could wound her most right now.

She crossed the room, hand extended, and infused her voice with her truth. "Hello. I'm Marcie and I'm truly happy that I've found my sister. I'd like to get to know you."

She didn't know what Monica saw on her face and why she trusted her now and never before, but slowly she reached out and took Marcie's hand. "Hi. I'm Monica. And I would like to try."

It was more than she had hoped for. It was more than she deserved.

Next stop, her father and asking his forgiveness.

MONICA STOOD IN front of the small unassuming headstone, a profound sadness suffusing her. In not knowing her mother, she had missed so much.

They could have shared laughter, tears and Monica's many firsts. How much easier would her life have been had she been able to talk to her mother when she got her first period, rather than being directed to one of Dad's female friends?

So, if Mom had been there, what would you have said to her?

I don't know. Maybe I would have wanted her to commiserate with me in what a pain this new event was going to be in my life.

So, tell her.
What? Now?
Yes. Tell *her.*

"It was a pain." She felt foolish, talking out loud to a headstone. "It was *such* a pain. I was only fourteen and knew that I would be in for discomfort once a month for decades to come."

She sat down on the grass and rested her hand on the headstone.

"I wish you had been there to talk to." She sighed and it felt like it came from her heart instead of her lungs. Everything hurt. "I wish I'd known you."

That one sentence embodied all of her regrets. "I wish I had known you."

She sat for long minutes while the breeze played with her hair and a peace she'd never known before settled over her.

She was coming to accept she might never have the kind of relationship with her sister that she craved. They might never have a friendship.

But when Marcie had come to Monica's apartment to apologize, she'd seemed different and her sincerity real. Maybe there had been a turning point in her twin.

It remained to be seen whether they could have a relationship, though.

And Noah? How could they work it out after his betrayal? Maybe Monica was too used to being alone. Maybe she was a little like those poor monkeys who'd been experimented on, the ones who were deprived of touch as infants and then later in life could never take the affection they so desperately wanted.

She had never been deprived of touch—Dad had been wonderful—but she hadn't had enough company, enough social interaction with adults and with other children. It had left her feeling like an island in the midst of a colorful, roiling ocean.

Noah had brought her out of her shell, but where did they go from here?

What about Noah? What do I do about Noah?

If she couldn't trust him, if he couldn't trust her, it was over.

She would have to find her own joy. The emptiness inside of her was hers, and hers alone, to fill.

She would find joy in her new shop. She would love the work. She would be fine.

She stayed overnight in a cold motel room not far from where her mother was buried, curled into a ball under the covers.

How could she return to Accord and pass Noah on the street without wanting him? Yes, she was still full of anger, but it was abating.

Realistically, when Noah had seen Monica, or the woman he had thought was her, stealing and given his past experience, he was primed to overreact. Marcie had pushed all of the right buttons.

Could Monica forgive him? She just didn't know.

NOAH WATCHED A delivery van drive up to the house.

He trudged in from the fields to find out what the

guy jumping out from behind the driver's seat could possibly have for him. He hadn't ordered anything.

"Hey," he called.

"Hey, yourself. I've got a pretty big package for you."

He hauled it out of the back and Noah knew right away what it was.

"Sign here." The young guy handed him a clipboard. Noah signed. The truck drove off and Noah opened the box.

There, among a ton of wasteful packing materials—which he nonetheless thanked his lucky stars for at this moment—was his vintage bike, restored to better than its former glory.

All he had to do was put the front wheel on and align the handlebars properly and tighten them. He flexed the fingers of both of his hands. Earlier this morning, he'd finally had the cast removed. It felt great.

After putting the bike together, he rode it around the farm yard, in circles, his mind echoing his movements. His thoughts had been going in circles since he'd screwed up with Monica. How did he get her back? Around and around he rode on his new-old bike.

Getting it fixed must have cost Monica a small fortune. She couldn't have done anything more thoughtful for him.

She had said she would do it. When was he finally going to realize he could trust her?

Monica. He missed her as though a piece of his flesh had been torn from his body.

How many times could a man be the same fool? Couldn't he just once change his knee-jerk response to her?

He didn't have a clue how to mend what he'd broken. His distrust of Monica had destroyed something sweet and beautiful. All he knew was that he couldn't live the rest of his life without her.

Around and around he rode. How could he fix this? He wasn't about to find the answer in one of his many books. It had to come from within him…and that scared the daylights out of him. He was always so sure he knew the answer to everything. But what if he couldn't come up with the solution to healing Monica's heart?

He needed to do something heroic, but he wasn't a hero. He was an ordinary, simple guy—a farmer, not a hero.

While he rode his bike aimlessly, his thoughts consumed by Monica, he remembered every conversation they'd had, reviewed everything that had ever been said, that had ever been shared.

In a wild jolt of awareness, it came to him. He stopped cycling and stared at his dilapidated old farmhouse. He knew exactly what he had to do to win back his princess.

He needed to build her a castle.

He would have to hustle to get it all set up before she returned home tomorrow.

Would it be enough?

THE FOLLOWING DAY, after one more visit with her mother, Monica drove home. She didn't feel well. Even though she knew she could forge a new life in Accord without the love she'd thought she'd found with Noah, it would be hard.

All through the long drive, she fought sorrow over having come so close to a transcendent love only to have it destroyed so easily.

Tired, she unlocked her apartment door and dropped her keys onto the side table. She butted her suitcase against the wall then walked into the dark living room.

She reached for the lamp on the glass table just inside her door. It wasn't there. Where was it? Why wasn't it where it should be?

A lamp on the other side of the room flared to life. She blinked in the sudden brightness.

Noah sat in a chintz armchair, white with large pink and green cabbage roses. It sat at the corner of a rose-colored carpet, the exact same shade as the roses in the chair. On the other corner was a matching chair, empty.

A brass and stained-glass lamp sat on a small rosewood table with curled legs.

Noah looked good. Better than good. He looked

vital and big and colorful. The only thing missing was his usual confidence. He was unsure of her and her response. She didn't blame him.

She wasn't yet sure of her response.

He'd gutted her living room. Other than the cozy tableau he'd set up in front of the fireplace, the room was empty.

What she really wanted to do was cross the great distance separating them, and she wasn't talking about the bare room, but the gaping chasm of distrust.

A large black-and-white photograph of Noah's farm hung above the mantel. That's how it must have looked in her great-grandparents' time, the house still new and freshly painted.

"I found the photo in the newspaper's archives." He sounded oh-so-hopeful.

She didn't know what to say, so she opted for the first thing that came to mind. "Where's my furniture?"

"In storage. I can have it all moved back here tomorrow and the apartment returned to the way it was, if that's what you want."

No, that wasn't what she wanted.

"If what I did was wrong, I'm sorry. I needed to find some way to reach you, to break through your anger, and the pain of my betrayal. I'm not articulate enough to do this right by words alone."

He was doing all right so far. She wasn't ready to let him off the hook yet, though. There was so much more she needed to hear.

"Will you sit? Please?"

She did.

He kneeled in front of her. "I love you, Monica."

Yes. That was one of the things she wanted to hear. When she opened her mouth to speak, he stopped her.

"Hear me out, okay?"

She nodded.

"I will never doubt you again. I have come to realize you are the most trustworthy, honest person I've ever met."

He grasped the arms of the chair, caging her. "I like your morals. I like your ethics. I like how you take the high road."

"Not lately."

"Lately you've been provoked beyond reason."

She nodded. "I have."

"I have loved you forever. I've loved you since I realized how much I liked the differences between boys and girls."

He tucked a strand of hair behind her ear. He'd done that once before. She'd liked it then and she still liked it now.

"I have loved you since the day when I was a young boy and you walked past me on the street and I thought, she's the one. I've loved you since I was a gangly, awkward, stuttering teenage fool."

With his thumb, he rubbed her bottom lip. "I loved you while I chased all of those long-legged, blonde beauties who looked like you, but *weren't* you. I was disappointed every time. There is no one on this earth like you."

He cradled her cheek in his big palm. "Imagine my surprise now that I know you and find how truly good and kind and wonderful you are. You are perfect. I have always loved you and I will love you from now into eternity."

"Noah?"

"Yes?"

"Some day I want you to tell me about all of those women, but not now." She fished in her purse for an embroidered handkerchief and wiped her eyes so she could see his cherished face clearly. "Someday let's talk about your gangly years because, honestly, I don't remember you ever being gangly. I remember you as always handsome."

She touched the one freckle on his bottom lip. "Right now I don't want to talk anymore. I want to make love. Can we do that?"

"Oh, baby, we can do that until we're both crippled."

She launched herself into his arms and he caught her. They fell back onto the floor with her straddling him.

"While I love this position, you have to stop doing this. It's hard on my back." He tempered his criticism with a satisfied grin.

His hands roamed her back. Her eyes flew open. Hands! She squealed. "You got your cast off."

"Yeah. Feels great."

"Noah, I'm so, so sorry I ran you down that night."

"I'm not. If you hadn't, we wouldn't be here right now. I would have still been wandering around town too intimidated to talk to you."

"And I would have still been intimidated by you. But I'm still sorry I hurt you."

He tucked her hair behind her ear, ran his fingers along her jawline and down her throat, and to shivery parts beyond, leaving a trail of goose bumps.

"Oh, Noah, I do love you so."

They made love there on the floor, in the living room of her future. Noah had packed away the living room of her past for her and she couldn't be happier.

Much later, they showered then walked naked to her bedroom.

Noah directed her to the white lace bed.

"Lie down," he said. "Since the first day I saw this bed, I've wanted to make love to you here."

"Really?"

She stretched her lean body on top of the lace bedspread. The lace suited her. This room was warm, alive with who Monica was.

"How could we have imagined all of those weeks ago that we'd end up here?"

She reached for him and he lay down beside her. "I'm more happy than I've ever been in my life."

"Me, too. I didn't know this kind of happiness was possible. It's like I've lived my whole life with my eyes closed and now they're finally open."

"Yes, and everything's bright and vibrant."

He made love to her with all of her white lace embracing them.

Later, sated beside him, she asked, "How will we work out our lives?"

"Would you live at the farm?"

"Of course. I love it there. It would feel a bit like coming full circle."

"Will you marry me and bring this gorgeous bed to the farm with you?"

She giggled. "All you want me for is my bed."

He waggled his eyebrows. "All I want you for is what you do in bed."

"I have something for you." She rose up onto her elbow and leaned across him, brushing the tips of her nipples over his chest.

"Hallelujah and glory be."

He tried to reach for her breasts, but Monica avoided his roving hands and giggled again. She opened the bedside table and took out a small bottle. "Smell this. It's a cologne I designed for you."

He took it from her with wonder. "You made me my own cologne?"

He sat up and opened the bottle. The scent that greeted him was rich and complex. "Cinnamon? I like it!"

Monica combed her fingers through his hair. "I love your red hair. I thought the cinnamon suited you."

"Yeah, it does. I love this."

"May I ask you a favor? Can you grow back your hair and beard?"

"Honestly, I've been missing it. Why are you asking me to grow it back? I thought maybe you found it too scruffy."

"At first I did, but not anymore. Now I love it. You have a handsome face, and I *do* like to see it." She traced his freckles with her index finger. "But you are so *you* when you are covered with red hair."

He threw back his head and laughed. She kissed his bared throat.

"Ah, Monica, I'm going to enjoy loving you for the rest of our lives." He set about proving his point in the white lace of her bed.

Fifteen Years Later

STANDING AMID THE hustle and bustle swirling around her like a colorful carousel, Monica Accord thought back to when it all started. She wasn't a violent person, but she thanked her lucky stars that she had broken Noah Cameron's arm all of those years ago.

She stood in the farmhouse kitchen on the living-room side of the counter and felt Noah come up behind her, his energy preceding him.

He wrapped his arms around her from behind. She rested her head back against his shoulder.

"It's nice to have the family together, isn't it?" His voice rumbled, getting deeper with age. Every spring, no matter what else was happening in their lives, or in town, the family came together for a full weekend to help Noah plant his fields.

Monica closed up her shop, Hidden Treasures, and Marcie set aside her jewelry-making that Monica sold in her store. Both the shop and the gallery she opened all of those years ago had been a success. Her clientele had built slowly but steadily. Monica was her own businesswoman and she loved it.

A friendly argument at the kitchen table snagged her attention.

Two sets of teenaged twins, hers and Marcie's, played a board game with their aging grandfather, Milton Ian Accord.

Marcie bustled between the stove and the refrigerator, pulling together lunch. Her husband, John, not so dapper today after helping Noah outside all morning, his hair more salt-and-pepper than ever, did his best to keep up with Marcie.

Marcie had made her peace with Donna before her death years before.

Monica had made her peace with both her father and her sister before she married Noah. Since then, the rewards had been too great to count.

She had never figured out whether that hole in her core, that sense of something missing, had been about her mother or her twin, but now her life was so full it no longer mattered.

Noah's fingers slipped inside the buttons of Monica's dress to feather the sensitive skin of her stomach, sending shivery chills through her.

"Ah, Noah," she said. "How can you still do that to me after all of these years?"

Mouth close to her ear, he growled, "Where is it today?"

Leaning against his big, solid body, gloriously happy, fulfilled and safe in her husband's arms, Monica said, "You'll have to find it for yourself. Later."

His laughter rang through the old farmhouse.

* * * * *